THE BEE-MAN OF ORN

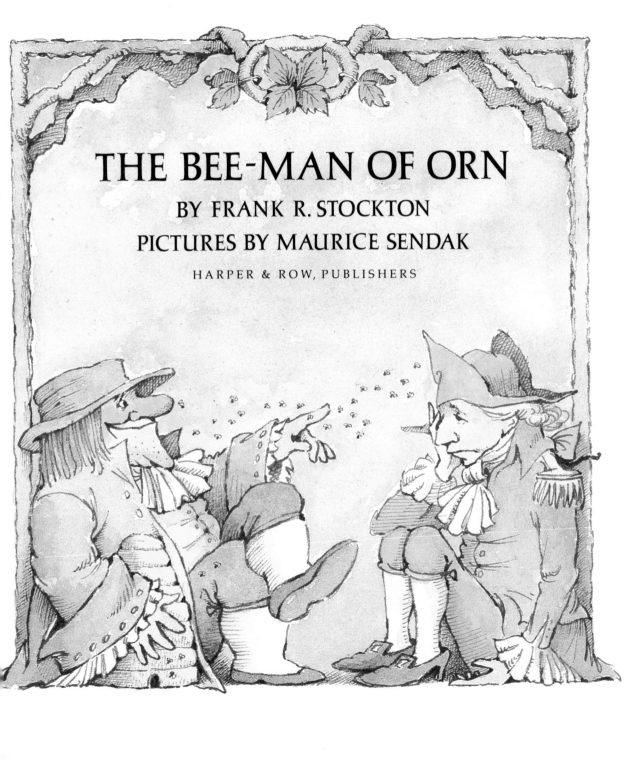

THE BEE-MAN OF ORN

BY FRANK R. STOCKTON

PICTURES BY MAURICE SENDAK

HARPER & ROW, PUBLISHERS

THE BEE-MAN OF ORN
Illustrations copyright © 1964 by Maurice Sendak
Printed in the U.S.A. All rights reserved.
LC 85-45813
Trade ISBN 0-06-025818-7
Harpercrest ISBN 0-06-025819-5
Designed by Maurice Sendak and Nonny Hogrogian

THE BEE-MAN OF ORN

IN THE ANCIENT COUNTRY OF ORN there lived an old man who was called the Bee-man, because his whole time was spent in the company of bees. He lived in a small hut, which was nothing more than an immense beehive, for these little creatures had built their honeycombs in every corner of the one room it contained, on the shelves, under the little table, all about the rough bench on which the old man sat, and even about the headboard and along the sides of his low bed.

All day the air of the room was thick with buzzing insects, but this did not interfere in any way with the old Bee-man, who walked in among them, ate his meals, and went to sleep without the slightest fear of being stung.

He had lived with the bees so long, they had become so accustomed to him, and his skin was so tough and hard that the bees no more thought of stinging him than they would of stinging a tree or a stone. A swarm of bees had made their hive in a pocket of his old leathern doublet; and when he put on this coat to take one of his long walks in the forest in search of wild bees' nests, he was very glad to have this hive with him, for, if he did not find any wild honey, he would put his hand in his pocket and take out a piece of a comb for a luncheon. The bees in his pocket worked very industriously, and he was always certain of having something to eat with him wherever he went. He lived principally upon honey; and when he needed bread or meat, he carried some fine combs to a village not far away and bartered them for other food. He was ugly, untidy, shriveled, and brown. He was poor, and the bees seemed to be his only friends. But, for all that, he was happy and contented; he had all the honey he wanted, and his bees, whom he considered the best company in the world, were as friendly and sociable as they could be, and seemed to increase in number every day.

One day there stopped at the hut of the Bee-man a Junior Sorcerer. This young person, who was a student

of magic, was much interested in the Bee-man, whom he had often noticed in his wanderings, and he considered him an admirable subject for study. He had got a great deal of useful practice by trying to find out, by the various rules and laws of sorcery, exactly why the old Bee-man did not happen to be something that he was not, and why he was what he happened to be. He had studied a long time at this matter, and had found out something.

"Do you know," he said, when the Bee-man came out of his hut, "that you have been transformed?"

"What do you mean by that?" said the other, much surprised.

"You have surely heard of animals and human beings who have been magically transformed into different kinds of creatures?"

"Yes, I have heard of these things," said the Beeman, "but what have I been transformed from?"

"That is more than I know," said the Junior Sorcerer. "But one thing is certain: you ought to be changed back. If you will find out what you have been transformed from, I will see that you are made all right again. Nothing would please me better than to attend to such a case."

And, having a great many things to study and investigate, the Junior Sorcerer went his way.

This information greatly disturbed the mind of the Bee-man. If he had been changed from something else, he ought to be that other thing, whatever it was. He ran after the young man and overtook him.

"If you know, kind sir," he said, "that I have been transformed, you surely are able to tell me what it is I was."

"No," said the Junior Sorcerer, "my studies have not proceeded far enough for that. When I become a Senior I can tell you all about it. But, in the meantime, it will be well for you to try to find out for yourself your original form; and when you have done that, I will get some of the learned Masters of my art to restore you to it. It will be easy enough to do that, but you could not expect them to take the time and trouble to find out what it was."

And, with these words, he hurried away, and was soon lost to view.

Greatly disturbed, the Bee-man retraced his steps, and went to his hut. Never before had he heard anything which had so troubled him.

"I wonder what I was transformed from?" he thought, seating himself on his rough bench. "Could it have been a giant, or a powerful prince, or some gorgeous being whom the magicians or the fairies wished to punish? It may be that I was a dog or a horse, or perhaps a fiery dragon or a horrid snake. I hope it was not one of these. But whatever it was, everyone has certainly a right to his original form, and I am resolved to find out mine. I will start early tomorrow morning; and I am sorry now that I have not more pockets to my old doublet so that I might carry more bees and more honey for my journey."

He spent the rest of the day in making a hive of twigs and straw; and, having transferred to this a number of honeycombs and a colony of bees which had just swarmed, he rose before sunrise the next day; and, having put on his leathern doublet and having bound his new hive to his back, he set forth on his quest, the bees who were to accompany him buzzing around him like a cloud.

As the Bee-man pressed through the little village the people greatly wondered at his queer appearance, with the hive upon his back. "The Bee-man is going on a long journey this time," they said; but no one imagined the strange business on which he was bent. About noon he sat down under a tree, near a beautiful meadow covered with blossoms, and ate a little honey. Then he untied his hive and stretched himself out on the grass to rest. As he gazed upon his bees hovering about him, some going out to the blossoms in the sunshine and some returning laden with the sweet pollen, he said to himself, "They know just what they have to do, and they do it, but alas for me! I know not what I may have to do. And yet, whatever it may be, I am determined to do it. In some way or other I will find out what was my original form, and then I will have myself changed back to it."

And now again the thought came to him that perhaps his original form might have been something very disagreeable or even horrid.

"But it does not matter," he said sturdily. "Whatever I was, that shall I be again. It is not right for anyone to keep a form which does not properly belong to him. I have no doubt I shall discover my original form in the

same way that I find the trees in which the wild bees hive.
When I first catch sight of a bee tree I am drawn toward
it, I know not how. Something says to me: 'That is what
you are looking for.' In the same way I believe I shall find
my original form. When I see it, I shall be drawn toward
it. Something will say to me: 'That is it.'"

15

When the Bee-man was rested, he started off again, and in about an hour he entered a fair domain. Around him were beautiful lawns, grand trees, and lovely gardens; while at a little distance stood the stately palace of

the Lord of the Domain. Richly dressed people were walking about or sitting in the shade of the trees and arbors; splendidly equipped horses were waiting for their riders; and everywhere were seen signs of wealth and gaiety.

"I think," said the Bee-man to himself, "that I should like to stop here for a time. If it should happen that I was originally like any of these happy creatures, it would please me much."

He untied his hive and hid it behind some bushes, and, taking off his old doublet, laid that beside it. It would

not do to have his bees flying about him if he wished to go among the inhabitants of this fair domain.

For two days the Bee-man wandered about the palace and its grounds, avoiding notice as much as possible but looking at everything. He saw handsome men and lovely ladies; the finest horses, dogs, and cattle that were ever known; beautiful birds in cages, and fishes in crystal globes; and it seemed to him that the best of all living things were here collected.

At the close of the second day the Bee-man said to himself: "There is one being here toward whom I feel very much drawn and that is the Lord of the Domain. I cannot feel certain that I was once like him, but it would be a very fine thing if it were so; and it seems impossible for me to be drawn toward any other being in the domain when I look upon him, so handsome, rich, and powerful. But I must observe him more closely, and feel more sure of the matter, before applying to the sorcerers to change me back into a lord of a fair domain."

The next morning the Bee-man saw the Lord of the Domain walking in his gardens. He slipped along the shady paths and followed him, so as to observe him closely and find out if he were really drawn toward this noble and handsome being. The Lord of the Domain walked on for some time, not noticing that the Bee-man was behind him. But suddenly turning, he saw the little old man.

"What are you doing here, you vile beggar?" he cried, and he gave him a kick that sent him into some bushes that grew by the side of the path.

The Bee-man scrambled to his feet and ran as fast as he could to the place where he had hidden his hive and his old doublet.

"If I am certain of anything," he thought, "it is that I was never a person who would kick a poor old man. I will leave this place. I was transformed from nothing that I see here."

He now traveled for a day or two longer, and then he came to a great black mountain near the bottom of which was an opening like the mouth of a cave.

This mountain, he had heard, was filled with caverns and underground passages, which were the abodes of dragons, evil spirits, horrid creatures of all kinds.

"Ah me!" said the Bee-man with a sigh, "I suppose I ought to visit this place. If I am going to do this thing properly, I should look on all sides of the subject, and I may have been one of those horrid creatures myself."

Thereupon he went to the mountain, and, as he approached the opening of the passage which led into its inmost recesses, he saw, sitting upon the ground and leaning his back against a tree, a Languid Youth.

"Good-day," said this individual when he saw the Bee-man. "Are you going inside?"

"Yes," said the Bee-man, "that is what I intend to do."

"Then," said the Languid Youth, slowly rising to his feet, "I think I will go with you. I was told that if I went in there I should get my energies toned up, and they need it very much; but I did not feel equal to entering by myself, and I thought I would wait until someone came along. I am very glad to see you, and we will go in together."

So the two went into the cave, and they had proceeded but a short distance when they met a very little creature, whom it was easy to recognize as a Very Imp. He was about two feet high and resembled in color a freshly polished pair of boots. He was extremely lively and active, and came bounding toward them.

"What did you two people come here for?" he asked.

"I came," said the Languid Youth, "to have my energies toned up."

"You have come to the right place," said the Very Imp. "We will tone you up. And what does that old Bee-man want?"

"He has been transformed from something and wants to find out what it is. He thinks he may have been one of the things in here."

"I should not wonder if that were so," said the Very Imp, rolling his head on one side and eyeing the Bee-man with a critical gaze.

"All right," said the Very Imp, "he can go around and pick out his previous existence. We have here all sorts of vile creepers, crawlers, hissers, and snorters. I suppose he thinks anything will be better than a Bee-man."

"It is not because I want to be better than I am," said the Bee-man, "that I started out on this search. I have simply an honest desire to become what I originally was."

"Oh! That is it, is it?" said the other. "There is an idiotic moon calf here with a clam head which must be just like what you used to be."

"Nonsense," said the Bee-man. "You have not the least idea what an honest purpose is. I shall go about and see for myself."

"Go ahead," said the Very Imp, "and I will attend to this fellow who wants to be toned up." So saying, he joined the Languid Youth.

"Look here," said the Youth, "do you black and shine yourself every morning?"

"No," said the other, "it is waterproof varnish. You want to be invigorated, don't you? Well, I will tell you a splendid way to begin. You see that Bee-man has put down his hive and his coat with the bees in it. Just wait till he gets out of sight, and then catch a lot of those bees and squeeze them flat. If you spread them on a sticky rag, and make a plaster, and put it on the small of your back, it will invigorate you like everything, especially if some of the bees are not quite dead."

"Yes," said the Languid Youth, looking at him with his mild eyes, "but if I had energy enough to catch a bee I would be satisfied. Suppose you catch a lot for me."

"The subject is changed," said the Very Imp. "We are now about to visit the spacious chamber of the King of the Snap-dragons."

"That is a flower," said the Languid Youth.

"You will find him a gay old blossom," said the other. "When he has chased you round his room, and has blown sparks at you, and has snorted and howled, and cracked his tail, and snapped his jaws like a pair of anvils, your energies will be toned up higher than ever before in your life."

"No doubt of it," said the Languid Youth, "but I think I will begin with something a little milder."

"Well, then," said the other, "there is a flat-tailed Demon of the Gorge in here. He is generally asleep, and, if you say so, you can slip into the farthest corner of his cave and I'll solder his tail to the opposite wall. Then he will rage and roar, but he can't get across his cave; I have measured him. It will tone you up wonderfully to sit there and watch him."

"Very likely," said the Languid Youth, "but I would

rather stay outside and let you go up in the corner. The performance in that way will be more interesting to me."

"You are dreadfully hard to please," said the Very Imp. "I have offered them to you loose, and I have offered them fastened to a wall, and now the best thing I can do is to give you a chance at one of them that can't move at all. It is the Ghastly Griffin, and is enchanted. He can't stir so much as the tip of his whiskers for a thousand years. You can go to his cave and examine him just as if he were stuffed, and then you can sit on his back and think how it would be if you should live to be a thousand years old, and he should wake up while you are sitting there. It would be easy to imagine a lot of horrible things he would do to you when you look at his open mouth with its awful fangs, his dreadful claws, and his horrible wings all covered with spikes.

"I think that might suit me," said the Languid Youth. "I would much rather imagine the exercises of these monsters than to see them really going on."

"Come on, then," said the Very Imp, and he led the way to the cave of the Ghastly Griffin.

The Bee-man went by himself through a great part of the mountain, and looked into many of its gloomy caves and recesses, recoiling in horror from most of the dreadful monsters who met his eyes. While he was wandering about, an awful roar was heard resounding through the passages of the mountain, and soon there came flapping along an enormous dragon, with body black as night, and wings and tail of fiery red. In his great foreclaws he bore a little baby.

"Horrible!" exclaimed the Bee-man. "He is taking that little creature to his cave to devour it."

He saw the dragon enter a cave not far away, and, following, looked in. The dragon was crouched upon the ground with the little baby lying before him. It did not seem to be hurt, but was frightened and crying. The monster was looking upon it with delight, as if he intended to make a dainty meal of it as soon as his appetite should be a little stronger.

"It is too bad!" thought the Bee-man. "Somebody ought to do something." And, turning around, he ran away as fast as he could.

He ran through various passages until he came to the spot where he had left his beehive. Picking it up, he hurried back, carrying the hive in his two hands before him. When he reached the cave of the dragon, he looked in and saw the monster still crouched over the weeping child. Without a moment's hesitation, the Bee-man rushed into the cave and threw his hive straight into the face of the dragon. The bees, enraged by the shock, rushed out in an angry crowd and immediately fell upon the head, mouth, eyes, and nose of the dragon. The great monster, astounded by this sudden attack, and driven almost wild

31

by the numberless stings of the bees, sprang back to the farthest corner of his cave, still followed by the bees, at whom he flapped wildly with his great wings and struck with his paws. While the dragon was thus engaged with the bees, the Bee-man rushed forward, and, seizing the child, he hurried away. He did not stop to pick up his doublet, but kept on until he reached the entrance of the cave. There, he saw the Very Imp hopping along on one leg and rubbing his back and shoulders with his hands, and stopped to inquire what was the matter and what had become of the Languid Youth.

"He is no kind of a fellow," said the Very Imp. "He disappointed me dreadfully. I took him up to the Ghastly Griffin, and told him the thing was enchanted, and that he might sit on its back and think about what it could do if it were awake; and when he came near it the wretched creature opened its eyes, and raised its head, and then you ought to have seen how mad that simpleton was. He made a dash at me and seized me by the ears; he kicked and beat me till I can scarcely move."

"His energies must have been toned up a good deal," said the Bee-man.

"Toned up! I should say so!" cried the other. "I raised a howl, and a Scissor-jawed Clipper came out of his hole and got after him; but that lazy fool ran so fast that he could not be caught."

The Bee-man now ran on and soon overtook the Languid Youth.

"You need not be in a hurry now," said the latter, "for the rules of this institution don't allow creatures inside to come out of this opening or to hang around it. If they did, they would frighten away visitors. They go in and out of holes in the upper part of the mountain."

The two proceeded on their way.

"What are you going to do with that baby?" said the Languid Youth.

"I shall carry it along with me," said the Bee-man, "as I go on with my search, and perhaps I may find its mother. If I do not, I shall give it to somebody in that little village yonder. Anything would be better than leaving it to be devoured by that horrid dragon."

"Let me carry it. I feel quite strong enough now to carry a baby."

"Thank you," said the Bee-man, "but I can take it myself. I like to carry something and I have now neither my hive nor my doublet."

"It is very well that you had to leave them behind," said the Youth, "for bees would have stung the baby."

"My bees never sting babies," said the other.

"They probably never had a chance," remarked his companion.

They soon entered the village, and after walking a short distance, the Youth exclaimed: "Do you see that woman over there sitting at the door of her house? She has beautiful hair, and she is tearing it all to pieces. She should not be allowed to do that."

"No," said the Bee-man. "Her friends should tie her hands."

"Perhaps she is the mother of this child," said the Youth, "and if you give it to her, she will no longer think of tearing her hair."

"But," said the Bee-man, "you don't really think this is her child?"

"Suppose you go over and see," said the other.

The Bee-man hesitated a moment, and then he walked toward the woman. Hearing him coming, she raised her head, and when she saw the child she rushed toward

it, snatched it into her arms, and screaming with joy she covered it with kisses. Then, with happy tears, she begged to know the story of the rescue of her child, whom she never expected to see again; and she loaded the Bee-man with thanks and blessings. The friends and neighbors gathered around, and there was great rejoicing. The mother urged the Bee-man and the Youth to stay with her, and rest and refresh themselves, which they were glad to do, as they were tired and hungry.

They remained at the cottage all night, and in the afternoon of the next day the Bee-man said to the Youth: "It may seem an odd thing to you, but never in all my life have I felt myself drawn toward any living being as I am drawn toward this baby. Therefore, I believe that I have been transformed from a baby."

"Good!" cried the Youth. "It is my opinion that you have hit the truth. And now would you like to be changed back to your original form?"

"Indeed I would!" said the Bee-man. "I have the strongest yearning to be what I originally was."

The Youth, who had now lost every trace of languid feeling, took a great interest in the matter, and early the next morning started off to tell the Junior Sorcerer that the Bee-man had discovered what he had been transformed from and desired to be changed back to it.

The Junior Sorcerer and his learned Masters were filled with delight when they heard this report; and they at once set out for the mother's cottage. And there, by magic arts, the Bee-man was changed back into a baby. The mother was so grateful for what the Bee-man had done for her that she agreed to take charge of this baby and to bring it up as her own.

"It will be a grand thing for him," said the Junior Sorcerer, "and I am glad that I studied his case. He will now have a fresh start in life, and will have a chance to become something better than a miserable old man living in a wretched hut with no friends or companions but buzzing bees."

The Junior Sorcerer and his Masters then returned to their homes, happy in the success of their great performance; and the Youth went back to his home anxious to begin a life of activity and energy.

Years and years afterward, when the Junior Sorcerer had become a Senior and was very old indeed, he passed through the country of Orn, and noticed a small hut about which swarms of bees were flying. He approached it, and, looking in at the door, he saw an old man in a leathern doublet, sitting at a table, eating honey. By his magic art he knew this was the baby which had been transformed from the Bee-man.

"Upon my word!" exclaimed the Sorcerer. "He has grown up into the same thing again!"

Perhaps best remembered for his adult story, *The Lady or the Tiger?*, Frank R. Stockton was also the creator of many distinctive tales for children, tales of such unusual quality that Alice M. Jordan in *From Rollo to Tom Sawyer* includes his work as a significant contribution to the golden decade of the 1880's, "a brilliant period in American children's literature."

Born in Philadelphia in 1834, Mr. Stockton was originally trained as an engraver, but his great interest was in writing; and from 1873 until 1881, he worked on the staff of the notable *St. Nicholas Magazine,* serving as assistant editor to Mary Mapes Dodge. Until his death in 1902, Mr. Stockton was one of the magazine's most loved contributors.

Maurice Sendak could never be advised by the Junior Sorcerer that he had been transformed from something other than his present being—that of one of the best-known, best-loved illustrators in the field of children's literature—for there is no other Maurice Sendak.

Winner of the 1964 Caldecott Award for the classic *Where the Wild Things Are*, Mr. Sendak knew he wanted to write and illustrate books when he was very young. He is now the distinguished author-artist of a number of books of his own, including *In the Night Kitchen* and *Outside Over There,* and the illustrator of many books by other writers. His first "collaboration" with Frank R. Stockton, *The Griffin and the Minor Canon,* gave him an appreciation of the writer's whimsical imagination that is reflected, too, in his pictures for THE BEE-MAN OF ORN.

ENVIRONMENTAL
PSYCHOLOGY

ENVIRONMENTAL
PSYCHOLOGY

NORMAN W. HEIMSTRA
LESLIE H. McFARLING
The University of South Dakota

BROOKS/COLE PUBLISHING COMPANY
MONTEREY, CALIFORNIA

A Division of Wadsworth Publishing Company, Inc.

ISBN: 0-8185-0122-7
L.C. Catalog Card No.: 74-76749
Printed in the United States of America
1 2 3 4 5 6 7 8 9 10—78 77 76 75 74

Manuscript Editor: Grace Holloway
Production Editor: Meredith Mullins
Interior Design: Bernard Dix
Cover Design: Linda Marcetti
Typesetting: Datagraphics Press, Inc., Phoenix, Arizona
Printing & Binding: Colonial Press, Clinton, Massachusetts

PREFACE

Everywhere about us we see a concern for the quality of our physical environment. This concern has been translated into action at many levels, ranging from the housewife who uses a laundry detergent that is supposedly less harmful to the water, to Boy Scout campaigns to clean up river banks, to stringent federal regulations concerning a variety of pollutants. While much of the interest in the relationship between man and the physical environment has dealt with the ways in which man affects his environment, there has also been a growing interest concerning the manner in which the physical environment influences man's behavior.

The purpose of this book is to present a brief overview of basic concepts and major research concerns in the field that has become known as environmental psychology. The central issue of this newly emerging field is the various relationships between the physical environment and man's behavior. Underlying this issue is the assumption that behavior is profoundly shaped by the physical environment—both the "built" and the "natural" environment— and that a knowledge of this shaping process is necessary to more fully understand why man behaves the way he does and to more effectively design the environment with which man interacts.

A primary objective in writing this book was to develop a text that is readable to students in a variety of different disciplines, since there are few fields of study that do not, at least to some degree, touch upon the relationship between man and the environment. Although the book is not all-inclusive, the content areas discussed provide an introduction to the discipline of environmental psychology for readers in psychology, sociology, other social sciences, urban planning, environmental studies, architecture, design, engineering, and related areas. Rather than develop an encyclopedia of studies, we have selected a variety of topics that are representative of major concerns in the field of environmental psychology; at the same time we have avoided the overuse of psychological jargon.

As is the case with any emerging field of inquiry, there is some question regarding the subject matter that is appropriately considered part of the field of environmental psychology. As will become apparent in the text, the definition of the subject matter is far from precise, and what one researcher thinks of as being appropriate to environmental psychology may not seem so to another investigator. However, certain types of man-environment relationships have received more attention than others, and most researchers would agree that the kinds of relationships discussed in this book are particularly relevant areas of investigation for environmental psychologists.

Considerable attention has been given to the effects on behavior of the built environment (such as rooms, buildings, institutions, and cities). Similarly, the natural environment and its effects on behavior have also been subjected to research, although on a more limited scale. Typically, however, the relationships that have received the most attention have been negative ones —for example, the effects of pollution or overcrowding on behavior. However, positive relationships, such as those involved in many types of interactions that man has with his natural environment, have also been studied, and many are discussed in this book.

We wish to express our appreciation to the staff of Brooks/Cole Publishing Company and to the following individuals for their helpful reviews of our manuscript: Evan Brown of the University of Nebraska, Carolyn Toepfer of Slippery Rock State College, Robert Sommer of the University of California at Davis, and Edward L. Walker of the University of Michigan.

Norman W. Heimstra
Leslie H. McFarling

CONTENTS

ENVIRONMENTAL
PSYCHOLOGY

CHAPTER ONE

INTRODUCTION

Not too many years ago, only a few scientists and public officials were concerned about the effects that advancing technology and population growth were having on the quality of our physical environment. Only rarely was the word "environment" mentioned in the media, and few, if any, legislators were making any concentrated effort to pass laws to protect the environment. But now environmental problems are discussed in newspapers and magazines, on television specials, and in other media that reach millions of Americans. Public awareness of the problem has resulted in numerous local, state, and federal laws and in the creation of the Environmental Protection Agency. The relationship between man and his environment is of interest to individuals in many areas, including architecture, urban and regional planning, civil and sanitary engineering, forest and parks management, geography, biology, sociology, and psychology, to name only a few. As Wohlwill (1970) says, "there are few, if any, fields that do not at some points touch on the relationship between man and his environment" [p. 303].

We hear a great deal about pollution of air and water, destruction of the natural environment, noise, and overcrowding. Considerably less is heard about positive actions, such as restoration of natural areas, renewal of slum areas, and progress in environmental design. Yet all too often we have been concerned with the effects of man's behavior on the environment at the expense of studying how the environment and man's changes in it affect behavior. Behavioral scientists are now beginning to show an interest in this area, for, as Proshansky, Ittelson, and Rivlin (1970) point out:

> This is precisely the task that the environmental sciences have set for themselves—the study of the consequences of environmental manipulations on man. As this study progresses, our ability to predict and control these consequences will increase. We will know what results will follow a particular environmental manipulation, and we will understand the consequences of environmental change [p. 3].

We will be concerned with both the relationship between man and his physical environment and the effects of environmental manipulations on man. Much of the research that has been conducted in this area has been subsumed under the heading of *environmental psychology,* although, as we shall see, the problem areas that constitute this discipline are not clearly defined.

SOME PROBLEMS OF DEFINITION

It would be difficult to arrive at a consensus among environmental psychologists on just how their discipline should be defined. Indeed, Proshansky et al. (1970) question whether it actually can be defined:

> Is there, at present, an adequate definition of environmental psychology? We think not. There are, in general, two ways in which the definition of a field of study may be stated. One—and in the long run, the only really satisfactory way—is in terms of theory. And the simple fact is that as yet there is no adequate theory, or even the beginnings of a theory, of environmental psychology on which such a definition might be based.
> The second approach to definition—a much less satisfying but much more feasible one—is operational; environmental psychology is what the environmental psychologists do [p. 5].

Essentially, in this book we will use the latter type of definition. Although the topics covered are quite diverse and represent contributions from investigators in a variety of disciplines, these researchers have in common an interest in the relationships between man and the physical environment. Thus, for purposes of definition, we will consider environmental psychology as *the discipline that is concerned with the relationships between human behavior and man's physical environment.* To clarify this definition, however, it is necessary to discuss several aspects of it in more detail. Thus, in this section we will be concerned with a more precise explanation of what is meant by the physical environment, by human behavior, and by the relationships that exist between the two.

THE PHYSICAL ENVIRONMENT

Psychologists and other behavioral scientists have always talked about the role of the environment in shaping behavior. Usually, however, they have thought of the environment as social or interpersonal and have considered other people to be the major determinants of human behavior. When behavioral scientists have referred to other environmental influences, they have generally done so in nonspecific terms, with the concept of environment "used to refer to the most diverse set of conditions of experience, ranging from attendance in nursery school to socialization practices of the parents; from the provision for practice or training on a task to the role of culture or society in a global sense" [Wohlwill, 1970, p. 304]. Although behavior is also influenced by its physical environment, until recently the relationship between the two has received little attention.

In its broadest sense, "physical environment" connotes everything that surrounds a person. As used in environmental psychology, however, the term has a more limited meaning—although, as will become apparent, it is still quite broad. Environmental psychologists divide the physical environment into two types, the *man-built* or *man-modified* and the *natural.*

Obviously, the man-built or man-modified physical environment encompasses a great deal. Of particular interest to researchers, however, has been the relationship between man's behavior and such features of the built environment as the rooms of buildings in which the behavior occurs, the relationship between various types of housing and behavior, the design of institutions and how design characteristics may modify behavior, and the effects on behavior of living in cities. Man-built features of the environment have also resulted in pollution, overcrowding, and other undesirable consequences; the effects of these conditions on behavior have been of considerable interest to environmental psychologists. It is these aspects of the built environment with which we will be primarily concerned in this text.

The distinction between the man-built or man-modified environment and the natural environment is primarily one of convenience, since very little of the natural environment has not been modified to some extent by man. However, many national parks and wilderness areas are still thought of by many as being natural, and there has been some research on the relationship between behavior and these kinds of environments. Researchers have also been interested in another kind of natural environment, the *geographic,* which includes climate, terrain, and such natural hazards as floods, earthquakes, and hurricanes, all of which influence behavior.

It should be pointed out that use of the term "natural environment" in this way is somewhat different from the manner in which it is often used by psychologists. They may use the term simply to refer to a situation or setting that has not been modified by the experimenter. Thus, a psychologist studying the behavior of schoolchildren in a classroom would report that their behavior was observed in a natural environment.

To study the relationships between human behavior and the many features of the physical environment, the behavioral scientist is confronted with a challenging task. It is difficult, if not impossible, to isolate one feature of the environment and study its effects on behavior without having the behavior modified, at least to some extent, by other features. For example, suppose a researcher is interested in the relationship between the shape of a room and the behavior of its occupants. He could design his study in any one of several ways, and various types of behavior could be involved. In addition, however, the room is only one unit of a building, and various other characteristics of buildings influence behavior. The building, in turn, might be one of several in a complex, the complex forming part of a neighborhood. The neighborhood is part of a city, having hot or cold weather, and the potential of natural hazards, such as floods or earthquakes. The environment can be composed of subsystems—climatic conditions, cities, buildings, and so forth—all interacting and influencing behavior. Consequently, it is difficult to isolate one of these features, or subsystems, and determine the relationship between it and human behavior. As we shall see in the following chapters, this is a problem in much environmental psychology research.

HUMAN BEHAVIOR

We have defined environmental psychology as the discipline concerned with the relationships between human behavior and the physical environment. As Craik (1970) points out, "While the everyday physical environment is its unifying theme, the subject matter of environmental psychology is human behavior *as it relates to,* for example, rock formations, downtown streets, and corners of rooms, not the rock formations, downtown streets, and corners of rooms themselves" [p. 13]. Thus, although the environmental psychologist may spend a good deal of time and effort describing and defining characteristics of the physical environment, his ultimate objective is relating these characteristics to human behavior.

When we speak of human behavior, we are, of course, referring to an almost limitless range of activities. As Skinner (1953) states:

> Behavior is a difficult subject matter, not because it is inaccessible, but because it is extremely complex. Since it is a process, rather than a thing, it cannot be easily held for observation. It is changing, fluid, and evanescent, and for this reason it makes great technical demands upon the ingenuity and energy of the scientist [p. 15].

As we shall see, because of the nature of the relationships between behavior and the physical environment, the demands on environmental psychologists are often more severe than those on other behavioral scientists.

Behavior, then, is any form of activity that is observable either directly or with the aid of instruments. Elaborate equipment is required to observe some kinds of behavior—electrical changes within the brain, for instance. Various types of tests can be used to detect mental and psychological processes. Still other kinds of behavior are overt, and the researcher need only jot down what he sees or hears. The point to keep in mind is that behavior ranges from very subtle forms of activity to overt activities that are easily observable.

Later in this chapter the kinds of behavior that have been of particular interest to environmental psychologists will be discussed, together with the methods used to measure the behavior.

RELATIONSHIPS BETWEEN BEHAVIOR AND THE ENVIRONMENT

Human behavior is, in many ways, functionally related to attributes of the physical environment. Wohlwill (1970) has distinguished among three forms of this relationship, and in this section we will consider them in some detail.

Wohlwill points out that behavior takes place in a particular environmental context. This context imposes major restrictions on the kinds of behavior that can occur in it and "frequently serves to determine in a more positive sense particular aspects or patterns of an individual's behavior" [p. 304]. For example, the behavior that a person living on a farm or in a small town can engage in differs considerably from the behavior that a city dweller can engage in. One kind of relationship, then, is that the environment determines the range of behavior that can occur in it.

In the second type of relationship, certain qualities associated with a particular environment may have a broad effect on the behavior and personality of the individual. Wohlwill cites as examples the "wonted brusqueness of the typical New York City bus driver on the job [and] the proverbial 'mad cabbie' of Manhattan." He suggests that, at least to the extent that these stereotypes hold true, "it seems plausible to relate them to the conditions of stress and tension to which these individuals are subjected in their daily battle with urban traffic and congestion" [p. 304]. This type of relationship may also explain reported differences between urban and rural incidences of mental disease and various physical disorders, as well as bystander apathy in the face of violence.

The third kind of relationship is one in which the environment serves as a motivating force.

> Individuals give evidence of more or less strongly defined attitudes, values, beliefs, and affective responses relating to their environment. . . . They develop diverse forms of adjustment and adaptation to environmental conditions. They exhibit temporary and permanent responses of approach to and avoidance of or escape from given environmental situations, ranging all the way from recreation and tourism to migration to the suburbs, or to a different part of the country [p. 304].

This last type of relationship thus has three important facets: (1) affective and attitudinal responses to environmental features, (2) approach and avoidance responses to various attributes of the environment, and (3) adaptation to environmental qualities. As Wohlwill (p. 305) points out, not only are these kinds of relationships directly connected with many current environmental problems, but they also can be analyzed in terms of existing principles or hypotheses in psychology.

Much of the research conducted by environmental psychologists has dealt with the first of these relationships, the environment as a source of affect and attitudes. As we shall see in the following chapters, the physical environment can elicit strong feelings and attitudes, both positive and negative. The physical environment may also result in approach or avoidance behavior. Thus, a person may move from an area that he dislikes for some reason—cold climate or overcrowding, for example—to a region that he finds more attractive. This kind of behavior is also involved when a person selects one vacation spot over another, selects one building site over another, and so forth. This aspect of the behavior-environment relationship is now beginning to be investigated.

The question of how a person adapts to his physical environment is also of considerable interest to environmental psychologists. We know that man is capable of adapting both behaviorally and physiologically to a wide range of environments. Although much of the research in this area has been conducted in the laboratory and deals with adaptation to temperature, light, and so forth, man also adapts to life in the ghetto, to noise from jet aircraft and freeway traffic, to pollution, and to other features of the physical environment. We will discuss this adaptive process at several places in the text, since it raises a number of intriguing questions for the researcher studying man in relation to his physical environment.

Although we will not discuss it in any detail in this text, the counterpart of the effect of the environment on behavior is, of course, man's effect on the environment. Thus, instead of studying the effects of air pollution on behavior, we might have wished to study the kind of behavior that results in air pollution. The point to keep in mind when we define environmental psychology as the study of the relationships between behavior and the physical environment is that these relationships are a two-way street; the physical environment influences man's behavior, but man also modifies his physical environment.

We have attempted to define "environmental psychology" and to discuss some of the types of relationships between human behavior and the environment. In the rest of this chapter, we will examine how environmental psychologists study these relationships.

RESEARCH METHODS IN ENVIRONMENTAL PSYCHOLOGY

Scientific research is designed to find the answer to a question by scientific techniques. The question that the investigator seeks to answer depends upon many factors. Sometimes the question is generated by a practical problem encountered in our technological society. At other times the question is abstract. Regardless of the type of question, the same commonly accepted methods may be used by researchers in their attempts to arrive at an answer.

Although any classification of these research methods is somewhat arbitrary, one scheme is based on the control that the investigator exerts over the situation in which the behavior occurs and the conditions that influence the behavior. In this classification scheme, the researcher uses what is called the *experimental method* when he has direct control over the behavior and can manipulate the appropriate variables or conditions. At the other end of the spectrum is the *naturalistic observation method,* in which the researcher makes no attempt to manipulate or control variables. Between these two extremes are a number of other methods, several of which will be discussed later in this section.

THE EXPERIMENTAL METHOD

Basically, the experimental method of studying behavior involves manipulating certain aspects (*independent variables*) of a behavioral situation and observing the effect of the manipulation on behavior (*dependent variable*). For example, suppose a researcher is investigating the effects of noise level on the ability to concentrate. In this study noise is the independent variable, while ability to concentrate, a form of behavior, is the dependent variable.

In an experiment the investigator generally uses several levels of the independent variable to determine whether changes in its level will result in changes in his measure of the dependent variable. Thus, in the noise study the investigator might use four levels of the independent variable, noise. A group of subjects would be tested under a no-noise condition (the control group), another group under 70 decibels (db), another under 80 db, and the fourth group under 90 db. Under each of these conditions, the subjects would be required to proofread an article containing a number of typographical errors. A composite score involving length of material completed and number of errors missed would serve as the measure of concentration, the dependent variable. If the subjects' performance on the proofreading task differed under the various noise conditions, the investigator would use a statistical test to determine whether the differences were due to chance alone or were statistically significant.

The experimental method is generally used in laboratory studies because they can be conducted under carefully controlled conditions. As will be apparent, relatively little research in environmental psychology has been conducted in laboratories. The experimental method, however, can be used in field experiments in many natural settings, such as a school, a city, and a forest or wilderness area.

Although the experimental situation in a field study often cannot be as tightly controlled as in the laboratory, the field study has several virtues that make it a useful method for researchers interested in the effects of the built or natural environment on behavior. One important advantage of the field study is that the setting is much more realistic than the laboratory. This realism usually makes generalizations from the research findings more valid. Finally, many kinds of behavior, ranging from relatively simple reactions to complex social processes, that are difficult to study in the laboratory can be studied in the field. For example, the effects of classroom size or design on learning would be difficult to determine in a laboratory setting but could be studied in the field setting.

THE NATURALISTIC OBSERVATION METHOD

The researcher using the naturalistic observation method observes behavior in a natural setting and, in some fashion, records what he considers as the relevant behavioral events that take place. Although he may be interested in the effects of certain variables on the behavior that he is observing, he does not attempt to manipulate these variables or influence the behavior in any way.

Many specific techniques are associated with the naturalistic observation method. The observer may use equipment ranging from a notepad and pencil for recording observations to elaborate photographic or videotaping systems. The researcher may be concealed from the subjects he wishes to observe, or he may actually become a member of a group in whose behavior he is interested. Similarly, the behavior studied by this method may range from simple motor responses to elaborate types of social behavior. The important feature, of course, is that the observer typically does not attempt to influence or control the behavior in any fashion.

This method is popular with investigators in many different areas. For example, much of what we know about animal behavior, particularly that occurring outside laboratory settings, has been obtained by researchers observing animals in their natural habitats. Psychologists have often studied the behavior of children by naturalistic observation techniques. This approach has frequently been used to analyze behavior in specific settings, such as small towns, urban areas, and schools and other institutions. For studying naturally occurring human behavior in these and other types of settings, psychologists interested in this type of research (often referred to as *ecological psychology*) must usually rely on some form of the naturalistic observation technique.

THE TESTING METHOD

"Testing method" includes several approaches used by environmental psychologists in their studies. Typically, when using one of these approaches, the researcher is investigating a particular characteristic of a group of individuals. A standard stimulus situation (called a test) is designed to measure the characteristic. Tests have been designed to measure intelligence, personality, aptitude, and affective states. Interviews, questionnaires, opinion surveys, and attitude surveys also are tests. Although the actual instruments used in testing may differ, they all involve a controlled stimulus situation designed to elicit responses that reveal something about the individual in which the researcher is interested.

The testing method is frequently employed by environmental psychologists interested in attitudes of groups of people about an environmental problem, such as air or water pollution. To obtain this kind of information, the researcher typically uses a special testing method called *survey research.*

We are frequently exposed to information gathered by surveys; indeed, before an election, the public is bombarded with the results of one kind of survey research—public opinion polling. In survey research the investigator attempts in some systematic fashion to obtain data from a population (more typically, samples of a population) in order to assess some characteristic of it.

Conducting a survey so that results are meaningful is a complex procedure that we cannot discuss in any detail. Several aspects of the procedure are, however, of particular importance. One is that only on rare occasions can an entire population be studied by a surveyor. Consequently, in most studies the researcher draws samples from the population and, from these samples, attempts to infer its characteristics. How the sample is selected is critical. There are a number of methods for selecting the sample to be used in a survey, and the investigator must use a correct procedure if his generalization of his findings from the sample to the population is to be valid.

Another critical feature of survey research is the construction of the interview questions. It is relatively easy to get almost any kind of response from a person if the question is worded in a particular fashion. For example, virtually everyone asked the question "Does smog bother you?" would be likely to reply in the affirmative, so that the researcher might conclude that smog is really a matter of great concern to the people he has interviewed. He might get quite a different response if the question were "What do you consider to be the most serious environmental problem in this area?" The interview instrument must be constructed so as to get at what the investigator is interested in and also to avoid distortion or feigning of responses. That is often difficult to accomplish.

Much more could be said about the methods of studying behavior that are commonly used by researchers in many different fields. However, in the remainder of this chapter, we will be concerned with how these methods are used by environmental psychologists in their work and with some of the problems they encounter.

13

VARIABLES IN ENVIRONMENTAL RESEARCH

We have emphasized that the experimental method of studying behavior involves manipulating certain aspects (independent variables) of the environmental situation and observing the effect of the manipulation on behavior (dependent variable). In the testing method and the naturalistic observation method of studying behavior, the independent variables are not manipulated.

The experimental method has not been employed as frequently in environmental psychology studies as it has in other areas of behavioral research because of the nature of the independent variables involved. Many of the variables do not lend themselves to manipulation, and it is difficult, if not impossible, to use different levels of the independent variable, as is required in the experimental method. For example, suppose an investigator is interested in the effects of air pollution on some form of behavior. It would be difficult for him to exert any control over the level of pollution that his subjects would be exposed to at any given time. Similarly, it would be difficult to manipulate the level of pollution in a stream, the population density in an urban area, noise pollution near an airport or a lake, and so forth.

Keeping in mind, then, that it is difficult for a researcher to manipulate many types of environmental independent variables, let us consider some of the variables that are of interest to environmental psychologists and the ways in which they study the relationship between these variables and behavior.

INDEPENDENT VARIABLES

Virtually any aspect of the built or natural environment with which man interacts can influence his behavior and, consequently, could be selected as an independent variable. Because there are so many potential independent variables, we will make no effort to discuss them in any exhaustive fashion. Rather, we will briefly mention some of the types of variables that have been studied, many of which will be taken up in much more detail in later chapters.

For many years researchers have been interested in how various aspects of the built environment influence certain types of behavior. For example, psychologists and engineers have systematically studied the effect on work efficiency and comfort of such variables as lighting, noise levels, heating, ventilation, and machine design and position. Although studies such as these can certainly be considered to be environmental research, they are more appropriately dealt with in books on industrial or engineering psychology and will not be discussed in any detail in this text.

Architects, engineers, urban planners, behavioral scientists, and others have recently become interested in variables of the built environment that influence behavior and so are now trying to take the "human factor" into consideration. Among the variables that can influence behavior are such features as size and arrangement of rooms and passageways, number and size of windows and doors, and arrangement of furniture; interior illumination, temperature, and noise; community layout, recreational facilities, and shopping convenience; and transportation facilities, including location and speed of public transport, parking space, and street layout (McCormick, 1970, p. 575).

Similarly, numerous features of the natural environment may affect behavior. Among these are the physical characteristics of a natural environment, such as the presence or absence of trees, mountains, streams, or lakes. Features such as accessibility, perceived "wildness," cost, and many others are also variables that must be considered. Climate and such natural hazards as floods, droughts, and earthquakes are additional features of the natural environment that may influence behavior.

As the level of technology in our society has increased, so has the deterioration of the environment. Thus, air pollution, water pollution, noise pollution, and desecration of the landscape have become major issues to large numbers of people. These features of the environment, then, are another important class of independent variables having an effect on behavior.

The independent variables we have listed can be thought of as physical, nonliving influences on behavior. It is important to keep in mind, however, that when a person is exposed to these variables, he is generally not in isolation but rather is in the company of other people. Consequently, the individual not only reacts to these variables but also interacts with other individuals, and this interaction may modify the effects of environmental variables. In many cases the existing social condition may be an important environmental variable in its own right. For example, one variable of particular interest to researchers is the effects of varying levels of population density on behavior. We will consider this variable in some detail in a later chapter.

It should be apparent, then, that a wide variety of environmental features can serve as independent variables. It should also be kept in mind that they are not the neat, easily quantifiable, readily controlled and manipulated variables that make for a tidy experimental design of research projects.

Presenting the Independent Variable

Because the environmental researcher studies the effect of some feature of the environment on a particular type of behavior, that feature must, of course, be exposed in some fashion to the persons in whose behavior he is interested. In much of the environmental research that has been conducted, the persons whose behavior is being studied have already been exposed to the environmental feature of interest. For example, most of the research dealing with attitudes toward air, water, and noise pollution is of this type. Researchers also frequently compare attitudes or other forms of behavior of persons exposed to different types of environmental features. Thus, the attitudes toward pollution of persons living in polluted areas may be compared with the attitudes of those living in "clean" areas, the behavior of people living in high population density areas compared with that of people living in low density areas, the attitudes toward earthquakes or other natural disasters of people living in regions where these events occur compared with the attitudes of people in areas where they do not, and so forth. In studies such as these, the exposure (or lack of exposure) to the environmental feature has occurred, so that the investigator does not have to be concerned with how the independent variable is presented to his subjects.

In many other types of environmental psychology studies, however, presenting the environmental feature to the subjects is an important consideration for the researcher. Moreover, the manner in which it is presented is critical to the success of the investigation. The exact methods used will, of course, depend upon the particular variable or variables that the investigator is concerned with, and we cannot attempt to describe all the possible approaches. However, as Craik (1970) has pointed out, several methods of presenting environmental features encompass, with some modifications, many of the approaches used by environmental psychologists; and we will discuss these general techniques.

When referring to the environmental feature that is to be presented to a subject, Craik uses the term "environmental display" [pp. 65–66]. An environmental display may include virtually all the independent variables that we have discussed in this section. Thus, a room, a building, a forest glade, a crowded street, and a smoggy atmosphere are all examples of environmental displays. Craik discusses three general methods by which environmental displays can be presented to subjects: *direct presentation, representation,* and *imaginal presentation.*

Direct Presentation. In this type of presentation, subjects are exposed to the actual environmental feature, or display, and can view it, possibly touch it, perhaps walk or drive around or fly over it. For example, suppose an investigator is interested in the effect of a badly polluted stream on the mood or feelings of people who view it. He might take a group of subjects to an area near the stream, measure their mood (techniques for doing this will be discussed later), then have them walk along the stream, look at it, perhaps even taste it, and finally again measure their mood to see whether it was changed by exposure to the stream. Although there are a number of environmental displays to which subjects can be exposed by the direct presentation method, obviously in many studies it would be difficult actually to get subjects to the display. Consequently, for those studies the representation method is more feasible.

Representation.   As Craik points out, "The various representational media offer attractive alternatives to direct presentation, being less expensive, more convenient, and more standard methods" [p. 68]. An experimenter might choose to employ any of a number of devices in lieu of direct presentation. Drawings, maps, models, and replicas of the environmental feature can be presented to subjects and their responses to these representations studied. Photographs, movies, and television can also be used.

With this approach, the investigator interested in the effect of a polluted stream on the mood of observers could conduct his study in a laboratory and not have to worry about transporting his subjects to the actual stream. In this case he might measure the mood of the subjects, show them a movie or some other representation of the stream, and then measure the subjects' mood again to see whether the environmental display had any effect. Obviously, the pollution would not be as "real" to the subjects as a direct presentation would, and one drawback of this method is that we do not know whether people respond to a representation of an environmental display in the same manner as they respond to a direct presentation of it.

Imaginal Presentation.   The researcher using this technique asks his subjects to visualize a display. This method is a convenient one because the researcher does not have to take his subjects to the display or prepare representations for his study. The researcher using imaginal presentation to gauge reaction to a polluted stream might measure the mood of his subjects, ask them to imagine a polluted stream (he might describe such a stream in some detail to the subjects), and then again measure their mood. Imaginal presentation has been used in a number of environmental studies, some of which will be described later.

DEPENDENT VARIABLES

Exposing subjects to some feature of the environment of interest to the researcher is only one aspect of investigation. The researcher must also be concerned with selection and measurement of the behavioral response that he wishes to study.

Behavior involves many activities, some easily observed by the experimenter, some observed only by sensitive electronic equipment, and some "observed" by tests and interviews. The exact behavioral response selected by a researcher will be determined by the question he wishes to answer. In the following chapters we shall see that even though environmental psychology is a new field, researchers have already studied a number of behaviors.

In some studies these variables involve overt behavioral responses. Movement through a room served as the dependent variable in one study about the effects of room color. In other studies the dependent variable has been the number of people visiting a particular national park. Reaction time, detection of infrequently appearing signals, eye irritation as a function of smog level, and performance on a task under crowded conditions—these are only a few of the variables used. Typically, measurement of these variables is relatively straightforward and poses no great problem for the investigator.

Most work in environmental psychology involves variables more difficult to deal with than the type described above. Frequently, the researcher is concerned with how a person feels about a particular environmental feature rather than with how the feature affects his overt behavior. Since feelings, judgments, and similar reactions are more difficult to measure in a reliable fashion than are reaction time, locomotion, and other dependent variables of this type, and since they are so common in environmental research, we will consider these in some detail.

There are several ways of eliciting and recording these types of responses to the environment. Craik categorizes these responses as *descriptive responses, global responses, inferential responses, attitudinal responses,* and *preferential responses.* Though all of these have been used in environmental research, some are more common than others; and these will be emphasized in the following discussion.

Descriptive Responses

In some instances subjects are asked to describe, either verbally or in writing, their reaction to an environmental display. The researcher using this technique, called *free description,* makes no effort to structure his subjects' responses; he only analyzes what is said or written. A disadvantage of this technique is that it is difficult to quantify and compare the responses obtained with it. Consequently, most researchers who wish to elicit descriptive responses use a *standardized description* technique instead. The numerous standard descriptive formats include rating scales and adjective check lists.

Rating Scales. Although rating scales exist in a variety of forms, all have certain features in common. Typically, the subject is presented with several categories from which he selects the one that he feels best characterizes the environmental display or feature of the display. The categories are usually assigned numbers, which can be directly used in statistical analysis. If a researcher wished to measure, for example, reactions to air pollution, he might ask his subjects to select on the scale shown below the category best describing their feelings about air pollution. The subjects' answers to a number of such rating scales, each with different descriptive categories, would give the researcher a relatively broad picture of his subjects' feelings about air pollution.

Very Harmful	Harmful	Not Very Harmful	Not at All Harmful

One rating scale method that has been used a great deal in behavioral research is the semantic differential. With this technique, which was developed by Osgood, Suci, and Tannenbaum (1957), the subjects are asked to make a judgment about an environmental display on a scale with opposing adjectives—such as pleasant-unpleasant, comfortable-uncomfortable, or friendly-unfriendly—at opposite ends. For example, assume that an investigator wishes to determine how people view two rooms in a building that are identical except for wall and carpet color. The researcher shows each room to his subjects and asks them to complete semantic differentials like the ones shown below. If each position on the scales from left to right is numbered from 1 to 7, then the individual who completed the scales shown felt that this room should be rated as a 3 on the pleasant-unpleasant scale, a 5 on the comfortable-uncomfortable scale, and a 4 on the friendly-unfriendly scale. Normally, many more scales than are shown in our example would be administered. The numbers assigned to the judgments would then be averaged to determine whether the subjects viewed the two rooms differently.

Room A

Pleasant	__	__	X	__	__	__	__	Unpleasant
Comfortable	__	__	__	X	__	__	Uncomfortable
Friendly	__	__	__	X	__	__	__	Unfriendly

Rating scales have some definite advantages in behavioral research. Usually, they require less time than other methods, have a wide range of applications, are typically interesting and easy for the subjects to use, and in most cases are more economical than other measures.

Adjective Check Lists.   An adjective check list consists of a long list of adjectives (sometimes several hundred) that the subject checks as being applicable or not applicable to an environmental feature. Thus, the researcher who is interested in how people view the two rooms with different colored walls and rugs could use the list of adjectives shown below (together with many others) instead of the semantic differential. He would then ask his subjects to view the rooms and check whether each adjective is or is not applicable to them. Check lists of this type are easy to administer and can be used effectively with many kinds of environmental displays.

Room A

	Yes	No
Pleasant	X	
Comfortable	X	
Friendly		X
Cold	X	
Large	X	
Coherent	X	

A common response to certain kinds of environmental features is a change in affective state. For example, viewing a mountain stream may make a person feel happy; if the stream has been polluted, he may feel sad. One form of adjective check list that has been developed to enable persons to describe their mood in a quantifiable fashion is the Nowlis (1965) Mood Adjective Check List (MACL). The MACL consists of a group of adjectives that describe eight mood factors, such as anxiety, fatigue, aggression, and concentration. For each of the adjectives, a subject rates how he feels at the moment on a four-point scale like the one below. He circles "VV" if he definitely feels relaxed at the *moment,* "V" if he feels slightly relaxed, "?" if he cannot decide, and "No" if he definitely does not feel relaxed. Analysis of the responses (which can be assigned numbers) gives the experimenter a comprehensive picture of the subject's mood.

Relaxed   VV   V   ?   No

The MACL can be used in a number of ways in environmental research. By administering the check list both before and after the presentation of an environmental display, the researcher can determine the effect of the display on the subject's mood. Sometimes, different environmental displays are presented to different groups of subjects, with members of each group completing a MACL. In this way the researcher can compare the effects of various environmental displays on the mood of viewers.

Other techniques for eliciting descriptive responses that can be used in environmental research have been developed. However, rating scales and adjective check lists such as those described are the most common techniques used.

Global Responses

Although the simple descriptions of reactions to the environment provided by rating scales and adjective check lists are useful, recording subtle responses to environmental displays may require different techniques. For example, as Craik (1970) points out, "One seemingly implicit reaction to displays such as buildings, rooms, rural valleys, and urban alleys is an automatic scanning response answering the question 'What might go on here?'" [p. 73]. To elicit this reaction, subjects could be asked to write a brief story about the display they were shown. Readers familiar with some of the personality tests commonly used by psychologists will recognize the similarity between this procedure and the use of the Thematic Apperception Test (TAT). Global responses, then, typically involve little structure on the part of the researcher. Subjects respond to an environmental display by telling a story about it, by describing how a display makes them feel, by interpreting what effects a display might have on other persons, and so forth.

Another technique for obtaining global responses requires that subjects draw environmental displays. In studies of urban areas, subjects have often been requested to sketch maps to convey their concepts of cities. In a later chapter the results of this "cognitive mapping" technique will be discussed in some detail.

Inferential Responses

We continually make inferences about features of the environment and gradually build up notions about them. These beliefs may or may not correspond to reality. There are several ways to elicit and record these inferential responses. Suppose, for example, that we are interested in finding out how people in a small town in South Dakota view people living in New York City and vice versa. Persons in each locale could be given adjective check lists on which to describe what they think the kinds of people living in the other locale are, what they do for a living, how they entertain themselves, and so forth. Inferences about an environmental feature can also be elicited by having people list as many consequences as they can imagine that might be associated with the presence of some environmental display (such as a new lake formed by a dam) or the removal of some display (a wooded area being destroyed for a new housing development).

Although these and similar approaches entail some difficulties in quantification and analysis, they can show the investigator a dimension of behavior that is important in better understanding man-environment interactions.

Attitudinal Responses

Much of the research in environmental psychology has been concerned with measuring people's attitudes toward such features of the environment as air and water pollution, aviation and other transportation noise, and outdoor recreation areas. Sometimes the surveys have been aimed at the public in general, sometimes at more restricted populations, such as wilderness campers or persons living near an airport. Attitudes can be measured in several ways, but most researchers use detailed questionnaires.

Although the term "attitude" means different things to different psychologists, an attitude can be thought of as a mental readiness to respond that is organized through experience and will influence behavior. Attitudes, however, do not always modify behavior; as we shall see later, people have very strong negative attitudes toward air, water, and noise pollution but, apparently, do very little about it.

As pointed out earlier, measuring attitudes toward an environmental feature requires considerable care on the part of the investigator. It is particularly important that questions be constructed in such a way that they do not put words in a respondent's mouth. For example, a person who lives near an airport may not be bothered by the noise enough to complain about it or even be particularly concerned. However, if he were asked, "Do you think aircraft noise is the most serious neighborhood problem?" he would probably answer in the affirmative.

Although attitude measurement is an important area of research in environmental psychology, too much emphasis may have been placed on it. Consequently, other kinds of research, which might result in more useful information, may have been neglected.

Preferential Responses

Eliciting and recording preferential responses are relatively simple procedures. A subject can, for example, give his preference after simply looking at photographs of environmental displays, whether landscapes, neighborhoods, wilderness areas, or camping facilities. The researcher with a number of photographs of, say, different camping facilities can ask his subjects to choose between paired alternatives, to rank the photographs in order of preference, or to rate them. After the subjects have expressed their preferences, the researcher can analyze the displays in some detail to determine what features may be associated with high or low preference ratings.

Our discussion of various kinds of responses has not by any means exhausted the possible responses that have been and could be used as dependent variables in environmental research. The natural and built environments influence man's behavior in so many ways that virtually any aspect of behavior can be considered an appropriate variable for study.

SELECTION OF SUBJECTS IN ENVIRONMENTAL RESEARCH

We have emphasized that two critical decisions that the investigator must make have to do with the selection and manipulation of independent variables and the selection and measurement of dependent variables. A third decision deals with the selection and assignment of the subjects to be used in a study.

In some instances the investigator must decide whether to use human subjects or some species of lower animal in his research. As we shall see in Chapter 6, much of the research on the physiological and behavioral effects of population density has been conducted with rats and mice as subjects. Generally, though, researchers in environmental psychology are interested in the effects of environmental features on human behavior and recognize that generalizations of findings from studies with animal subjects can be made to humans only with a great deal of caution. Thus, although the researcher who plans to use animal subjects is confronted with some problems of selection, we will be concerned here with selection and assignment of human subjects.

SAMPLES AND POPULATIONS

In nearly all studies in the behavioral sciences, the number of subjects that an investigator actually uses is relatively small. Nonetheless, the researcher can often generalize the findings of his study to a larger number of people if he selects a sample of subjects from a population that possesses the characteristics in which he is interested. For example, suppose an investigator wants to determine the attitudes toward aircraft noise of the inhabitants of a small city where, each day, overflights by military jets produce sonic booms. In this case the population is all the inhabitants of the city—perhaps 40,000 people. Because interviewing all of them would not be feasible, the researcher would select a sample. If the sampling strategy was adequate, the views held by the persons making up the sample would very closely reflect the views of the entire population. This procedure, of course, is the one followed by the various professional survey groups, who, on the basis of information obtained from a sample of only a couple of thousand people, can quite accurately determine what the nation thinks about a particular topic.

The researcher studying behavior in a laboratory setting must also be concerned with the manner in which subjects are selected and assigned to experimental conditions. Though all too often the subjects in laboratory research are college students in introductory psychology courses who may or may not be willing participants, the investigator can take steps to make the generalizability of his data more valid. Normally, his strategy involves some type of random selection of subjects as well as random assignment of the subjects to the different levels of the independent variable.

The selection of samples is often a complex procedure and is beyond the scope of this text. Detailed discussions of sampling strategies can be found in Ellingstad and Heimstra (in press) and in Babbie (1973). The point to keep in mind is that the subjects for a study, whether it is a large-scale survey or a small laboratory experiment, must be selected carefully if the researcher hopes to generalize his findings.

CHARACTERISTICS OF THE SUBJECTS

The characteristics of the subjects selected obviously depend upon the research question that the investigator hopes to answer. If he is interested in the effects of aircraft noise on children's classroom performance, his sample would consist of children drawn from a noisy area. Similarly, if he is interested in the attitudes of wilderness campers toward a new highway being built through a wilderness area, his sample would consist of persons who camp in the area. In some instances subjects are selected on the basis of a personality characteristic, such as extroversion or introversion, and their responses to various types of environmental displays compared. Because so many questions about the effects of the environment on behavior remain to be answered, virtually any person could be a member of a group with some characteristic of interest to environmental psychologists.

Often, however, the subjects are drawn from what Craik (1970) refers to as *special competence groups* and *special user-client groups.* In the former groups are engineers, architects, city planners, landscape architects, and others with competence in a particular area. In special user-client groups are elderly persons, hospital patients, inmates of prisons or other types of institutions, wilderness area campers, and so forth. The type of special competence group or special user-client group selected depends, of course, on the objectives of the study.

A last category from which subjects are drawn is the large number of people who happen to live in areas where some aspect of the environment is deteriorating. In many areas air pollution has reached an extremely high level, or the residents are bombarded with aircraft or other transportation noise, or the population density is very high. A single area often has all these environmental features. Much of the research in environmental psychology has been an attempt to determine how the environmental deterioration affects these people's behavior.

CHAPTER TWO

THE BUILT ENVIRONMENT:
ROOMS AND HOUSING

The two principal types of physical environments are the built environment and the natural environment. They should not, however, be thought of as mutually exclusive but as part of a continuum on a number of dimensions. For our purposes, the most important of these dimensions is the relative contribution (in number or in space occupied) of man-designed and man-built structures in a particular physical setting. Consider, for example, the difference in the composition of the overall physical setting between a suburb or a classroom and a campground or a trail through a national park. Both types of settings contain man-designed structures or features, but man-designed and man-constructed features are dominant in the composition of the suburb or classroom setting. A built environment, then, is one that has been designed and formed, to a large degree, by man.

According to this general concept of what is meant by the term "built environment," much of our behavior occurs in built environments of one type or another. Obviously, then, the built environment has great potential for influencing our activities.

   As mentioned previously, the built environment can be considered to be a system made up of many subsystems. Although these subsystems vary tremendously in physical size, function, and amount of social interaction taking place within them, each can be broken down into elements that may affect human behavior in the system. By the same token, the human element in different built environments also varies, providing unique behavior-environment relationships in each built environment. Thus, behavior in a room in a house may differ substantially from the types of behavior that occur in a large airport terminal. We will therefore first consider interactions between man and the built environment at the relatively simple level of rooms and their furnishings and then consider more complex man-environment systems, such as houses, large buildings and facilities, and social institutions.

   It is important to keep in mind that even though each level of the built environment will be discussed as if it were an entity in itself, each level is a component of some larger system. As shown in Figure 2-1, although we may be interested in the physical features of a room that influence the behavior of the person in that room, it is but one room in a specific building in a neighborhood of a city in a geographical region—in this instance, the West Coast. Each of these systems (the building, the neighborhood, the city, and the

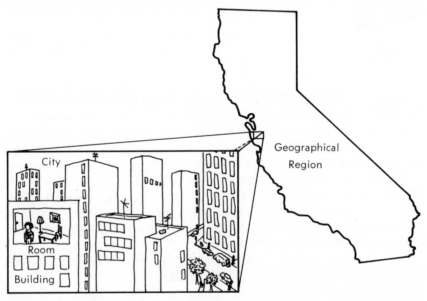

Figure 2-1.   An example of the levels of the physical environment that may affect behavior.

geographical region) possesses unique physical features that may influence the behavior of the individual in the room. Moreover, these same physical features affect other persons in each level of the system and thus may promote social behavior that involves the single person under consideration.

ROOMS

The most significant influence of a room on behavior is the purpose of the room. In many cases a room's function is partially defined by the purpose of a larger system—a single classroom in a school building, for example. That this room is part of a school typically places constraints on the behavior occurring there. The type of influence on behavior depends on whether the room is a lecture hall, a chemistry laboratory, or a small seminar room. Moreover, for each type of room, we expect a certain shape, certain furnishings, and certain ambient conditions, all of which affect behavior.

In other cases the purpose of a room is not so explicit. An example of such a room is a family room in a private home. Because many different kinds of behavior may occur in this room, the specifications for its physical structure and contents are not nearly so clear as for a particular type of classroom.

When, however, a room is to encourage specific kinds of behavior, certain design considerations must be kept in mind. For a classroom the most obvious consideration is provision for student learning. Thus, if a classroom is to serve as a lecture hall, the seating should be arranged so that each student has as clear a view as possible of the instructor and the teaching aids he will use. This consideration means that all the students will typically be facing the professor in some type of desk or table arrangement. Associated with this type of classroom are implied social behavior regulations; for example, student interaction must be minimized in order not to interfere with the lecturer. This behavioral prerequisite means additional specifications for the seating arrangement.

From these examples, it should be apparent that there exist two potential modes of physical design that affect behavior. The first is those aspects of the built environment that must be incorporated into the design of a room if it is to fulfill its function; for example, room for laboratory tables must be provided in a chemistry lab. The second mode is the physical attributes of a room that are not directly required by its function. Both categories of physical design contain independent variables that exert considerable influence on behavior. One such variable in the latter category is color.

COLOR

Color is probably the one physical dimension of a room that suffers least from the restrictions imposed by the planned function of a room, even though wall and ceiling color are frequently chosen to complement window and lighting fixture placement in reducing glare and increasing reflected light. Accordingly, the color scheme of a room is generally left to the architect or interior decorator. His decision should not, however, be purely an aesthetic one; as shown in the research discussed below, colors elicit affective states and influence overt behavior.

Characteristics of Color

Colored light has three dimensions, *brightness, hue,* and *saturation.* Brightness is intensity of the color, and hue is simply the color of an object, or the wavelength in the color spectrum that predominates in the composition of the color. Saturation is the amount of white present in any color; the more saturated a particular color, the less white it contains. For example, red is more saturated than pink.

In specifying colors composed of pigments rather than light, the term "hue" is retained, but the term "chroma" is often substituted for "saturation," and the dimension of *value* is added. Value is "the degree of lightness or darkness of the color relative to a white-to-black scale" [Woodson & Conover, 1966, pp. 2–211]. Because one or more of these dimensions can be varied in planning color layouts for rooms, designers have considerable latitude in attempting to produce desired subjective reactions in the people who use the rooms.

Studies of Room Color and Behavior

One of the most common notions about room color is that colors toward the red end of the spectrum (yellows, oranges, and reds) are warm, while colors at the other end (blues and greens) are cool. This idea was probably arrived at by commonsense associations. Blue water and green forest glades suggest cool temperatures; yellows, reds, and oranges provoke thoughts of the sun or fire. These kinds of associations have led to the seemingly intuitive hue-heat hypothesis "that an environment which has dominant light frequencies toward the red end of the visible spectrum feels warm and one with dominant blue frequencies feels cool" [Bennett & Rey, 1972, p. 149].

These authors tested a logical extension of the hue-heat hypothesis: The perceived warmth obtained from the color of a room and the actual temperature in the room may interact to differentially affect the thermal comfort of room occupants. The room used for the investigation was an environmental chamber, a room with strict controls over humidity and temperature. The temperature in the chamber was changed by circulating hot or cold fluid through coils attached to the walls, which were aluminum. Color, the other independent variable, was controlled by requiring each subject to wear successively red, blue, and clear goggles. Under each color condition the wall temperature was increased to 101 degrees and then decreased to 58 degrees. The subjects, who were seated close to the walls, were required to rate periodically their feelings of thermal comfort. Temperature readings were obtained at the points at which the subjects shifted from one thermal comfort condition to another—for example, from "slightly warm" to "warm"—in each of the color conditions. The investigators' analysis revealed that red did not affect the subjects' feelings of thermal comfort any differently than did the blue or the clear conditions. Bennett and Rey suggest that the hue-heat hypothesis is only intellectual, a pervasive belief that some colors make rooms seem warmer than do others.

Evidence of this intellectual effect was also obtained by Berry (1961) in a similar investigation. The subjects in his study were placed in a room under different colors of illumination and, as the experimenter raised the air temperature in the room, asked to report when they felt too warm. Although no differences between colors and the point at which the subjects stated a feeling of discomfort were discovered, the participants indicated that the warmer colors (usually amber and yellow) conducted more heat than did the cooler colors (green and blue).

These two studies illustrate an important point. Although no behavioral effect of room color on thermal comfort could be established, the subjects in the studies still maintained that cognitive perception of warmth varied as colors were changed. Thus, this perceptual effect of color may be as important as actual behavioral indications of comfort in color choice for a room.

Color affects perception of not only a room's warmth but also such qualities as its spaciousness, complexity, and social status. Acking and Küller (1967, 1972) asked subjects to rate colored slides of rooms on an extensive list of adjectives that could describe an environment. The ratings were used by a team of architects and psychologists to select a set of adjectives that would best describe the pleasantness, social status, complexity, unity, and enclosedness of a room. Using this derived rating list, the participants in the second investigation evaluated slides of room sketches in which the colors of walls and some of the room details varied. The social evaluation of the rooms was found to vary as a function of lightness; as the darkness of the room color and its detail increased, the subjects thought rooms more rich or expensive. The dimension of value also accounted for the perceived spaciousness of a room. As the room colors became lighter, the rooms were generally judged to be more open. The effect of openness was also achieved by increasing the chromatic intensity of the room's details while leaving the color of the walls relatively weak in saturation. The room's judged complexity was also found to depend on the chromatic strength of the hues, with the more saturated room colors receiving higher complexity ratings. The room's pleasantness rating varied from individual to individual, with no firm color preferences being established.

Up to this point our discussion of color as an independent variable has dealt with the effects of different dimensions of color on perceptions of a room. Although a person's perceptions of warmth or spaciousness can be considered behavior of a sort, they are difficult to measure. Another approach to studying the effects of color attempts to link a person's perception of a room to behavior that is more observable, or at least more subject to objective assessment. However, such behavioral measures become increasingly difficult to obtain as a man-environment relationship becomes more natural.

An ingenious device that measures "locational" behavior and how it is affected by environmental features has been developed at the Environment Research Foundation in Kansas. This apparatus records the locational behavior of unknowing subjects in a museum room at the University of Kansas. The device, referred to as a *hodometer* (*hodos* is a Greek term for pathway), consists of a network of square switchmats similar to those used for automatic doors. The mats are laid on the floor, covered by a carpet, and wired to counters placed in a side room unnoticeable to people in the museum viewing room. The number of places where visitors go in the room, the time they spend at a particular location, and other kinds of behavior can thus be measured. Betchel (1967) has used this hodometer to establish correlations between locational behavior and picture preference in art displays.

Of more immediate interest, however, is a study by Srivastava and Peel (1968) using the hodometer to measure the exploratory behavior of museum room visitors. In each of the two conditions in the study, the color of the carpet concealing the switchmats and the color of the walls were changed. When the walls and carpet were light beige, the subjects explored less (used less of the available floor space) than did the subjects in the room when the carpet and walls were chocolate colored. The subjects under the latter condition took more steps, covered nearly twice as much area, and spent less time in the room.

This section has provided at least a preliminary statement of the effects of color perception on other forms of behavior. Unfortunately, the studies discussed here do not represent a small sample of the research conducted on this topic; they constitute most of the reported research. In addition to providing important information on man-environment interactions, such thought-provoking studies suggest future research directions. The study by Srivastava and Peel suggests that color in rooms should not be disregarded or relegated to fulfilling purely aesthetic functions in future design considerations.

AMBIENT ENVIRONMENT

The experience of color in a room is visual. Other aspects of a room impinge on different sensory modalities. These aspects, known as the *ambient environments,* are noise, temperature, illumination, and odor. Traditionally, these have been given more consideration in discussions of work environments, such as offices and factories, or of special environments, such as hospitals. The concept of noise as an environmental stressor will be covered in detail in a later chapter, as will the ambient environmental aspects of offices and special-purpose building systems. However, a few general statements about the effects of the ambient environment on persons' perceptions of rooms can serve to provide an awareness of their existence in the scheme of any room environment.

An acceptable ambient environment is a prerequisite for aesthetic satisfaction. According to Fitch (1965), "the aesthetic process only begins to operate maximally, i.e., as a uniquely human faculty, when the impact upon the body of all environmental forces is held within tolerable limits. . . . A temperature of 120 degrees F or a sound level of 120 decibels can render the most beautiful room uninhabitable" [pp. 707–708]. Thus, not only must all ambient conditions be acceptable, but no one stimulus should be allowed to dominate the others even though that stimulus may be tolerable. If the stimulus is extreme, sensory overload can result, which constitutes a stressful situation for the individual. The concept of the environment as a creator of stress will be examined in depth in a later chapter. Although the examples presented in that chapter deal with pollution, overcrowding, and other stress-creating attributes of the physical environment, it should be kept in mind that stressful aspects of the ambient environment in a room can elicit much the same type of behavior. Even if not stressful, an excessive amount of one or more aspects of the ambient environment in a room may cause an individual to perceive the room as unpleasant, which may lead to a more active behavior—avoiding the room in the future, for example.

The ambient conditions required for satisfaction and appreciation vary from room to room because they are a function of the purpose for which a room was designed. Thus, depending on the purpose of a particular room, different aspects of the ambient environment can be manipulated to produce an atmosphere that, in turn, will elicit the desired behavioral state in the occupants of the room. The following examples of common rooms, together with an examination of their ambient environments and the desired behavior, are illustrations.

In a discotheque two ambient conditions, lighting and sound, are highly manipulated. Music and other sources of sound often reach a sustained overall level of more than 100 decibels. Although the overall lighting level is often quite low, the lights may be in unusual places—for instance, under a plexiglass floor—and may be programmed in flashing or blinking sequences in an attempt to produce an exciting visual experience. Moreover, the temperature in establishments of this sort is likely to be higher than the occupants would consider pleasant in other situations.

In a dentist's office, light and sound are usually manipulated to help give the impression of a pleasant atmosphere. Sound levels are much lower than in a discotheque, although soft music is likely to be played. Lighting, on the other hand, is at a higher level, not only because the dentist needs it for his work but also because it seems cheerful. Such ambient conditions help to create an environment that is advantageous for both patient and dentist. From the point of view of the dentist, the more pleasant the atmosphere of his office, the greater the chance of a favorable impression on the patient. The impression that the patient receives may influence his returning or his referring his friends. The patient appreciates a soothing, cheerful office while he is waiting for and undergoing treatment.

Obviously, other conditions are also operating in these two situations, and among the most prevalent may be social conditions. Social interactions and how they are affected by various aspects of a room will be discussed later in this chapter.

SIZE AND SHAPE

If we think of the various features making up a room as either fixed or flexible, size and shape are undoubtedly the most rigid. Although, as we shall see later, the nature of rooms can be altered by rearranging their furnishings, the physical dimensions of a room do not lend themselves to change without considerable effort and expense. Thus, the size and shape of any particular room have been largely accepted as fixed, and researchers have concentrated on manipulating other aspects of the room environment, such as color, ambient conditions, and arrangement of furnishings.

The primary reason for the lack of research on the effect of room shape on behavior is our almost total lack of variety in shapes. For the most part, the American room is rectangular; it is difficult to remember seeing a room that does not consist of 90-degree angles. Only in futuristic architecture and in other cultures—the igloo in Eskimo culture and the tepee in Indian culture, for example—do rooms have different shapes. Indeed, the rectangular room is so common that we tend to believe that a particular room is rectangular even though cues from objects within the room tell us that it is not. Ittelson and Kilpatrick (1951) provide an excellent example of this phenomenon's occurring in a distorted room:

> . . . the floor slopes up to the right of the observer, the rear wall recedes from right to left and the windows are of different sizes and trapezoidal in shape. When an observer looks at this room with one eye from a certain point, the room appears as if the floor were level, the rear wall at right angles to the line of sight and the windows rectangular and of the same size. Presumably the observer chooses this particular appearance instead of some other because of the assumptions he brings to the occasion [p. 55].

The relevance of this study for environmental psychology is that the viewer's perception of the distorted room is influenced by his previous experience with rooms. Unfortunately, little research has been reported on different behavioral effects of various room shapes. Ittelson and Kilpatrick's study suggests that the findings of such research would be of considerable interest.

The size of most rooms is determined by their function. Generally, the size of a room is the minimum required to serve its function. For example, if the function of a classroom is to hold 30 people, it is doubtful that the room will comfortably accommodate a class of 50. Here economic considerations take priority over possible psychological benefits of larger size.

Because size is to a large extent dependent upon room function, the effect of size on behavior can be thought of as an interaction with other independent variables, such as the number of persons in a room. In this context size becomes important as a potential determinant of behavior. For example, the presence of many persons in a room may result in overcrowding, which can have behavioral consequences. (Overcrowding is discussed in Chapter 6.) Thus, size can be viewed as the amount of space available for each person in a room. The different ways in which people use space to ensure privacy, to declare ownership or status, and to influence social interaction are discussed later in this chapter.

FURNISHINGS AND THEIR ARRANGEMENT

So far in this chapter, we have emphasized the effects of some aspects of a room—size and shape, color, and ambient conditions—on the perceptions, appreciation, and locational behavior of the individual. In this and the following sections, our emphasis will shift to the effects of various aspects of rooms on persons interacting with one another. One reason for this change in emphasis is that the effects of room furnishings on the individual are generally confined to his perceptions of their efficiency, comfort, beauty, and value. When two or more persons are interacting in an educational, work-related, recreational, or other setting, however, the behavioral effects of furnishings and their arrangement can be more readily observed (Mehrabian & Diamond, 1971; Sommer, 1959, 1962). Another reason for focusing on group behavior rather than on that of the individual is that, as we shall see later, certain variables associated with an individual can be studied only in social interactions. For example, a person's territorial behavior and his need for privacy are best observed in situations involving actual or potential contact with others. Finally, much of our knowledge of the effects of environment on behavior has been obtained through observing people engaged in a variety of activities in such places as classrooms, libraries, lounges, and dormitories.

As stated at the beginning of this chapter, many components of the built environment are designed to meet both functional and behavioral objectives. The function of a chair, for instance, is obviously to provide something to sit on. At the same time, however, a chair may be designed to affect behavior. Sommer (1969) reports that a Danish furniture designer was contracted to design a chair that would become so uncomfortable after a short time that an occupant would be forced to get up. This design was requested by restaurant owners who did not want their customers lingering over coffee. Sommer (1969) also describes similar design considerations in the seating arrangements at a typical airport:

> In most terminals it is virtually impossible for two people sitting down to converse comfortably for any length of time. The chairs are either bolted together and arranged in rows theatre-style facing the ticket counter, or arranged back-to-back, and even if they face one another they are at such distances that comfortable conversation is impossible. The motive for the arrangement is the same as in hotels and other commercial places—to drive people out of the waiting areas into cafes, bars, and shops where they will spend money [pp. 121–122].

If the objective of the seating arrangements in airports is actually to discourage social interaction and promote financial gain, the arrangement is highly appropriate. In a series of experiments, Sommer (1959, 1962) investigated the seating preferences of persons engaged in conversation. In the first study pairs of subjects were asked to sit on two couches in a lounge and discuss a prepared topic. The couches were placed across from each other at distances depending on the experimental conditions. Sommer found that up to a distance of about three feet between couches, his subject pairs preferred to sit across from each other. When the distance was greater, they preferred to sit on the same couch.

Using the findings from this experiment, Sommer conducted a second study in which the couches were replaced by four chairs to allow greater variety in side-by-side distance. The experimental situations were constructed so that the distance between side-by-side and facing chairs could vary from one foot to five feet. Again pairs of subjects were given a topic to discuss and assigned to an arrangement of chairs. As in the previous study, the subjects generally preferred to sit across from each other if the distance was equal to or less than the maximum side-by-side distance (see Figure 2-2). In interpreting these findings, however, Sommer cautions that they were obtained in one room and in one structured interaction. He emphasizes that manipulation of

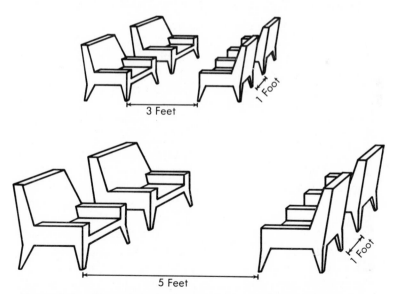

Figure 2-2.   Research indicates that chair arrangement influences the seating choice of two persons who wish to converse. People prefer to sit across from each other while talking if the chairs are close enough, as they are at the top of the illustration. If the distance separating the chairs is too great for comfortable conversation, as it is at the bottom of this illustration, people will sit beside each other.

other environmental variables, such as room size and function, as well as the social situation may elicit different responses.

The classroom and what happens in it have always been of much interest and concern to administrators, teachers, and parents. New educational techniques, such as modular scheduling and the open classroom, with broadly defined goals of increasing the quality of the educational experience have accelerated this interest substantially. However, not nearly so much attention has been directed toward the contribution of the physical classroom environment to the educational process. More often than not, if the classroom environment is altered in any way, it is altered to promote some behavioral objective —for instance, to increase class discussion. Researchers then are confronted with a host of independent variables. If class discussion is shown to have increased, was it due to the new teaching technique, or was it possibly due to arranging the furnishings in a manner more conducive to student-teacher interaction? Research designed to answer this type of question is rare. However, Sommer (1969) and Richardson (1967) provide some insight into the question of physical classroom conditions and student behavior.

Richardson maintains that the traditional physical arrangement of the classroom—students' desks in straight rows facing the instructor—may not be the best way to encourage student involvement and satisfaction. She cites a number of reasons: (1) Students may not be able to see the instructor or what he is doing because other students may inadvertently block their view. (2) Many students may be so far from the instructor that they feel isolated from the class and its subject matter. (3) Students have difficulty seeing and hearing other students. If a person in the front row answers a question, his voice may not carry to students in the rear. Moreover, it is difficult for the front row student to gauge the class's reaction to his answer. Students in the rear answering a question also cannot see and hear their classmates' reactions. (4) The dominant role of the instructor is accentuated by the use of furniture different from that of the students and by the distance between class and instructor. (5) The row-by-row arrangement inhibits "action" types of lessons.

Richardson offers several alternatives to the traditional classroom furnishings arrangement that would encourage class participation. One suggestion is to arrange desks in one or more circles or semicircles. She also notes that substituting large tables for desks would enhance class unity and cooperation. Although Richardson's opinions were derived from observation and represent no more than anecdotal evidence, her basic ideas are supported by Sommer (1969), who investigated seating arrangements, room properties, and class participation.

Sommer used six rooms in his study. Four of the rooms had the traditional arrangement of straight rows. Two of these rooms were student laboratories containing the usual equipment in addition to the fixed tables. The other two traditional rooms differed in another dimension: One was window-less, and a wall of the other consisted of windows. The remainder were seminar rooms, with tables in a square in one of the rooms and on three sides in the other. Observation of students during regular classes showed that a higher average number of students per session in the straight row arrangements participated in class discussions. However, the absolute number of statements per session was higher for the classes held in the seminar rooms. Sommer also notes that students said that they did not like to have their classes in the laboratories and the windowless room. The results of this investigation suggest that the physical characteristics of a classroom are important determinants of the behavior occurring there.

PERSONAL VARIABLES AND ROOMS

At this point we will shift our emphasis from the physical vari-ables of rooms to properties, or variables, inherent in the persons who use the rooms. Personal factors are important because (1) every individual has these characteristics to some degree and (2) they influence interaction with a room's physical properties as well as with other people in the room.

These personal variables have a number of different sources. A person's attitude about the social and physical function of a room may be the result of past experience in the same or a similar room. For example, Richard-son (1967) reports that an innovative instructor decided to move the tradi-tional straight rows of desks in his classroom into the grouping typical of a seminar room. His secondary level students did not like the new arrangement. Apparently their past experiences with conventional classrooms had formed attitudes about how a classroom should be arranged. The results of the previ-ously discussed study on perceptions of a distorted room also reflect the effect of past associations on an individual's expectations, or set.

An individual's social learning is an equally important determi-nant of his behavior in certain environments and will tend to elicit the behavior that is expected in a particular situation. The discotheque mentioned previ-ously is such a behavior setting, for a person's accumulated knowledge about typical behavior in a discotheque, plus the cues he receives from the environ-ment, determines his behavior there.

Some personal factors, such as the inherent need for privacy, are not so easily influenced by past experience. These are more universal variables that determine certain aspects of social behavior in nearly all socioenvironmen-tal settings. Two of these variables are the need to establish territory and the need to preserve personal space.

PERSONAL SPACE

Personal space can be thought of as an envelope around an individual that forms his portable territory. Personal space is social because its existence can be directly observed only when one person unwittingly or purposefully intrudes into the personal space of another. The phenomenon can easily be seen in many situations. Sommer (1969) uses as an example a city park where a person is seated alone at one end of a bench. Another person approaches the bench and sits down, not at the other end, but in the center. The victim of this circumstance (the one whose personal space has been invaded) will usually change his posture, fidget, or show some other sign of uneasiness. This sort of behavior is a precursor to the victim's moving slightly away from the intruder or possibly leaving the bench altogether. The observer of such a scene may be surprised at the actions of the victim, but if he were in a similar situation, he probably would react in much the same way. The time it takes him to react might, however, be different, depending on his own personal space requirements.

Besides differing among individuals, personal space requirements have been shown to be different across cultures and population subgroups. For example, Horowitz, Duff, and Stratton (1964) explored the possibility that the personal space requirements of "normal" persons are different from those of persons in mental institutions. The mental patients, who were classified as schizophrenics, were asked to approach an object and other persons at three different angles—walking forward, walking backward, and walking sideways. After each subject had stopped moving toward the object or person, the distance between the subject and the object or individual was measured. The same experimental conditions were used for the unhospitalized subjects. The investigators then plotted their data around a drawing of each subject's body. The lines connecting these points were determined to be the boundaries of the subject's zone of personal space. By comparing the average size of these plots for the two groups of subjects, the researchers found that the schizophrenic patients possessed a greater zone of personal space than did the nonpatient subjects.

Many of the ideas that North Americans have about people from other countries or cultures derive from differences in requirements for personal space. The common stereotypes of the aloof Englishman and the pushy or aggressive Latin American may have arisen from North Americans' personal interactions with natives of these countries. For example, a North American may be taken aback when he converses with a Latin American, for the latter's need to be very close to carry on a comfortable conversation may seriously violate the North American's space boundaries. If this situation is repeated a number of times, the North American could easily arrive at the conclusion that Latin Americans are aggressive (Hall, 1966).

Personal space also varies as a function of the social situation. The boundary for close friends is different from that for strangers, as it is for members of the opposite sex and members of the same sex. Requirements for personal space have been shown to vary in crowded situations, although the nature of the crowd may also be of considerable importance. If the reason for the formation of the crowd is a common one—for instance, commuting on the subway or waiting in line—personal boundaries essentially collapse. People accept the situation and stand very close together, showing little discomfort at another individual's being what would otherwise be considered unreasonably close. However, this spatial adaption results in discouraging social interaction among the members of the crowd. When a crowded situation is the result of limited space, the same kind of behavior occurs. In investigations simulating conditions in emergency shelters, for example, the subjects gradually exerted more care in moving about the shelter in addition to moving only when necessary (J. W. Altman, 1960).

Unfortunately, detailed study of personal space must await the development of more sophisticated methods of measurement unless the experimental situation can be highly controlled, as it was in the investigation by Horowitz and his co-workers. In less rigid social situations we can only make inferences from simple observation.

TERRITORIALITY

Another aspect of human spatial behavior, one that is often difficult to separate from maintaining personal space, is territoriality. The relationships between numerous variables and territorial behavior have been reported by I. Altman and co-workers (Altman & Haythorn, 1967; Altman, 1970; Sundstrom & Altman, 1972; Lett, Clark, & Altman, 1969), Esser (1971), and Sommer (1969).

A person delineates a territory by using existing aspects of his environment or by modifying his environment to establish markers or boundaries. These lines of demarcation are understood and respected by other individuals. This behavior is strikingly similar to that of lower animals. Bears, for instance, establish the boundaries of their territory by leaving claw marks on trees. A dog may use his master's fence (a human territorial marker) as his own territorial marker and become aggressive if a stranger comes inside it. Groups of people also establish territories, as is evident in the activities of adolescent gangs in cities.

These examples of territorial behavior involve areas larger than personal space. The importance of every family's having an established territory will be considered in our discussion of housing. However, the study of human territorial behavior in public places, where actual ownership of space is denied, also provides interesting information about the use of the immediate environment to extend personal space.

Sommer (1969) has engaged in considerable research on the defense of personal space and territory under different social and environmental conditions in public libraries. The results of his efforts offer valuable information on library room design and furnishings as well as a better understanding of territorial behavior.

One of Sommer's investigations concerned the seating position people would choose when attempting to maintain an active or a passive defense of the area they were using. The subjects were given diagrams of rectangular tables with three, four, and five chairs to a side. The subjects in the active spatial defense condition were asked, "If you wanted to have the table to yourself, where would you sit to discourage anyone else from occupying it?" [p. 49]. The subjects in the passive spatial defense conditions were asked, "If you wanted to be as far as possible from the distraction of other people, where would you sit at the table?" [p. 49]. These two questions yielded a substantial difference in the seating preferences of the experimental groups. The subjects who were asked the active defense question consistently chose the middle chairs on a side, while those asked the question for a passive defense regularly chose an end chair. Thus, the subjects' choice of seating depended upon their concern for their control over the immediate spatial environment.

Sommer was also interested in whether a person can successfully "defend" an entire room by mere occupancy. He positioned a female student in one of several small rooms in a heavily used refreshment area. Each room contained a number of tables, with four chairs per table. Because of the large number of people in the area, the student was never able to discourage other persons from using the room, although in all but one of the ten experimental sessions she was successful in maintaining her control over the table where she sat. This finding indicates that an individual can successfully defend his immediate physical territory when the number of other people about is low to moderate, but that when the number of people increases, his territory is more likely to be used by others.

Other observations led Sommer to suggest that room shape and size can be important variables in determining defensibility. He states, "Avoidance [passive defense] works best in a room with many corners, alcoves, and side areas hidden from view" [p. 47]. On the other hand, defending an entire irregularly shaped area is more difficult than defending one of regular proportions. Size can also be a handicap; "a large homogeneous area, lacking lines of demarcation, barriers, or obstructions, makes it difficult to mark out and defend individual territories" [p. 51].

The investigations by Sommer and others have shown that different room environments produce different strategies and levels of success in establishing and maintaining control over the immediate environment. This knowledge should prove helpful to planners of rooms where privacy is a consideration.

HOUSING

The logical next level in our discussion of the built environment is housing. Here rooms become components of a larger system and are bound by the system's objectives: providing physical shelter for the family, places for family activities, and psychological shelter from the pressures of the outside world. Each individual dwelling is in turn a component of a larger housing system, whether in a suburban neighborhood or an apartment house.

Houses and housing units are considered to be important factors in the investigation of environment-behavior relationships for reasons ranging from the commercial to the social. Interest in the effects of housing on behavior has grown with the recognition of the tremendous need for new housing to allay current and projected shortages. A conservative estimate is that the nation's current total number of housing units should double by the end of the century. New dwellings of all types will be required: suburban developments to satisfy the demands of the growing middle class, additional public housing projects for the economically deprived, and increased numbers of structures aimed at enticing people to remain in the cities. Spokesmen for the construction industries indicate that it is impossible to meet new housing needs by using conventional methods. Thus, factory-fabricated housing is rapidly expanding to fill the gap left by on-site construction methods. Advocates of both types of construction, however, lack knowledge about the behavioral correlates of present design and construction methods, not to mention the possible influences of new housing concepts on behavior.

For example, an idea that has been considered for military housing is a modular unit consisting of a fiberglass shell, with various plug-in room components to adapt the shell to different size families. Some of the concepts embodied in these units—for instance, the materials used in construction and the shape of the units themselves—are radical departures from those associated with housing construction in the past. Some questions that researchers interested in the environment and behavior might ask are these: Will this home be as satisfactory to the family as one built of more conventional materials? Will typical noise levels be increased or reduced by the new materials and the plug-in components? Will the house's looking virtually identical to every other house in the complex have any behavioral effects? These and other questions need answers before any type of housing is implemented on a large scale.

Equally relevant questions can be raised about the effects of multiple family dwellings on behavior. Such questions are especially important in view of the population growth in our cities coupled with the decrease in available land surrounding them. Moreover, the increasing urban renewal programs involve moving many persons to large housing complexes, which their occupants often dislike and which appear to encourage antisocial behavior. All these considerations should be kept in mind during the following discussion.

SINGLE FAMILY DWELLINGS

Our society places considerable value on living in individual houses, and a major goal of many families is owning their own homes. However, research on the effects of single housing units on their occupants is limited. One of the reasons is that it is hard for the investigator to determine whether the attractiveness of single family housing is due to cultural or social norms or to psychological needs. Another obstacle to determining the aspects of single family dwellings responsible for their inhabitants' satisfaction or dissatisfaction is the relative independence of the population the researcher attempts to study. If a home does not prove satisfactory, the family usually modifies it or moves to another. Thus, the researcher is confronted with a population that is generally satisfied with its existing housing. For these reasons we can make only general statements about some features of the single dwelling that suggest reasons for its appeal.

One primary attribute of the single family dwelling and its environment is the treatment of space. Typically, the family is assured a space where it can engage in activities without interference from neighbors. Although we have little data showing that space other than that within the house itself contributes to resident satisfaction, denial of this type of space has proved to be detrimental to family relations and activities in multiple family dwellings.

Michelson (1970) provides evidence from a survey that desired life style to some extent determines the quest for family space. He notes that a substantial number of families who moved from cities to suburbs indicated that the primary reason for their move was to break away from intense relationships with relatives outside the immediate family. Apparently, these people perceived the suburban single family dwelling environment as a means of changing their emphasis from extended-family to nuclear-family activities. Thus, the space provided by the single family dwelling, as well as the increased distance from their relatives, served as a source of satisfaction with their new life style.

Another factor which may be partly responsible for the choice of single family dwellings is the typical role of the man in the household as keeper of the physical plant and all-around "pioneer" handyman. Evidence for the importance of space to play this role is again provided indirectly by pointing out the negative aspects of multiple family dwellings:

> When a man lives in a multiple dwelling, particularly when he is surrounded on all sides by other tenants, he can't perform any activity which is violent inside his own dwelling without provoking his neighbors—not unless there is adequate soundproofing, an expensive proposition. He can by no means alter the interior of his dwelling to any major extent without typically invoking the wrath of his landlord and probably a lawsuit.
>
> But where else can he perform this role? Private outdoor space provides a suitable outlet. The man who has just completed an active job and stands talking with his neighbor, foot on split-rail fence, is out of the American dream. Yet most multiple dwellings, particularly high rise apartments, have no provision for private open space for such purposes [Michelson, 1970, p. 81].

Michelson also cites Kumove (1966), who conducted a study comparing high rise apartment buildings and town houses. An informal visitor in a high rise generally sees no men about, whereas in town house complexes, where each unit has direct access to ground level, the males are observed to be engaged in a variety of activities, mostly recreational. Kumove felt that these activities help fulfill the man's expected social role.

Although such sociological variables influence choice of a home, more personal variables are also involved. The desire for single family dwellings and the space they provide can be considered to be an extension of the need for territory. The possession of a house and lot can satisfy the need to exert territorial influence. An additional advantage of territorial possession in the form of home ownership may be a reduction in the social tension that can exist when possession of a space is ambiguous, as in the case of public areas used for family activities. This concept is supported to some extent in the previously cited studies by Sommer.

Michelson's study also investigated relationships between individuals' values and their judgments of different types of housing. From the results of a standard inventory designed to determine a person's value structure, Michelson obtained measures of his subjects' instrumentalism, expression, group-indebtedness, individualism, and activity-mindedness. Each of his subjects was then asked to rank photographs of four different types of housing, ranging from a single family house to a high rise apartment, on the same types of value dimensions as were used in the inventory. Each subject was also asked to sketch a map of his ideal environment, including the position of his ideal home in relationship to neighbors' houses and commercial establishments. From these sketches and the responses to the photographs, Michelson attempted to distinguish relationships between the individual's value structure and his housing preference. For instance, if a person valued group activities, which type of housing environment seemed group-minded to him? Although Michelson's overall results were inconclusive, a number of suggested relationships did emerge. In general, the subjects who expressed a desire for large lots in their sketches were high in individualism. Also, the single family dwelling was thought by subjects to be highly related to the pursuit of family activities, much more so than any of the other housing types presented. Moreover, regardless of whether the subjects expressed a desire for a large or a small lot in their sketches, they consistently stressed that the purpose of the lot was to provide for family and individual activities they felt could not be undertaken in a public area. The findings of this investigation provide some indication of the importance of single family housing and the kinds of behavior that its space fosters.

Environments of Single Family Dwellings and Social Behavior

In this section we expand our discussion to the residential areas that are made up of varying numbers of single family dwellings. These areas are much smaller than what could be considered a suburb or an urban neighborhood, which are discussed in a later chapter. The present discussion focuses on the role that the physical properties of a residential environment play in determining social interaction among the people who live there.

One aspect of the residential environment that affects behavior is socioeconomic. The planners and builders of a particular development often purposely minimize cost variation from dwelling to dwelling. The result of this practice is that the families who live there are fairly homogeneous in income, social and educational background, and occupational status, and they generally have compatible, if not similar, interests. Although the overall behavioral ramifications of this fact are sociological and beyond the scope of this text, that socioeconomic factors exist in any housing area should be kept in mind while examining the physical aspects of these environments that also influence behaviors.

Two primary features of residential environments shown to affect behavior are spatial: *distance between houses* and *relative locations of houses.* A number of investigators have studied the relationship between residence proximity and the social relations of the occupants. An early study by Festinger, Schachter, and Back (1950) surveyed friendship patterns of students in a university housing project consisting of single family detached homes grouped around public yards. The study revealed a direct relationship between interhouse distance and friendship. In general, families were more likely to establish social contact with others living in the same residential grouping. Moreover, the probability of friendship tended to increase as the distance between houses located in the same courtyard decreased. The authors point out, however, that the relationships revealed in their investigation may be due to social homogeneity.

Taking this factor into consideration, Yoshioka and Athanasiou (1971) interviewed 300 residents of single family dwellings who lived in a variety of differently planned sites. The subjects varied considerably in income and occupation, so that any relationships discovered between the residential environment and social behavior could be interpreted with more confidence than was the case in the study by Festinger and his co-workers. The subjects were asked about their family's life styles, attitudes, and social, educational, and occupational backgrounds. Each subject was also asked to draw a map of his residential area, including the location of friends whom he saw on a regular or an occasional basis.

Among the number of relationships discovered was that the distances to friends' homes were a function of the particular site plan. Generally, the families living on culs-de-sac, or dead end streets, lived closer to their friends than did the subjects living on through streets. The authors suggest that two features of residential arrangement may contribute to this pattern of social interaction. The first is that the lower population density of the through street may require its residents to travel further to satisfy their needs for social interaction. The second suggestion is that a main street may act as a barrier to social contact, whereas a cul-de-sac does not.

Other investigators provide evidence of yet another feature of the residential environment that influences social behavior: door placement. Caplow and Forman (1950), in a study of university housing, observed that friendships were likely to develop among residents whose doors opened onto a common sidewalk. This finding held even for doors that were closer together but opened onto different sidewalks. Thus, the orientation of the doors, in addition to the shared public space, was shown to affect friendship patterns.

One of the most significant studies of residential environment and behavior is presented by Whyte (1956), who conducted a survey of part of a new, fast-growing suburb south of Chicago. The residents of this suburb were generally homogeneous; most were young, in managerial or professional positions, and quite mobile in both social status and location of residence. Thus, the suburb was subject to substantial annual turnover in residents. Whyte was interested in whether certain social activities were related to the locations of houses with respect to one another or to characteristics of the residents. He found, as might be expected from the research previously discussed, that people living close to one another engaged in the same social activities. For example, people who lived next door to each other or across the street from one another met regularly to play bridge. Three years later Whyte returned to the area and again surveyed the residents. He found that although many of the families had moved and the nature of some activities had changed, by and large the residents in the same houses or locations were still involved socially regardless of the identity of the people there at the time. Whyte concluded that house-to-house distance and orientation of houses influenced significantly the retention of social interaction patterns even when the individuals involved had changed.

From the research thus far discussed, we have obtained an idea of the important environmental features of the single family unit, particularly the space it provides for private family activities and its fulfillment of the territorial need. The results of these studies have also shown the importance of interhouse distance, relative locations of houses, and orientation of doors in determining friendship formation and social interaction. Much of the research also reveals that the residents are highly satisfied with their housing.

Although the same concepts of privacy, space, residence arrangement, and dwelling component orientation have been considered in research on multiple family dwellings, the results often reveal resident dissatisfaction or antisocial behavior. Before discussing the possible reasons for the differences reported in resident satisfaction and behavior between single and multiple family dwellings, however, one important point should be noted. The socioeconomic status of residents of single family dwellings is often vastly different from that of residents of multifamily housing. The typical subjects of studies on the multifamily dwelling live in public housing projects. These people are usually economically deprived, often exposed to racial or ethnic prejudice, and generally live in such places out of necessity, not choice. Undoubtedly, these factors, as well as the physical aspects of the environment, significantly influence behavior.

MULTIPLE FAMILY DWELLINGS

Multiple family dwellings allot, of course, less land area for each family than do single family dwellings. Whether the family has access to a private land area for family activities depends on the type of multiple dwelling. In any event, they are almost certain to be closer to their neighbors than are people living in single family dwellings. Another feature of multiple family dwellings is the sharing of walls, ceilings, and floors. The number of shared partitions increases from single walls in garden apartments and town houses to walls, floors, and ceilings in walk-up and high rise apartment buildings. Clearly, as the number of common partitions increases, privacy decreases.

Lack of privacy is heavily emphasized in a report by Kuper (1953), who conducted an extensive survey of Braydon Road, a housing complex in Coventry, England. Built in the late 1940s of prefabricated steel, the semidetached units were based on a standard plan employing both through streets and culs-de-sac. Figures 2-3, 2-4, and 2-5 show the interior arrangement, the orientation of units, and the entire complex. As can be seen from these illustrations, the physical relationships within, between, and among the housing units, in addition to the unusual structural material, provided Kuper with a host of environmental features potentially affecting behavior.

One of the major sources of dissatisfaction on the part of the residents was a pronounced lack of privacy. The common walls between units resulted in nearly constant annoyance of each family by the other. Because both living areas shared the partition, much of the activity of one family in their living room was heard by the other family and vice versa, whether the noise was a result of daily routines or of boisterous celebrations. This infringement of privacy also existed at a more personal level, because the units shared bedroom walls as well. Many residents expressed embarrassment at being able to overhear clearly what they considered private conversations and activities. Since the residents were aware of the problem, most attempted to keep noise at a minimum. However, doing so often meant curtailing the normal play of children, keeping radios, televisions, and musical instruments very low, and hurrying through daily cleaning chores if the neighbor was asleep. Kuper expresses concern about the possible long-term effects of such enforced behavior on the development of healthy intrafamily relations.

Invasion of privacy was not restricted to the auditory dimension in Braydon Road. The arrangement of the doors between the buildings pro-

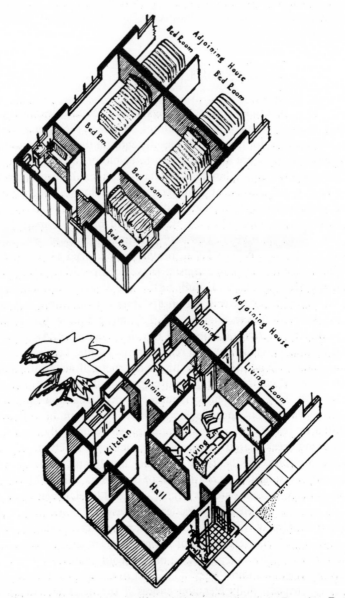

Figure 2-3. The first and second floors of a unit in Braydon Road.
Common partitions can be a source of annoyance between neighbors.
From *Living in Towns,* Leo Kuper (Ed.). Copyright 1953 by The Cresset
Press. Reprinted with permission of the publisher, Barrie & Jenkins,
Ltd., London.

voked considerable annoyance in a number of residents. Although the arrangement of the side doors encouraged social relations between residents of the units, a resident of one unit could easily see into the next if both doors were open. Even more detrimental to privacy was the arrangement of the buildings in the culs-de-sac. Anyone entering or leaving any dwelling could be seen by others. Residents also stated that it was difficult to look out their living room

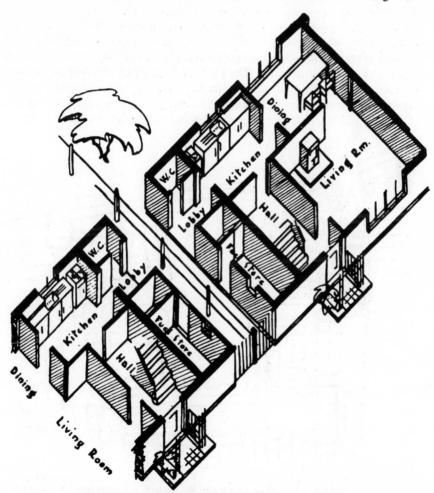

Figure 2-4.   The first floor of two adjacent units in Braydon Road. The short distance between the lobbies provides for intense social relationships, either positive or negative. From *Living in Towns,* Leo Kuper (Ed.). Copyright 1953 by The Cresset Press. Reprinted with permission of the publisher, Barrie & Jenkins, Ltd., London.

or bedroom window without inadvertently looking into the units across the court.

Another fault cited was the fences between the backyards and gardens of each dwelling. Solid fences would have ensured each family considerable privacy in their yards, but these fences were little more than symbolic, consisting of only wires. In brief, privacy in Braydon Road was highly desired but scarce.

If we were to rely on the previously cited research findings on single family dwellings, we would assume that a number of environmental features of the Braydon Road complex were conducive to friendship formation and healthy social interaction. The placement of doors, the culs-de-sac, and the informal lines of demarcation in the backyards all increased visual contact between residents, which is assumed by some to increase social interaction (Michelson, 1970). However, Kuper notes that although the neighbors with a

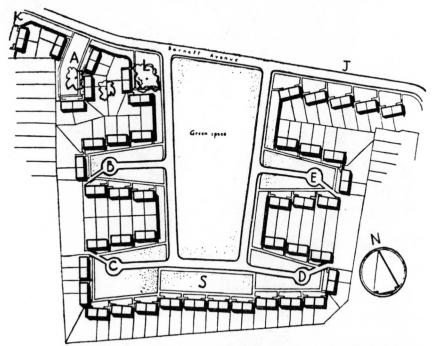

Figure 2-5.   Diagram of the Braydon Road complex. The cul-de-sac arrangements of B, C, D, and E provide an opportunity for increased social interaction but also allow for visual invasion of privacy. From *Living in Towns,* Leo Kuper (Ed.). Copyright 1953 by The Cresset Press. Reprinted with permission of the publisher, Barrie & Jenkins, Ltd., London.

common wall were physically closest, he observed very little social interaction between sets of these neighbors. One reason for this situation may be the considerable involuntary contact between the sets of neighbors, which can result in mutual avoidance. Another possible reason is the orientation of the doors of each unit. As can be seen in Figure 2-4, the main entrances to the two units in each building are at opposite ends of the structure. In terms of social interaction, this distance (referred to by some investigators as the *functional distance*) is actually much greater than the physical distance separating the two apartments. Even if the mutual violation of privacy is ignored, this feature of the environment would tend to discourage social interaction within the buildings. On the other hand, this same arrangement of side doors provides for maximum neighbor contact *between* the structures. However, depending upon the nature of the relationship between the neighbors, this door placement could encourage either friendly conversation or hostile confrontation. Kuper observed both kinds of behavior at Braydon Road.

Behavior in Public Housing

As mentioned previously, the occupants of public housing complexes typically are more handicapped socially and economically than are residents of other types of dwellings. A substantial number of persons living in public housing projects are welfare recipients. Absent fathers are common, so that many mothers must sacrifice full-time supervision of their children to earning a living. Many projects are managed by whites, though the tenants are nonwhites, a situation that contributes to racial tensions.

Another factor that may have an undesirable effect on behavior is that public housing is generally constructed with one objective: providing low cost accommodations for the maximum number of families. Consequently, to the builder space is usually at a premium, both within the buildings and around them. This strictly budgeted, high density housing environment combines with the characteristics of the project's residents to produce a setting unparalleled for adverse reactions.

As will be discussed in a later chapter, residents of slums often staunchly defend them as suitable places to live, yet urban renewal programs have often resulted in razing slums and erecting housing projects in their place. A critical question is whether the public housing projects provide more satisfaction to the residents than did the slum neighborhoods. Generally, the reverse has been found to be true.

Lewis (1970) provides an account of an interview with a woman who had moved from a slum neighborhood to public housing at the suggestion of her social worker. Although the subject indicated overall satisfaction with her apartment, she expressed distaste for other people living in the project, fear for her children's safety, desire for the informal interaction of the old slum, and general regret at having moved.

More objective accounts of resident surveys are presented by Yancey (1972) and Hollingshead and Rogler (1963). Yancey reports the results of a survey querying residents of Pruitt-Igoe, a large public housing project in St. Louis, and residents of a nearby slum about their satisfaction with various aspects of their environments. Seventy-eight percent of the Pruitt-Igoe residents indicated general satisfaction with their apartments, while 55 percent of the slum dwellers felt the same about their dwellings. However, when asked if they were satisfied with the neighborhood, 74 percent of the slum residents answered affirmatively, in contrast to 53 percent of the Pruitt-Igoe residents. The reasons most often cited for dissatisfaction in the public housing complex were inability to survey children's activities, mistrust of others in the building, and fear of being assaulted or robbed outside the apartment.

Hollingshead and Rogler's findings support those of Yancey. Comparing slums and public housing in Puerto Rico, they found that 7 percent of the men in public housing felt that it was a suitable location for raising a family, while 38 percent of the slum dwellers stated that their area was adequate for this purpose. The proportion of public housing residents expressing overall satisfaction with their situation was approximately 25 percent, in contrast to over 60 percent of the slum residents. These are typical findings of research on resident satisfaction with public housing.

According to current research, the physical design of public housing is a major contributor to resident dissatisfaction. This conclusion is based on two factors. The first is that the physical characteristics of the buildings do not foster either social relations among the residents or normal family activities —children's play, for example. The second factor is a result of the first: Because of the inadvertent discouragement of informal group relationships by the design process, certain types of public housing promote a disproportionate amount of undesirable behavior. The remainder of the chapter will center on the research support for this conclusion.

A typical structure in public housing is the high rise apartment building. This type of structure appears to have the largest number of design features that produce resident dissatisfaction and fear. One of these features is the height of the building itself. Mothers of children in high rises are quick to express concern about their lack of control over their children's whereabouts and activities. (See Figure 2-6.) Yancey (1972) relates one mother's answer to questions about her satisfaction with living in a high rise:

Figure 2-6. According to mothers living in multistory apartment buildings, the situation in the top photograph is much preferred for the supervision of children's play. Photos by Sam Sprague and John Tesnow.

"Well, I don't like being upstairs like this. The problem is that
I can't see the kids. They're just too far away. If one of them gets
hurt, needs to go to the bathroom, or anything, it's just too far
away. And you can't see outside. We don't have any porches"
[p. 131].

Hall (1959) supplies a similar comment from another high rise resident: " 'It's
no place to raise a family. A mother can't look out for kids if they are fifteen
floors down in the playground' " [p. 159]. The results of a survey by Kumove
(1966) suggest that the problem of control in high rises over a child's activities
increases with the child's age. He observed that after the age of 7, children
living in high rises tend to spend much more time outdoors than do their
counterparts living in single family dwellings.

An indirect result of rearing families in high rises is the mother's
reduced opportunities for social interaction. If, for example, the family has a
young child, his play will be restricted to the apartment rather than to an
enclosed yard of a single family dwelling, where the mother has more opportunity for informal contact with neighbors. Similarly, if the mother is occupied
in the apartment, she will not go down to ground level to supervise her older
children's play. Thus, the mothers in two adjacent apartments are denied the
opportunity for social interaction by the greater functional distance involved.

We have already pointed out that designers of public housing
units are forced to use the space as economically as possible. This emphasis
often results in the double loaded corridor, a straight hallway with apartments
on both sides. This corridor is considered by residents and administrators alike
to be public space, since many persons must use it to reach their apartments.
Thus, because of the traffic in the rather limited space and the implied function
of the hallway (if a resident is in it, he should be going somewhere), informal
social interaction is unlikely to occur there. Another disadvantage of this type
of corridor is the lack of symbolic or physical boundaries to act as territorial
markers for individual or small groups of apartments.

Two final features of high rises and their surroundings are also
thought to weaken the resident's social cohesion. One is that the typical high
rise building has stairways to satisfy fire regulations as well as a central
elevator. Thus, residents can enter or leave at a number of different points, and
this lack of a common entrance reduces social interaction. The second feature
is that the buildings often have large open spaces between them. The frequent
lack of fences or walls there serves to discourage residents from engaging in
activities within the boundaries of their building's territory.

However, a more serious behavioral result of the physical features
mentioned above is crime. In discussing this problem, Newman (1973a, 1973b)
presents the concept of *defensible space,* defined as:

a term for the range of mechanisms—real and symbolic barriers, strongly defined areas of influence, and improved opportunities for surveillance—that combine to bring an environment under the control of its residents. A defensible space is a living residential environment that can enhance the inhabitants' lives while providing security for their families, neighbors, and friends [1973b, p. 57].

Newman implies that the provision of defensible space fulfills two objectives that may in turn discourage criminal behavior. First, defensible space encourages social interaction, which hopefully promotes feelings of group cohesion, resulting in mutual aid by group members. Second, it provides for increased visual contact or surveillance, both informally by residents and formally by members of policing units.

Another physical feature of public housing that has been shown to have a significant relation to the incidence of crime is building height. From data on crime occurrence in New York City's public housing, Newman (1973a) reports substantial differences in crime rates between buildings of six stories or fewer and those of seven stories or more. In projects involving structures with six stories or fewer, the crime rate was approximately 46 per 1000 dwelling units, whereas the rate was approximately 59 per 1000 dwelling units in projects with higher buildings. An analysis of the felonies committed in or near the buildings of the projects revealed an equally dramatic difference. Figure 2-7 shows the felony rate for four different categories of building height. The rate for buildings in the shortest category (two or three stories) was about half that for buildings in the tallest category (16 stories or more).

Newman points out a number of factors that can account for the increased crime in high rise buildings. One is the number of persons living in each of the building types. By nature the larger building contains more people, thereby resulting in more anonymity. It is difficult for residents of a high rise to identify another person as a resident of the building.

Another factor is stairwells and elevators. Larger buildings have more of each than do shorter structures. As might be expected, Newman found a direct relationship between building height and crime rate when crimes committed in elevators were given separate consideration. Newman's defensible space hypothesis may explain why these differences exist. In most public housing the stairs are closed off from the hallways, thus eliminating not only any claims of territory by the residents of the nearby apartments but also the opportunity for informal surveillance. Consequently, stairways are notorious for the frequency of criminal acts. This situation is also noted by Yancey (1972), who relates that the residents of high rises in his study expressed great fear of using the stairways. Even more obvious, however, is the privacy afforded an offender in a closed elevator.

Another physical feature of public housing discussed by Newman is hall size. Recall that a common occurrence in public housing units is the double loaded corridor, which may serve as many as 20 families. Newman hypothesized that halls serving small numbers of apartments would tend to inhibit criminal behavior because of possible increased informal surveillance and the establishment of territorial behavior. Conversely, the absence of these kinds of behavior in larger halls would increase crime. This hypothesis is supported when crime rates are computed for different types of hallways; less crime is reported to occur in halls leading to five or fewer apartments.

Newman suggests that large projects (those containing 1000 dwelling units or more) composed of high rises were found to have the worst overall crime rate not only because of the problems of the structures themselves but also because of project layout. High rises require, of course, much

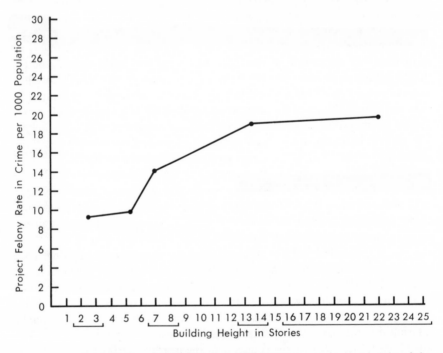

Figure 2-7. Felony rate in public housing projects and height of the buildings in the projects. From O. Newman, *Architectural Design for Crime Prevention.* Washington, D.C.: National Institute of Law Enforcement and Criminal Justice, U.S. Department of Justice, 1973.

less land than do lower buildings to provide the same number of dwelling units. Consequently, high rise projects often have large open areas between the buildings. These areas are not easily observed by the buildings' residents, and they usually feel no particular attachment to the grounds. Lower buildings, on the other hand, are thought to better define areas of informal resident control and promote feelings in the residents of responsibility for particular territories around their buildings.

Unfortunately, more complete treatment of the research reported by Newman is beyond the scope of this book. However, the points discussed here indicate the role that aspects of the physical environment can play in fostering or inhibiting certain kinds of behavior.

CHAPTER THREE

THE BUILT
ENVIRONMENT: BUILDINGS
AND SOCIAL INSTITUTIONS

In our earlier discussions of built environmental systems, we stressed the importance of a system's function in determining the major physical features of structures. In this chapter, function again determines the characteristics of built structures as well as the behavior that occurs in them. However, we will deal here with built environments designed for occupational and service-related activities or for the modification of behavior. These different functions result in a number of differences between the characteristics of these systems and those of the systems discussed previously.

One major difference is the number of persons involved. In Chapter 2 we were concerned primarily with the environmentally influenced behavior of individuals and families. Structures such as offices and hospitals typically contain more persons interacting to accomplish a general objective, whether the management of business affairs or the provision of health care to a large number of patients. Such common objectives do not exist in public housing projects, which may contain more people; the residents have no binding common interest aside from involvement in their own families. Large numbers of individuals are also brought together to achieve a common purpose in the environmental systems constructed to produce behavioral change in certain segments of the population—those in penal institutions and mental hospitals, for example. Obviously, the functions of these institutions are important determinants of the physical features incorporated in any given structure.

A second difference between the built environments discussed in this chapter and those considered earlier is the types of behavior of interest to the researcher and his reasons for studying them. For example, wall color in an office is likely to be an important independent variable to consider. Although the researcher may be interested in the overall aesthetic appeal of a particular color layout to employees, he is more likely to be concerned with its effect on job performance. Moreover, the kinds of behavior that would give him information on aesthetic satisfaction and job efficiency would differ markedly. In a hospital, however, color is likely to be considered aesthetically for its contributions to a pleasant atmosphere and the alleviation of unnecessary patient discomfort and dissatisfaction. In penal institutions color may be used to provide inmates with a source of environmental variety.

The last difference has to do with the variety of persons involved in these larger systems and their varying needs in a particular structure. The two major factions in the systems discussed in this chapter are clients, patients, or inmates and staff or employees. The needs of these two factions are often nearly opposite. Moreover, different segments of the same faction may have different needs.

Thus, a particular system is designed to support persons engaged in fulfilling the system's objectives. The extent to which these efforts have been successful and the physical features that have proved important in determining success or failure are the topics of this chapter.

OFFICES

Typically, behavior in offices is geared toward one purpose—maximum output within reasonable cost limitations. To make achieving this goal possible, the designer of an office building must provide for, among other considerations, optimal communication between departments, work flow within and between various groups, supervisor-subordinate relationships, and allocation of jobs between men and machines. An integral part of these considerations is the continuous provision for individual worker efficiency, whether he is a clerk or an executive.

Factors important for maximum individual efficiency are job design, adequate training, and effective employee-task matching. These factors have received considerable research attention and management interest for many years. Until recently, however, the relationships between the physical features of office environments and job performance have received comparatively little attention from researchers. The reason may be that if the other factors mentioned have been provided for, the physical environment may have so little effect on job performance that its consideration is not economically feasible. Nonetheless, the small but growing body of research on office equipment and accommodations, ambient conditions, office layout, and general employee satisfaction suggests that these factors deserve further research and design emphasis.

FURNISHINGS AND ARRANGEMENTS

The immediate office environment of an employee often consists of a desk, chair, typing table and typewriter, and possibly a more specialized piece of furniture or equipment, such as a drafting table or a computer card punch machine. Because the employee presumably spends most of his time here, it would seem reasonable to study the effect of the equipment design and arrangement on comfort and efficiency.

For a number of years, investigators in the field of ergonomics, the study of human performance in work situations, have collected data and formulated standards on the acceptable dimensions for desks, chairs, and other office equipment. These standards are based on measurements taken from several thousand men and women to determine, for instance, how far from the floor a chair's seat can be and still permit the average person's feet to touch the floor. These standards are useful only in preventing unnecessary gross bodily movements and positioning resulting in fatigue, inconvenience, or injury. More recent investigations have included an additional furnishing design consideration, that of comfort. Grandjean, Hunting, Wotzka, and Scharer (1973) had 50 judges evaluate 12 different chairs of the types used for general seating in offices for various aspects of comfort. The rating method was paired comparisons in which each chair was compared for comfort with every other chair. The judge rated each chair on how comfortable it felt to the neck, shoulders, back, legs, and arms while leaning forward and while sitting back in the chair. The investigators also took detailed measurements of each chair's seating angle, width, height, and curvature and noted the type of chair and its upholstery. From the judges' ratings the researchers determined what features contributed to maximum comfort and incorporated these features into one design recommendation, shown in Figure 3-1. If the designers and suppliers of office equipment use these types of standards for furniture dimensions and comfort, they may improve worker efficiency.

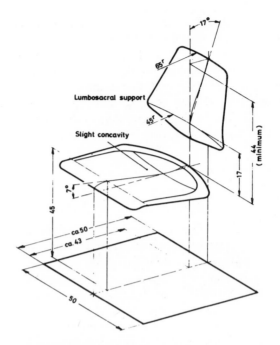

All measurements in cm.

Figure 3-1.   The use of design recommendations for office furnishings as illustrated in the figure can contribute to increased employee comfort and efficiency.. From E. Grandjean, W. Hunting, G. Wotzka, & R. Scharer. An ergonomic investigation of multipurpose chairs. *Human Factors,* 1973, **15**(3), 247–255. Reprinted by permission of the Human Factors Society.

Another factor in the individual's immediate work environment is the arrangement of furnishings. Although furnishing arrangement has remained much the same, it has been proposed that different arrangements can facilitate different work activities and consequently enhance overall efficiency. Propst (1966) designed an office that he labeled the "Action Office," whose furnishings and arrangement he considered conducive to better efficiency, alertness, and creativity. Figures 3-2, 3-3, and 3-4 present examples of offices that he thought appropriate for a plant manager, a research specialist, and a physician.

Fucigna (1967) attempted to evaluate the effectiveness of the Action Office. As Fucigna points out, among the number of features of the Action Office that are thought to induce maximum performance are these:

Figure 3-2.   An Action Office for a plant manager. From Robert L. Propst. The Action Office. *Human Factors,* 1966, **8**(4), 299–306. Reprinted by permission of the Human Factors Society.

Figure 3-3.   An Action Office for a research specialist. From Robert L. Propst. The Action Office. *Human Factors,* 1966, **8**(4), 299–306. Reprinted by permission of the Human Factors Society.

Figure 3-4. An Action Office for a physician. From Robert L. Propst. The Action Office. *Human Factors,* 1966, **8**(4), 299–306. Reprinted by permission of the Human Factors Society.

1. Both a sit-down and a stand-up work surface to give relief from the seated position.
2. File wells at the rear of desks as well as flip-up display panels to facilitate storage and retrieval of information.
3. Roll-top desks and flip-down panels to provide privacy of information. These also keep work surfaces neat.
4. A communications center, with a phone, dictation equipment, and so forth.
5. A variety of information racks for coded data folders to be reviewed. Portable box drawers, shelves, and bins limit blind accumulation [p. 593].

Fucigna's criterion for evaluation of the Action Office was the degree to which it facilitated activities assumed to be important in planning and decision making. He suggests that a process like that described below is involved in planning and decision making.

From information *received,* the individual *determines* that a decision must be made. He then *identifies* the information necessary for an effective decision. The next step is *retrieval* of the information from various sources and by various means and temporary *storage* of some of it until all the pertinent facts have been collected.

The information is then *processed,* which may include discussions with other personnel, reading, writing, modifying the information, comparing it, and so forth. This step may, of course, take a long time, so again *storage* and *retrieval* may be involved. Finally, the information is put into suitable form for making a *decision* and taking appropriate *action.*

To evaluate the Action Office, Fucigna asked office workers to keep logs of the time spent on each of the above activities, the work station used, the data used, the location of the data, and the involvement of other individuals. The workers were observed for one month in their conventional offices, given time to adjust to the Action Office, and then studied in the Action Office condition.

No differences between the two office layouts were found in the percentages of time spent on each activity (reading, writing, visiting, storing and retrieving information, and so on). Analysis of conferences and phone calls revealed that in the Action Office they were fewer but lasted longer. The presumed reason is that more information was readily available in the Action Office, so that the worker accomplished in one conference or phone call what might have taken more in a conventional office. Although efficiency did not improve, many subjects said that they liked the Action Office organization, information availability, neatness, and physical convenience. Fucigna concludes that, although the structure of the office did not affect activities, the workers' perception of the Action Office as more efficient and convenient should not be ignored.

AMBIENT ENVIRONMENT

Another factor that can affect behavior in offices is ambient environmental conditions. Temperature, humidity, illumination, and noise can produce comfort or annoyance, thus affecting performance. These behavioral effects may be either a direct or an indirect function of some ambient condition. For example, inadequate light may directly affect the efficiency of an office worker engaged in a demanding visual task. If, however, planning for noise reduction was inadequate, one worker may be annoyed and distracted by a conversation between two fellow workers. The noise thus affects not only the worker's emotional state but also his efficiency. This effect is indirect, the result of an interaction between a physical feature of the office environment and the people in the office.

Providing for at least satisfactory ambient conditions may seem relatively simple, but that impression is erroneous. One reason is that some individuals' preferences in ambient conditions may be different from those of other people. These sets of physical and psychological needs, coupled with the constraints of actual office design, interact with ambient conditions to produce unique behavioral situations in the office setting.

Relatively little attention has been paid to the effect of temperature in offices on employee behavior. Surveys (Manning, 1965; Nemecek and Grandjean, 1973) have shown that office temperatures are generally comfortable. Nemecek and Grandjean measured the temperatures in several large Swiss office buildings and obtained employees' attitudes on the best temperature. The majority of the temperatures measured (from 71 degrees F to 75 degrees F) were within the range that the employees considered acceptable. They did think, however, that anything above 75 degrees was too warm. Both surveys report some dissatisfaction among the employees with the air-conditioning systems. Although the temperatures supplied by the systems were satisfactory, complaints about the drafts caused by the systems were frequent even though in some cases measurements by the investigators indicated that air movement was within the range of comfort. Other complaints were directed at the great difference between indoor and outdoor temperatures in summer and the necessity of keeping windows closed during the warmer months. The attitudes expressed in these surveys can be considered to be behavioral states. Unfortunately, however, nothing can be said about the effects of these dimensions of ambient conditions on employee efficiency because no performance measures were taken.

The question of light in office environments has resulted in some controversy even though standards for light levels and the amount of glare (light reflected from work surfaces, walls, and ceilings) are well established and can be met in any office. The argument is over whether the light should be natural or artificial. The results of one investigation (Wells, 1965) suggest that light obtained from windows is considered an important office feature by employees. Wells obtained estimates from personnel in a large office building of what percentage of the light available at their desks was supplied through the windows. He discovered that the further people were seated from the windows, the more they tended to overestimate the proportion of daylight available to them. Wells also notes that when the subjects were questioned about the quality of daylight compared to that of artificial light, nearly 70 percent stated that daylight was better to work by than artificial light.

This concern for daylight in an office seems to have little to do with actual lighting conditions; it appears to be a function of a psychological desire for windows. Wells reports that almost nine out of ten persons in the offices felt it important that they be allowed to look out of a building regardless of the quality of artificial light. Manning (1965) provides anecdotal evidence obtained from interviews that people do not necessarily want a pleasant view —merely the opportunity to see out.

The apparent need for windows in offices is not particularly surprising. Recall from the previous chapter that the students in the Sommer study did not like the windowless room. Moreover, large buildings almost always have windows even though they are expensive and make insulation and ventilation more difficult than in windowless buildings. Thus, cost reduction is often sacrificed to the common need for windows to look out of. This design decision is, of course, a marked contrast to many other decisions we have encountered in our discussions of the built environment.

Our discussion of noise as an independent variable in the office environment must begin with a qualification. The majority of recent research on office environments that includes noise aspects has been conducted in large open plan offices. These offices are quite different from the small, more personal types having only a few occupants. The characteristics of open plan offices probably determine the types of sounds that are ultimately labeled noise and whether these noises are considered disturbing. The same sounds may not be disturbing (or may be more disturbing) in small offices. This qualification should be kept in mind during our discussion.

Two major facts emerge from the investigations of noise in large offices. The first is that, generally, noise levels are very close to being within acceptable standards in the offices studied. In their survey of several large offices, Nemecek and Grandjean (1973) report background noise levels ranging from 47 to 52 decibels, with the highest noise levels (defined as "frequent peaks" in noise level) reaching from 56 to 64 decibels. These levels are well within the limits considered acceptable by design engineers. Yet when employees were asked whether they were disturbed by noise in these offices, 35 percent indicated that they were "greatly" disturbed by noise, with an additional 45 percent stating that they were slightly disturbed by noise of various types. When these people were further questioned about the specific source of their complaint, nearly half listed conversation as the primary offender and specified that content, not loudness, was the disturbing factor. This contention is a rather surprising contrast to the usual listed sources of office noise— typewriters, key punches, telephones, and so on. The reasons will become more apparent as we discuss the concept of large open plan offices.

THE LANDSCAPE OFFICE

A large office with an open plan design typically consists of one entire floor that has no internal floor-to-ceiling partitions. This type of office may encompass an area the size of a football field or larger, and its occupants may range from clerks to vice presidents. This kind of physical layout has the economic advantages of flexibility, low maintenance, and low initial cost. Moreover, the open plan office is thought to facilitate interdepartment communication and intradepartment work flow. Finally, the open plan office is claimed to have social and psychological advantages. Feelings of large group cohesiveness are supposed to develop due to the lack of walls between managers, supervisors, and clerks, in addition to retaining small group cooperation by the provision of low (36 to 48 inches) barriers between defined work groups. Also, the landscape office design is said to provide greater opportunity for an aesthetically pleasing environment because the designer can use planters as dividers and has greater latitude in color schemes. Thus, besides being economical, the large open plan office implies behavioral advantages in both job-related activities and feelings of well-being and aesthetic satisfaction on the part of all employees.

Because the open plan office is a relatively new concept in the design of office environments, the success of such offices in achieving these behavioral objectives has not been extensively researched. However, two recent investigations have attempted to provide information about the effects of these offices on job-related and personal behavior.

Brookes and Kaplan (1972) present a relatively rare type of environmental investigation: a before-and-after comparative evaluation. Their study involved evaluations by workers of an old-style office layout and its replacement, a landscape office. Initially, the subjects completed adjective rating scales on the old-style office and on what they considered an ideal office environment. The scales were constructed so that information could be obtained on a number of factors deemed important in assessing the quality of the office environment—for example, functionality, privacy, sociability, and aesthetics. These data were used as suggestions for the design of the new accommodations. After a time in the new office, the employees again evaluated their office design on the adjective rating scales and were also personally interviewed.

The comparisons of the ratings of the old office and those of the new revealed some rather surprising findings. Most surprising was that the landscape design was not judged to be any more functional or efficient than the old arrangement. On a more personal level, the majority of employees stated that privacy had declined on both visual and acoustic dimensions; noise of conversations was frequently cited as being annoying, and the new open arrangement was judged to substantially reduce privacy and security. On the other hand, the employees generally judged their new office as being more conducive to social relations and as having more aesthetic appeal than the old.

However, the increase in group cohesiveness resulting from the improved sociability was not found to increase efficiency.

Nemecek and Grandjean (1973), in their survey of offices in Switzerland, gave several hundred employees in 15 open plan offices questionnaires probing their attitudes about their working conditions. The results of the questionnaires reveal that the large offices involved in the survey had both advantages and disadvantages. Most frequently cited as major disadvantages were difficulty in concentrating on work and disruptions in confidential conversations. When questioned on their ability to concentrate in these offices compared to the offices they had previously occupied, over half the respondents indicated that concentration in the large offices was more difficult. However, this response was found to be a function of the number of people present in the old offices. Persons who had previously worked alone or with few people were the most disturbed by the open plan surroundings. The reasons for the disturbance (office machines, telephones, office traffic) suggest that these persons were more distracted from their work than hindered because of lack of privacy. The feeling of invasion of privacy was reflected more in the responses of management personnel, who felt that their confidential conversations could be overheard and so felt somewhat hindered in the performance of their roles.

On the positive side, employees in the lower occupational roles indicated that the open plan offices promoted more social activity than did the old arrangements. Management personnel indicated that job-related communication improved. Averaged over all job classifications, 63 percent of the respondents felt that their work was accomplished with less effort and more efficiency. This finding is important from the standpoint of the workers' attitudes toward their jobs. One might speculate that a feeling of improved efficiency would promote greater satisfaction. However, this possibility remains to be empirically tested. One final note about employee attitudes toward the open plan offices is that the majority of the persons initially dissatisfied with the offices stated that they had adjusted to their new working environments enough to feel general satisfaction with them.

HOSPITALS

The hospital has long been regarded as an institution in its own right. So firmly established and standard is its image that the mention of the word "hospital" conjures up a picture of a not particularly beautiful building with long hallways, green-tiled operating rooms, gleaming utensils, and bustling white uniforms where health care is provided. Even though the hospital is so standardized in its image and activities, it is still of interest to an environmental psychologist because it offers innumerable opportunities to study man-environment interactions.

Many of the activities in a hospital are highly specialized, requiring great amounts of skill and planning. An obvious example of such an activity is an extensive surgical procedure, such as a major organ transplant. Here the duties of many persons must be performed and coordinated with a high degree of precision if the venture is to be successful. Stringent demands are also placed on the operating room environment and its various components to provide maximum support. Thus, reliability and efficiency are of prime importance in the design of hospital environments.

A second aspect of the hospital setting is the variety of people there—patients, medical staff, administrative and maintenance personnel, visitors. Each of these categories makes different demands on hospital environmental features. Moreover, each category can be subdivided. For example, the two categories of patients and staff can be divided depending on patient age, type of illness or injury, specialties of the physicians, roles of the nurses, and so on. Similarly, each subcategory of patient or staff may have environmental needs in the stages of diagnosis, treatment, and convalescence different from those of the other subcategories. As will be seen, these needs frequently conflict, resulting in stressful situations for one or more of the people involved.

A prevalent practice in hospital design has been to attempt to maximize medical personnel efficiency by manipulating the environment. Implied in this effort is an increase in the patient's well-being (Ronco, 1972). The psychological ramifications of such a practice will be discussed later; for the moment we will consider some of the research on medical staff behavior in different types of hospital layouts and their effects on efficiency.

A current controversial issue among hospital designers and medical personnel concerns the relative merits and faults of different ward layouts in such areas as cost, manpower use, and patient satisfaction. In his comparison of various ward plans, Lippert (1971) used nurses' movement about the wards as the dependent variable. Travel was assumed to be an important factor in the evaluation of ward design because a substantial amount of a nurse's time is taken up by travel, and excessive travel has been cited as a source of dissatisfaction by ward nurses. In developing his measure, Lippert constructed what he termed a "tour model." In the model a tour was considered one trip by a nurse from her station to see a patient or patients and her return to the station. Various stops in her tour for fresh linen or other supplies were considered "utility stops" and were included as part of the tour. Thus, a nurse may leave the station, check one patient, make a utility stop, check two more patients, and return to her station.

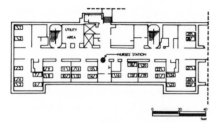

Fourth floor nursing unit, Pratt Diagnostic Clinic, New England Medical Center Hospitals

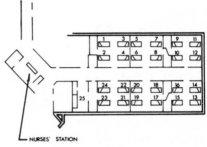

Yale University Hospital, 25-bed part of east wing nursing unit

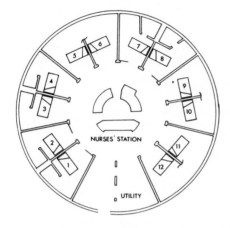

Rochester Methodist Hospital, 12-bed circular unit

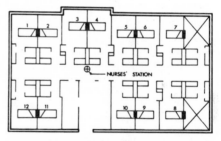

Rochester Methodist Hospital, 12-bed rectangular unit

Figure 3-5.   Hospital ward layouts used in the investigation of nurses' travel. From Stanley Lippert. Travel in nursing units. *Human Factors,* 1971, **13**(3), 269–282. Reprinted by permission of the Human Factors Society.

Lippert then applied his model to four hospital wards, three rectangular and one circular (see Figure 3-5), and attempted to arrive at relative measures of efficiency for each. Two efficiency measures obtained from application of the tour model were average utility stops per patient and average number of patients visited per tour. Lippert suggests that the most efficient ward design is one that allows for the most patients visited per tour, with the fewest utility stops. Table 3-1 lists the comparative results of the derived measures.

Although Lippert makes no inferences on the superiority of any of the ward arrangements over the others, he does note that because the circular ward and one of the rectangular ones were in the same hospital, the experimental situation was lent a measure of control in that the nurses were from the same staff, were under the same administration, and dealt with similar types of patients. The nurses did, however, use different tour patterns in these two wards, although the differences were not enough to provide much information on comparative efficiency. Nonetheless, Lippert's method was successful in that it reflected the different behavioral effects of the different wards.

As in other environmental settings, social and organizational norms in hospitals interact with features of the physical environment to produce predictable behavior. In fact, the strictly upheld status distinctions among doctors, residents, interns, medical students, registered nurses, surgical nurses, aides, and patients are firmly entrenched in the social structure of any hospital. An individual who occupies any one of these statuses maintains a quite rigid behavioral role. However, this role (and hence behavior) may change with the person's location in the hospital setting.

Table 3-1.   Summary of tour model findings. From Stanley Lippert. Travel in nursing units. *Human Factors,* 1971, **13**(3), 269–282. Reproduced by permission of the Human Factors Society.

Ward in Which Observations Were Made	Number of Utility Stops per Patient	Number of Patients per Tour
Pratt-4	0.375	2.00
Yale	0.50	2.00
Rochester Methodist, 12-Bed Rectangular Unit	0.125	2.67
Rochester Methodist, 12-Bed Circular Unit	0.22	2.25

Rosengren and DeVault (1963) observed the gamut of behavior and activities in an obstetrical ward of a large hospital, from the admitting room to the recovery rooms. Their approach was ecological in that virtually every activity was deemed to contribute to the overall behavioral setting. Thus, they viewed behavior not as strictly a result of the environment but as a result of the interaction of social and organizational variables with the persons in particular environmental settings.

Using this approach, Rosengren and DeVault related status to different components of the ward. The labor rooms, for example, were the domain of the nurses attending the patients there, and the nurses knew it and acted accordingly. Once they were in the delivery room, the attending physician was, understandably, the person with unquestioned authority. The researchers note, however, that interactions between the doctors and the nurses were more informal in locations where each person's role was ambiguous— for example, in the hallways. Other locations where status was reflected, both physically and behaviorally, were the respective lounges for residents and practicing physicians. Although both lounges served the same function, there were two of them, and they differed substantially in interior appointments. Moreover, the residents and interns were hesitant to use the private physicians' lounge even though they were entitled to do so at any time. Thus, it was evident to the investigators that something other than the features of the lounge environment was producing the behavior they observed.

We mentioned earlier that the most important design consideration for hospitals is thought to be the facilitation of medical staff activities, which in turn is thought to promote patient satisfaction and well-being. In other words, the needs of the patient are assumed to be met by fulfilling the requirements of the medical personnel. However, in some situations the needs of the patient and those of the staff conflict, so that one must be favored over the other. Fitch (1965) describes such a situation in the operating room:

> The surgeon and his staff will meet their greatest period of stress during surgery. At this juncture their requirements will be opposed to those of the patient. Where the latter requires warm moist air (and antiexplosive measures demand even higher humidities), the staff under nervous tension should ideally be submerged in dry, cool air. But since stress for them is of limited duration while any added load might be disastrous for the patient, the room's thermo-atmospheric environment is usually designed in the latter's favor. The staff sweats and suffers and recovers later [p. 713].

Although in this case the decision is made in favor of the patient to protect his physical well-being, to the discomfort of the staff, Ronco (1972) points out that psychological considerations involving the patients are frequently rejected in favor of enhancing staff efficiency. The result of one such decision is the physical and psychological confinement of the patient. Because of the crowded conditions of hospitals, patients are often discouraged from moving about in their rooms or wards, even though their illness or injury is such that they are able to do so. Ronco also notes that corridors are frequently so unappealing that patients avoid traveling in them. If they do move about in the corridors, they do so in a rigid fashion, to avoid infringing on other patients' privacy by inadvertently looking at them through the open doors. Moreover, patients have little control over the furnishings in their rooms and are not allowed to rearrange things to their liking.

Lack of privacy is yet another result of design for function rather than patient need. Ronco cites a study by Jaco (1967), who investigated psychological reactions to a radial nursing unit. Many patients reported a lack of privacy, presumably due to the ability of the nurse at her station to look directly into their rooms. The lack of privacy is especially evident during visiting hours; with no private visiting areas, most patient-visitor interaction is around the patient's bed and witnessed by others. As Ronco states, this situation is not conducive to frank or confidential conversations, especially in large multipatient wards.

Obviously, providing the comforts of home is functionally and financially impossible in any hospital. Yet ignoring patients' needs and denying them the opportunity to at least approximate various normal activities make the patients' burdens heavier, which in turn may result in need for increased care. Thus, any behavioral effects of hospital design for function without regard to patient needs will likely be deleterious.

SOCIAL INSTITUTIONS

In this section, on mental and penal institutions, our emphasis shifts from occupational types of environmental settings to settings in which a primary purpose is to change behavior deemed by society to be deviant. An examination of the rehabilitative methods used and of their recent criticism by sociologists and psychologists is certainly germane to any discussion of mental and penal institutions but is beyond the scope of this text. The following discussion is confined to whether certain physical features of these institutions may facilitate or hinder the rehabilitative process.

Both mental and penal institutions offer a unique opportunity for investigating the effects of the physical environment on the people in it. Either facility can be considered a microcosm, nearly free of any external influence or control. Although the staffs of both institutions have everyday contact with the "real world," the inmates or patients are captives in a single physical and behavioral environment. Thus, aside from occasional visits of family or friends and preinstitution experience, the influence of external variables is negligible.

This isolation allows the formation of stable man-environment relationships and makes their observation easier. However, due to the nature of the institutions and the reasons the inhabitants are there, any attempt to generalize the results of an investigation would be met, at best, with skepticism. Nonetheless, any links established between physical features of the institutional environment and occupant behavior can prove extremely valuable in designing for maximum rehabilitation.

MENTAL INSTITUTIONS

Social Behavior in Mental Wards

A prevalent notion in the treatment of mental patients is that they need to engage in social interaction both as a means of activity during their treatment period and as a preparation for social encounters once they leave the institution. Although social behavior is a function of many variables, such as therapeutic technique, administrative policy, and patient characteristics, features of the ward environment can be isolated as possible determinants of social activity. Among these features are the size of the ward, the size of ward components (bedrooms and day rooms, for example), and the components' internal arrangements. Typically, psychiatric wards contain all the features necessary to support patient activity: rooms for eating, sleeping, recreation and socializing, treatment, and personal hygiene. Thus, when the other variables mentioned are taken into consideration, the effects of wards differing in physical features can be compared by observing the activities taking place in them. Such investigations are reported by Ittelson, Proshansky, and Rivlin (1972); Gump and James (1970); and Barton, Mishkin, and Spivack (1971).

Although the major purpose of the study by Ittelson and his co-workers was to observe the stability of behavior patterns between psychiatric units, the report also provides information about the physical aspects of the wards and potential behavioral relationships. The investigators chose wards from psychiatric units in three hospitals. These wards varied substantially in size (both overall and in their components) and appearance as well as patient population.

The first ward consisted of a converted medical ward in a general hospital. Thus, it retained a hospital appearance, with tiled hallways, bright lights, and bustling activity. The bedrooms had either three or six occupants and were open to direct observation from the corridors. In addition to the standard day room, this ward contained a solarium for patient use.

Two more wards were in a state mental institution. This hospital was typical of many state mental health facilities in that it operated under rigid financial constraints. Both wards were utilitarian in structure and furnishings. Each contained a few private bedrooms and a mixture of three-bed, six-bed, and 20-bed, or dormitory type, rooms. Due to administrative policies, the wards did differ in one respect. One of the wards showed evidence of patient cooperation in keeping it neat and attractively decorated; the other had a considerably gloomier atmosphere.

The fourth ward was in a private hospital. The investigators report that this ward seemed more like an attractive hotel than a psychiatric ward. The color schemes were tasteful, and the furnishings were well appointed. All the bedrooms were either one-bed or two-bed rooms and had doors to seal off any corridor activity.

To observe and record the variety of behavior occurring in these wards, the investigators developed a technique called "behavioral mapping." To construct a map of each ward, trained observers were positioned at specific locations in the ward. At predetermined time intervals each observer recorded the types of behavior occurring in his area and the number and characteristics of the persons involved in them. For instance, at one time interval an observer in the day room might record that six male patients, two female patients, and one ward attendant were watching television; four male patients were playing cards; three female patients were reading; and one male patient was dozing in his chair. Thus, combining all the observers' data for one time interval gives an accurate description of the behavior occurring in the entire ward. Similarly, combining the data of all the observers at all time intervals establishes the behavioral patterns of the ward patients and staff. Such behavioral maps of a normal day's activities were constructed for each ward for extended periods.

For the purpose of meaningful explanation, the investigators put the locations of behavior into two major categories—bedrooms and public rooms. Places considered to be public rooms include the hallways, day rooms, eating rooms, and the solarium in the city hospital. The behavior was also categorized according to type of activity and types and amount of social encounters involved. These categories are isolated-passive (sitting or lying in bed alone, awake or asleep); active (personal duties, reading, and individual recreation); and social (patients interacting with other patients, visitors, or staff). Analysis of the data in these categories revealed differences among the wards as well as marked differences in the types of behavior as a function of location.

Comparison of the overall activities in the four wards showed that more active or social behavior occurred in the private hospital than passive behavior. In the state and converted city wards, isolated-passive behavior predominated. In the public places of the wards, behavior in the private hospital was again much more active or social than isolated-passive. Behavior

in the state and city wards, on the other hand, was relatively equally distrib-
uted among all behavioral categories. However, the researchers felt that these
differences were more the result of the differences in patient populations and
administrative policies than differences in physical environment.

The most intriguing findings of the study are the marked differences in behavior observed in the ward bedrooms within each unit. The investigators early noted overall differences among the wards and the behavior
occurring in the bedrooms. Although isolated-passive behavior was prevalent
in all ward bedrooms, a smaller percentage of the patients in the private
hospital engaged in this kind of behavior than in the state and city wards. This
difference was quickly traced to the presence of only one-bed or two-bed rooms
in the private institution. The researchers then discovered that the percentage
of isolated-passive behavior in bedrooms increased in all four wards with the
number of beds per room and, consequently, with bedroom size. At first glance
one might assume that these results would be expected; the larger the bedroom,
the more people occupying it and engaging in isolated-passive behavior at any
one time. However, the rate of use of the bedrooms did not increase with size
enough to account for the differences. The authors interpret this finding as
follows:

> ... the patient in the smaller room experiences the entire range
> of possible behaviors as open to him, he feels free to choose from
> the whole range of options, and he does, in fact, choose more or
> less equally from among all possibilities. This is [most] dramati-
> cally shown in the single rooms of the private hospital, where
> behavior is equally distributed over all categories.
> In contrast, the patient in the larger room is far more likely to
> be engaged in isolated-passive behavior than anything else and
> will spend anywhere from two-thirds to three-fourths of his time,
> while in his room, lying on his bed, either asleep or awake. He
> seems to see the range of options among which he can choose as
> severely limited and to be constrained to choose isolated-passive
> behavior over any other [p. 103].

Thus, if social interaction in psychiatric wards is desirable and does hasten
rehabilitation, one implication of this study for designers is that smaller bedrooms may be preferable.

In the previous chapter we discussed the work of Sommer (1969),
who established relationships between the arrangement of furnishings in classrooms and classroom activity and who showed that persons wanting to converse have strong preferences in seating arrangement and distances. Sommer's

research also provides evidence that the arrangement of furnishings in mental health facilities is important in determining the extent of social encounters among patients. He points out that the arrangement of chairs in the lounge areas of mental institutions is not unlike that in airport terminals. Typically, the chairs are in straight rows along the walls and back to back in the center of the room, with the distance between the center chairs and those against the walls far exceeding the limit for comfortable conversation. The reasons for this arrangement are ease of maintenance, neat appearance, and the unspoken tradition of what institutions are supposed to look like.

Sommer reports that in an investigation of such a ward arrangement in a Canadian institution, his observers recorded both one-way social communications (greetings or questions directed by one patient to another, for example) and reciprocal social communications lasting for two seconds or more. These data were gathered for use as baseline data for later comparisons with data gathered under different conditions. At the end of the baseline period, several square tables were moved into the lounge and the chairs along the walls were rearranged around the tables. This new arrangement provoked resistance from maintenance and other personnel, who complained that it disrupted their activities. Initial resistance also came from the patients. After allowing time for adjustment to the new arrangement, the observers again recorded the number of communications and found that both one-way communications and reciprocal communications increased.

The results of this investigation, coupled with the findings of Ittelson and his co-workers, provide relevant information to administrators and planners in the field of institutional design. Although the research is exploratory and a host of other variables may have influenced the results, it at least supplies a basis for alternatives to existing features in psychiatric wards.

Patient Needs

The emotional states of patients in mental institutions lead them to behave in ways considered abnormal in our society. Because of their behavioral disorders, these people have needs above and beyond those of a normally functioning individual. Thus, knowledge about these needs is important in the design of mental institutions, whether their ultimate purpose is considered to be rehabilitative or custodial.

In one study on the relationship between patient needs and institution design, Osmond (1970) cites the abnormalities in a schizophrenic's perceptions—visual, auditory, time, and self—and offers suggestions for institutional design that might help to alleviate, or at least not aggravate, these distortions. Sensory deprivation experiments have shown that a lack of changing visual stimulation may cause even normal people to experience visual hallucinations. Although not as extreme as in the experiments, somewhat analogous conditions exist in the majority of psychiatric hospitals; drab single color or uniform color schemes or barren walls, floors, and ceilings present the patient with minimally changing visual stimuli. Although we have no empirical evidence proving that the reduced visual stimulation in institutions causes hallucinations, the visual change in leaving an institution for the outside world has been a source of confusion and trauma in a number of persons (Wildeblood, 1959).

As mentioned in Chapter 2, the distorted self-perception of schizophrenics results in an expansion of their personal space requirements (Horowitz, Duff, & Stratton, 1964). This exaggerated need for personal space, in combination with a mental patient's desire to have a place to hide, leads Osmond to suggest that designers should provide for private spaces, or at least reduce the potential for unwanted personal contacts. These requirements could be met in a number of different ways—single occupancy bedrooms, small wards, alcoves, and landscaping the institution grounds for solace and seclusion.

Other patient disabilities requiring consideration by designers are the tendency toward rapid mood changes and the difficulty in making decisions. Osmond states that small groups who have had the opportunity to form understanding relationships are more resistant to mood swings than are larger, less cohesive groups. Thus, smaller wards and bedrooms again may serve a useful purpose. To alleviate decision-making difficulties, Osmond advocates reducing ambiguous situations (junctions of long, unmarked corridors, large dining halls and dormitories, for example) by using smaller units of these examples to reduce the number of alternatives present in each decision situation.

Throughout his article, then, Osmond contends that avoiding certain features now common to institutions (reduced visual stimulation, for example) and providing for other features (private spaces) may facilitate rehabilitative efforts. These efforts may also be enhanced if institutions are designed to require a minimum of adjustment on the part of new patients and so reduce potentially stressful situations.

PENAL INSTITUTIONS

The physical features of penal institutions are somewhat similar to those of mental health facilities. However, there are major differences between the two types of institutions that may affect the manipulation of physical features to help achieve institution objectives. Whereas the aim of mental institutions is to return the individual to society as quickly as possible, in penal institutions mandatory sentences and minimum time spent there before parole eligibility tend to emphasize the custodial function, not the rehabilitative function. However, providing a physical environment meeting the individual's personal needs may be as important in a prison as in a psychiatric ward. This consideration often conflicts, unfortunately, with society's demand for punishment.

Another difference between the two types of institutions lies in their populations. With the exception of some unusual cases, persons in mental institutions are not considered as being harmful to one another and are encouraged to engage in various types of social interaction. In prisons social interaction must be subjected to much more control for custodial reasons. Certain types of social interaction may also be discouraged for rehabilitative purposes —for example, keeping young first offenders separated from hardened criminals.

This need for control places additional restraints on the design of penal facilities. Obviously, one technique useful in controlling social interactions is the provision for physical separation of inmates. Equally obvious is that the construction of independent mini-prisons for individual inmates is probably far beyond economic limitations. Nonetheless, a general feeling among administrators and social scientists engaged in research on penal institutions is that the provision for inmate privacy is instrumental in rehabilitation. With a room or a cell of his own, an inmate can engage in such private activities as reading, writing, and studying without being disturbed by cellmates. It is also desirable to group inmates according to stage in the rehabilitative process. This concept has resulted in the compartmentalization now used in several newer prison systems.

In a study of the use of separate cells as a deterrent to criminogenic influences, Glaser (1972) conducted a survey of inmate activities in single occupancy cells and in dormitories in five institutions. Data were collected on the number of hours each inmate spent in everyday activities, such as working, eating, sleeping, talking with fellow prisoners, recreation, and reading. Although each institution differed from the others in administrative policy and treatment programs, time spent in reading and eating was consistently greater for occupants of single cells. Glaser attributes the increased time spent eating to the single cell inmate's need to socialize or to be away from the isolation of his cell. The results of this survey suggest that although occupants of single cells do have more opportunity for privacy, they do not take advantage of it as much as they might.

Glaser also obtained the same types of information for separate housing units in one prison setting. The housing units were organized according to different stages in the rehabilitative process and thus varied in physical features as well as in administrative policies on inmate supervision. Basically, the units at the bottom of this honor system consisted of dormitories, each with a supervisory officer. As an inmate advanced up the honor scale, his physical environment changed as well as the amount of supervision. The first significant change was from a dormitory to a single room, which was not locked in the "semihonor" units. From there the inmate's room increased in size, and in the "top honor" unit he could have his light on any time he wished. Associated with the changes in environment was decreasing supervision, which in the top honor unit was virtually nonexistent.

Although Glaser's activity analysis in these units reflects little influence of their physical characteristics on inmate behavior, some of the findings may provide grounds for future decisions in the design of penal institutions. One rather unexpected finding leads one to question the success of the honor system. Glaser's analysis of work and play activities of the inmates across housing units showed that work time increased while recreation time decreased until the inmates reached the two highest honor units. At that time the trend reversed, with play activities occupying substantially more time than in the other units and time spent working decreasing accordingly. In addition, the "intellectual quality" of the recreation activities seemed to decrease in the two top honor units. Records of enrollment in and completion of correspondence courses taken by the inmates also indicated that participation in courses decreased dramatically in the top honor units. Glaser thus concludes that "the 'honor units' may often contribute more to the comfort of both the inmates and staff than to the reformation of the inmates" [p. 112].

THE BUILT ENVIRONMENT—AN OVERVIEW

Thus far we have examined built environments and their various components, ranging from rooms to residences for the mentally disturbed. Each of these environments shares a common characteristic: physical aspects of the structure or its components may affect behavior. We will now briefly review some of the features of these environments and the behavior that occurs in them.

Earlier we discussed independent and dependent variables in psychological research. Recall that the independent variable is usually a condition or a situation in which a person is behaving; dependent variables are kinds of behavior that may vary with the independent variables. For purposes of review we will present the variables that have been most significant in the built environments we have considered so far.

The first category of independent environmental variables considered were integral structural features—size and shape of rooms and buildings; arrangements of walls, corridors, and rooms; placement of doors and windows; external arrangements. Various combinations of these structural features determine amount and type of indoor and outdoor space, an additional structural variable.

A second, more flexible category of physical aspects of the built environment was treated as comprising components of particular settings. Among these aspects are color scheme, furnishings, and their arrangement. In a similar category are the various dimensions of the ambient environment: temperature, noise, and illumination. These two categories include the majority of what we consider to be independent variables in research on the built environment and behavior.

In the studies discussed in Chapters 2–3, numerous kinds of behavior were observed to occur within or as a result of features of the built environments we have mentioned. These types of behavior, or dependent variables, differed substantially in kind and complexity.

Much of the behavior reported was perceptual. The expressions of thermal comfort, visual impressions of room color, perceptual confusion caused by experimental distorted rooms, and perceived noise level are examples of these types of behavior.

A variety of attitudes is also reported in the investigations discussed. The problem of satisfaction is repeatedly mentioned in many different contexts. Numerous surveys measured residents' attitudes toward their environment, their neighbors, and their jobs as well as nonverbal expressions of personal space and territoriality and of fear in particular situations.

Social behavior in physical environments was also commonly measured, ranging from casual glances or brief greetings to enduring friendships to crime. Such behavior was found to be encouraged or discouraged, depending on features of the physical environment.

Finally, more functional behavior was shown to be affected by features of the built environment. Classroom activities, movement in museums, and traffic patterns in hospitals all showed varying degrees of environmental influence.

Obviously, the examples of behavior listed here are not inclusive. Various aspects of physical structures can undoubtedly be linked to consumer behavior, children's play (or lack of it) in hospitals, guests' actions in hotels, reasons for home buyers' wanting sunken living rooms, and so forth. Unfortunately, research in these areas, as in most other areas of environmental psychology, is limited at this time.

CHAPTER FOUR

THE BUILT ENVIRONMENT: CITIES

We have seen in previous chapters how various aspects of environment—rooms, houses, buildings, neighborhoods, and so forth—may affect behavior. These kinds of built environments can be thought of as subsystems of the ultimate built environment, the city. Although in this chapter we will be discussing studies dealing primarily with the urban environment and behavior, the reader should remember that, directly or indirectly, the behavior studied is influenced by all the subsystems that make up a city.

LIVING IN THE CITY

As pointed out earlier, environmental attributes may elicit either approach or avoidance responses (Wohlwill, 1970). Nowhere is this more apparent than in cities. The individual living in a city is continually exposed to a tremendously diverse array of environmental attributes, some of which may have great appeal while others serve as a source of threat. Thus, although the urban environment may impose major restrictions on some types of behavior, it offers the opportunity for a variety of other kinds of behavior that no other environment permits.

It is impossible, of course, to begin to list all the environmental attributes that characterize life in the city and to discuss which of these serve as sources of satisfaction or dissatisfaction for those living there. The principal reason is that city dwellers are an extremely heterogeneous population, differing tremendously in virtually every characteristic—economic, educational, motivational, and so forth. Consequently, what a wealthy executive living in an expensive house in a suburb and commuting to a plush downtown office would consider satisfying or dissatisfying about life in the city might be quite different from what a welfare recipient living in a slum area would consider satisfying or dissatisfying. Because of this heterogeneity, researchers conducting environmental studies in urban areas must be careful to spell out the characteristics of the persons being studied.

Some features of urban environments, however, do have some effect on the majority of city dwellers. Unfortunately, these features are negative aspects of the urban environment and, in combination, have resulted in what has become known as the *urban crisis*. The complexity of the urban crisis is cogently spelled out by Arthur Naftalin (1970), whose background includes not only a Ph.D. in political science but also eight years as mayor of Minneapolis. He says:

> The subject is so broad and wide and deep, affecting us in so many different ways, it has come to be all things to all men. It involves concerns that are at once governmental, economic, social, psychological, technological, moral, and philosophical, and it covers all aspects of community life and individual behavior: human relations, law enforcement, housing, sanitation, health services, education, income distribution—name it and you name a part of the urban crisis.
>
> ... It involves the full sweep of our physical environment: growing congestion and pollution, the waste of our natural resources, especially our land, the critical lack of adequate housing, the failure to preserve open space, the growing problems of water supply, drainage, and waste disposal, and the baffling explosion of technology that has introduced speed and movement and change at a pace that confuses and bewilders almost everyone.
>
> On the social side the crisis is not only a matter of poverty, although this is certainly its single most critical element. It involves a changing value structure that is fundamentally altering

the nature of family life and the overall pattern of human relationships. It also involves an alarming increase in the use of alcohol
and drugs and mounting tensions that derive from growing inse-
curity and our inability to control or discharge hostility. It involves a general weakening of our major institutions of social
control, especially the family and education [pp. 108–109].

These factors as well as others contribute to the urban crisis and
have a profound impact on the lives of millions of city dwellers. Nonetheless,
we know very little about the behavioral responses associated with urban
problems. Environmental psychologists have investigated only a few of these
problems, so in most cases we can only speculate about the effects of a particular aspect of the urban crisis on behavior.

Although we have little data linking a specific urban problem
with specific types of behavior, we do have data showing that the problems
associated with the urban crisis contribute greatly to most persons' feelings of
dissatisfaction with urban living. Survey results differ according to the characteristics of the particular segment of the urban population sampled, but nearly
everyone lists the same environmental attributes as important contributors to
dissatisfaction with city life. High population density, leading to overcrowding,
is on most lists, as are crime, aggression and violence, poor housing, and
virtually all the other urban problems listed by Naftalin. Thus, determining
what factors appear to be important in contributing to dissatisfaction with city
life is not particularly difficult. It is more difficult to investigate the factors
contributing to satisfaction.

SOURCES OF SATISFACTION WITH CITY
LIVING

Obviously, cities appeal to a great many people for a great many
reasons. Cities offer varieties of experience that can be found nowhere else, and
many of these can serve as a source of intense personal satisfaction. As Milgram (1970a) suggests, "cities have great appeal because of their variety,
eventfulness, possibility of choice, and the stimulation of an intense atmosphere that many individuals find a desirable background to their lives"
[p. 1461].

More research has been conducted on the urban environmental
factors that contribute to dissatisfaction than on those contributing to satisfaction. In addition, much of the research that has dealt with the satisfactory
aspects of urban living centers on the factors in the immediate neighborhood

in which an individual resides and does not deal with attributes of the larger area—the community and region—that may be satisfying or dissatisfying. In other words, most of the concern has been with features of the microresidential environment as sources of satisfaction rather than with the attributes of the city of which the residential area is a part. Although it seems reasonable to assume that eliminating the problems associated with the urban crisis would result in a higher percentage of people being satisfied with urban life, there is little systematic research in this area.

In attempting to determine the satisfying aspects of a microresidential environment, researchers have generally concentrated on (1) the physical characteristics of the residences and the surrounding area and (2) the social interactions of the residents. Actually, of course, it is not feasible to separate the two; the physical characteristics to a large extent determine the types of social interactions. In previous chapters we discussed a number of studies that demonstrated the importance of such physical factors as location of doors and windows in determining friendship patterns and social interactions among residents of various types of housing developments. Also discussed was the importance of personal space and privacy in determining level of satisfaction or dissatisfaction. Although we will not consider these factors here, it should be kept in mind that they are important sources of satisfaction with city living. In this section we will discuss studies dealing with characteristics of neighborhoods that are found satisfying by two distinctly different populations, one made up of residents of high income suburban neighborhoods and the other of residents of a slum area.

Residential Satisfaction in an Urban Slum

In recent years a great deal of attention has been focused on urban slums and the problems associated with them. Residents of these areas have called attention to themselves not only by demonstrations and riots but also by becoming much more verbal and making themselves heard at local and national government levels. The result has been a number of government action programs, such as urban renewal. Although at the time of this writing funds for these and other programs are being withdrawn, interest in slum areas and the behavior of their residents is likely to continue.

Unfortunately, the available data do not present a very clear picture of slum areas and their populations. One reason, of course, is that no two slum areas are alike. As Fried and Gleicher (1972) point out:

> Slum areas undoubtedly show much variation, both variation from one slum to another and heterogeneity within urban slum areas. However, certain consistencies from one slum area to an-

other have begun to show up in the growing body of literature. It is quite notable that the available systematic studies of slum areas indicate a very broad working-class composition in slums, ranging from highly skilled workers to the nonworking and sporadically working members of the "working" class. Moreover, even in our worst residential slums it is likely that only a minority of the inhabitants (although sometimes a fairly large and visible minority) are afflicted with one or another form of social pathology [pp. 137–138].

Keeping in mind, then, that there are major differences among slum areas and that the findings of studies of one area may not be completely applicable to other areas, let us consider the study by Fried and Gleicher (1972) dealing with residents of Boston's West End. The data in this investigation were based on a probability sample of residents and included only households with a female between the ages of 20 and 65. Fifty-five percent of the residents in the sample had either been born in the area or had lived there for at least 20 years. The authors report that there was a marked residential stability and that the majority of residents had changed housing within the West End little if at all. This finding, of course, is contrary to the commonly accepted view of a slum area's having a highly transient population. Fried and Gleicher also found that, contrary to the popular view of slum dwellers' feelings about the area in which they live, 75 percent of the sample liked living in the West End while only 10 percent disliked living there.

In the exploration of the reasons for such a high rate of satisfaction, two major factors emerged. One is that the physical area has considerable meaning as an extension of home, and various parts of the area are delineated and structured on the basis of a sense of belonging. In other words, the local area around the dwelling unit is viewed as an integral part of the home. The strength of feeling of belonging in an area—that is, a sense of localism—was an important factor in determining whether the residents liked or disliked living in the area.

The second factor is that the residential area provides a framework for a vast and interlocking set of social ties, which serve as an important source of satisfaction. Fried and Gleicher found a strong association between the respondents' satisfaction with living in the West End and the social relationships they had established. The study revealed a variety of social relationships, but kinship ties (those involving the nuclear families of both spouses) appeared to be even more important than relationships with neighbors; "the more extensive these available kinship ties are within the local area, the greater the proportion who show positive feeling toward the West End" [p. 144].

However, Fried and Gleicher stress that the absence of these kinds of relationships does not necessarily mean that negative feelings about the area will be expressed. In many instances residents without strong social ties reported very positive feelings about the West End, so that alternative sources of satisfaction must exist for some people.

This study also revealed the importance of physical space and the special uses of the area made by the residents. A complete discussion of these factors would again involve us in such concepts as personal space, privacy, territoriality, and so forth. Basically, however, in working class areas, such as the West End, home is viewed as the local area rather than just the dwelling. The boundaries between the dwelling unit and its immediate environment are usually much more "permeable" in slum areas than in middle class areas. In the slum a great deal of activity occurs outside the dwelling: Children play in the streets, women go out in the street to talk with friends, families gather on steps and talk with neighbors, street corners serve as meeting places for social exchanges, and so forth. The external environment, in a sense, becomes an extension of the dwelling. Fried and Gleicher state:

> In conjunction with the emphasis upon local social relationships, this conception and use of local physical space gives particular force to the feeling of commitment to, and the sense of belonging in, the residential area. It is clearly not just the dwelling unit that is significant but a larger local region that partakes of these powerful feelings of involvement and identity. It is not surprising, therefore, that "home" is not merely an apartment or a house but a local area in which some of the most meaningful aspects of life are experienced [p. 151].

Apparently, then, life in a slum area furnishes enough sources of satisfaction that a high percentage of residents like living there. This fact has important implications, particularly for urban renewal projects. It has typically been assumed that altering the physical characteristics of slum areas by means of new dwellings or relocating the residents benefits not only them but the city as a whole. Perhaps so; we still know very little about the behavioral consequences of living in a slum. However, we also know little about the behavioral effects of massive changes in the physical characteristics of slums or forced relocation. Yet it would appear that the local area provides the framework for an extensive social integration that slum dwellers find highly satisfying. Programs that dislocate people and destroy social relationships may have deleterious effects that outweigh the expected benefits.

Residential Satisfaction in Suburbs

In an effort to determine the sources of community appeal, Zehner (1972) studied four suburban locations, each within 15 to 18 miles of a major metropolitan area and having primarily affluent, well-educated residents. The median home value was over $33,000 in each of the four areas and median family income was over $17,000. In two of the areas, the proportion of married couples with both husband and wife having at least a B.A. degree was over 40 percent; in the other two areas it was 17 percent and 20 percent. Obviously, the residents of these areas differed greatly from the respondents in the Fried and Gleicher study.

When asked to rate the community in which they lived as excellent, good, average, below average, or poor, over 80 percent of the residents in each of the suburbs rated their community as excellent or good. Among the reasons given for positive evaluations were well-planned and accessible physical facilities; good schools; friendly neighbors; relative safety from crime; good access to stores, jobs, and so on; good environmental quality in that trees, lakes, hills, and so on were available; plenty of space; and little congestion.

In addition to investigating the factors contributing to community satisfaction, Zehner gathered data on the factors involved in neighborhood satisfaction. He grouped these factors into five general categories: neighborhood density, accessibility of facilities, respondent's home, social compatibility, and neighborhood maintenance level.

Zehner found that respondents in the least dense neighborhoods, which are the quietest and furnish the most privacy, expressed a high level of satisfaction with the neighborhood. The lack of noise in neighborhoods with low densities seemed to be the most important variable in the neighborhood density category. Accessibility of facilities was not found to be highly associated with neighborhood satisfaction, although in families with children the adequacy and accessibility of playgrounds was important.

Social compatibility was a source of neighborhood satisfaction, just as it was in the slum study. However, Zehner found that his respondents felt it more important to have neighbors they felt were compatible than neighbors with whom they frequently interacted.

Neighborhood maintenance was most highly related to satisfaction in the communities studied. Maintenance level of the neighborhood had a correlation coefficient of .56, friendliness of .44, and similarity of neighbors .36. Neighborhood density, as it related to noise level, had a correlation of .34. The factors least related to neighborhood satisfaction were those involving accessibility of various community facilities.

The Fried and Gleicher and Zehner studies, as well as several others that have not been discussed, indicate that a significant percentage of city dwellers report being satisfied with life in the city. These studies have isolated several attributes of the urban environment that serve as sources of satisfaction. It should be kept in mind, however, that other attributes of the urban environment are viewed as threatening. (Some of these will be discussed in Chapter 6.) Possibly, the surveys conducted to determine the sources of satisfaction with city living do not sufficiently take into account the unsatisfactory aspects of city life in the questions asked of respondents. That several surveys show a high percentage of city dwellers reporting that what they would most like to do is to move to more rural areas may indicate that they are not as satisfied with city life as one might assume.

THE IMAGE OF THE CITY

Studies such as those by Fried and Gleicher and Zehner give the investigators some idea of how their respondents view the neighborhood or community in which they live. Other researchers have been more specifically concerned with the image that cities hold for their inhabitants or for visitors and have designed some ingenious techniques for studying these images. Typically, these methods are based on the assumption that inhabitants of a city acquire a "cognitive map" of the city and that this map results from both the personal characteristics of an individual and the physical characteristics of the city. The problem for the investigator, then, is to develop ways to "read" the maps carried around in the heads of the inhabitants. In this section we will discuss several of the procedures that have been developed and used by researchers interested in these cognitive maps of the city.

The Urban Atmosphere

One of the factors important in forming an image of a city has been referred to as the "urban atmosphere." Psychologists have found it hard to define just what an urban atmosphere is and to isolate its components. However, Heimstra and McDonald (1973) point out some of the components that may be important:

> Obviously, the look, or physical layout, of a city will have an effect on its atmosphere; some would argue that the look of Paris or London or New York can be equated with their atmospheres. There are undoubtedly many visual components of a city that

contribute and are therefore of interest to anyone who is concerned with urban atmosphere.

For example, the tempo, or pace, of a city contributes to its atmosphere. A visitor to a city is immediately impressed with the apparent hectic quality of the life. This may be an erroneous impression (empirical data are lacking), but it is certainly part of the atmosphere. Similarly, the density of the population, the types of people represented in the population, and the attitude and behavior of the people toward each other and toward visitors all contribute. It is a complex interaction of the inhabitants' characteristics and the city's characteristics that forms the "urban atmosphere" [p. 46].

Because the interaction between the inhabitants' characteristics and the characteristics of the city is complex, the urban atmosphere is difficult to quantify. For example, consider some of the personal characteristics that will determine an individual's impression of a city. Milgram (1970a) suggests that three personal factors can affect an individual's response to a city. First, a person's impression of a particular city will depend upon his standard of comparison. A Parisian who is visiting New York may have an impression of a frenetic city; to a native of Tokyo, New York may look relatively leisurely. Second, the perception of a city is affected by the status of the perceiver. A tourist, a newcomer to the city, an old-timer, and someone who is returning to the city after a long absence all may have different perceptions of the city. Finally, a person comes to a city with preconceived ideas and expectations about it. Even though these preconceptions may not be accurate, they contribute to the impression of the city.

Milgram (1970b) also describes a study he conducted dealing with "the atmosphere of great cities." Questionnaires were developed and administered to 60 persons who were familiar with at least two of three cities —London, Paris, and New York. The questionnaires were designed to elicit descriptions of the cities and, in general, to illuminate the character of the cities. For example, one item on the questionnaire asked the respondents to list several adjectives that they felt applied to a particular city. Analysis of these adjectives showed that New York elicited more descriptions concerned with its physical qualities, pace, and emotional impact than did Paris or London. For London, the respondents placed greater emphasis on social interactions than on physical surroundings. For Paris, the respondents were about equally divided in the emphasis placed on interactions with the inhabitants and on its physical and sensory attributes.

Another approach to studying the impressions created by a city is exemplified by the research of Lynch (1960).

The Lynch Studies

Kevin Lynch's book *The Image of the City* describes studies conducted in Boston, Massachusetts; Jersey City, New Jersey; and Los Angeles, California. Although we cannot begin to summarize Lynch's discussions of the characteristics of these cities and the findings of his studies in the space available, we will consider in some detail the methods used in his research. Lynch's book provides a detailed rationale for his approach, and his findings have important implications for urban designers.

Lynch used two principal methods in studying the image of these cities. In the first method a sample of citizens were interviewed about their image of their urban environment. In the second method trained observers made a systematic field reconnaissance of each city. Using information that had proved significant in the analysis of pilot studies, these observers mapped the presence of environmental elements, their visibility, their image strengths or weaknesses, and so forth. This approach allowed for a comparison of the data from the interviews with the data from the field analyses.

The interviews were lengthy, each taking about an hour and a half, and were tape recorded. According to Lynch, the subjects were greatly interested in the interviews and often displayed emotion. The subjects were asked to:

1. Tell what comes to mind when they think about their city and give a broad description of it.
2. Draw a quick map of the central area of the city as though they were sketching for a stranger the location of some point.
3. Describe in detail their trip from home to work. They were also asked to do the same for an imaginary trip along a route given by the interviewer. Their emotional reactions to each trip were requested together with the physical description.
4. Give what they thought were the distinctive elements of the central area of the city.

Essentially, then, the interview consisted of asking the subjects to sketch a map of the city, to give a detailed description of several trips through the city, and to give a brief description of the parts of the city they felt to be most distinctive or vivid. The analysis of the images obtained through these questions was limited to the effects of physical, perceptible objects, although

Lynch points out that there are other influences on the development of an image of an area, such as its social meaning, its history, its functions, and even its name. Lynch found that the physical elements of the city images could conveniently be classified into five types: paths, edges, districts, nodes, and landmarks.

Paths are streets, walkways, transit lines, railroads, and so forth. They are the channels along which the observer moves and for many people are the predominant elements in their images of a city. *Edges* are the "linear elements not used or considered as paths by the observers." They may be shores, railroad cuts, borders of developments, and so forth, but each serves to separate one region from another or to relate and join two regions. Edges are also important organizing features of a city for many observers. *Districts* are the "medium-to-large sections of the city, conceived of as having two-dimensional extent, which the observer mentally enters 'inside of,' and which are recognizable as having some common, identifying character." *Nodes* are important or strategic areas that a person can enter and that are foci to and from which he is traveling. These areas are junctions, places of a break in transportation, crossings or convergences of paths, and so on. They may also be such features as street corner hangouts and enclosed squares. As Lynch suggests, "Some of these concentration nodes are the focus and epitome of a district, over which their influence radiates and of which they stand as a symbol." In their images of a city, people almost always have nodal points, which in some cases are the dominant features of the image. Finally, *landmarks* are, like nodes, points of reference. However, landmarks typically are physical objects, not areas. Examples of landmarks are towers, signs, and stores [pp. 47–48].

The analysis of the images also showed that the elements discussed above did not exist in isolation; typically, districts were structured with nodes, defined by edges, penetrated in various ways by paths, and often had a number of landmarks sprinkled throughout. As Lynch points out, however, although his method allows for collection of adequate data about single elements, it does not yield much information about element interrelations, patterns, sequences, and wholes. He stresses that other methods must be developed to study these vital aspects of images of cities.

With some modifications, a technique such as that used by Lynch might make it possible to determine the image of a city quite accurately. For example, when residents are asked to tell what comes to mind when they think about their city and to give a broad description of it,

Some individuals may describe overcrowding, slums, pollution, characteristics of certain buildings that they find attractive or repellent, the design of streets and interchanges, and so forth. Some characteristics such as certain buildings, parks, and city squares may be viewed in a favorable light by many of the inhabitants whereas other characteristics may be almost uniformly disliked. Some characteristics would result in strong images; other characteristics of the city might be noticed by only a few individuals. When the information from a number of interviews is combined, the investigator will have a fairly comprehensive view of the occupants' image of the city [Heimstra & McDonald, 1973, p. 47].

Other Kinds of Psychological Maps

The psychological mapping technique used by Lynch is relatively unstructured; the persons interviewed responded to questions or instructions in an open-ended fashion. A method of psychological mapping used by Milgram (1972) is more structured. He showed his subjects colored slides of a variety of scenes in New York and asked them to identify the locations. The scenes were selected in an objective fashion by means of a coordinate grid system, with each intersection of a latitude and longitude line defined as a scene. For economy purposes the viewing points were narrowed down to 25 in the Bronx, 22 in Brooklyn, 31 in Queens, 20 in Staten Island, and 54 in Manhattan. The subjects were recruited through an advertisement in *New York Magazine*. Most of the 200 subjects obtained were in their twenties (mean age of 28.9), and a slight majority were women. The "median" subject held a job at the minor professional level and lived in his neighborhood five to ten years and in New York City more than 20 years.

The subjects, who were tested in groups, were each given an answer booklet and a neighborhood map and told to become familiar with the map. They were informed that the primary purpose of the study was to discover how well people can recognize various scenes of the city. The color slides of the various scenes were then projected on a screen. The subjects were asked to imagine that they were seeing the scenes from the window of a bus touring the city and to indicate in the answer booklet the borough where each scene was. They were also asked to identify the neighborhood and the street of each scene. The entire testing procedure took about an hour and a half.

By summing the percentage of correct responses for all scenes in a borough and dividing this figure by the number of scenes, Milgram determined the "index of recognizability," or mean, of the borough. The means of the boroughs were as follows:

Manhattan	64.12%
Queens	39.64
Brooklyn	35.79
Staten Island	26.00
Bronx	25.96

In considering these results, the reader should bear in mind that the scenes used were not selected because of the likelihood they would be recognized but were randomly sampled.

Milgram also found substantial differences according to borough in the proportion of scenes placed in the correct neighborhood. A scene in Manhattan was five times more likely to be placed in the correct neighborhood than was a scene in the Bronx or Staten Island and about three times more likely to be placed correctly than was a scene in Brooklyn or Queens. A similar pattern was found in street location identification.

Thus, as Milgram states:

> New York City, as a psychological space, is very uneven. It is not at all clear that such world cities as London, Paris, Tokyo, and Moscow have comparably uneven psychological textures. It would be extremely interesting to construct a similar psychological map of other cities of the world to determine how successfully each city, in all its parts, communicates to the resident a specific sense of place which locates him in the city, assuages the panic of disorientation, and allows him to build up an articulated image of the city as a whole [p. 200].

Among other recent studies of city images is that by Rand (1969), who used an approach similar to Lynch's. Rand interviewed airplane pilots and taxi drivers and found that images of cities known to both groups were markedly different. In another study Rozelle and Bazer (1972) interviewed residents of Houston, Texas, to determine how they assigned meaning and value to elements of their city by asking them what they regarded as important about the city, how they saw the city, and how they remembered it. Each type of question yielded a response. Rozelle and Bazer concluded that such verbal tasks can elicit the same kind of information as Lynch's sketch maps and have greater flexibility.

Studies using photographic techniques include those of Honikman (1972), who showed his subjects photographs to determine the relationship between qualitative evaluation and physical characteristics of an environmental display, and Kaplan and Wendt (1972), who studied urban environmental preference by means of a series of slides.

The findings of these and similar studies have important implications for urban design, but, unfortunately, little use has been made of them. As pointed out by Bell, Randall, and Roeder (1973) in discussing the work of Lynch:

> The original work by Kevin Lynch has had a significant effect on designers only because of the usefulness of his analytical methods as a tool of description. Because Lynch has been required reading for every design student for a decade, and because of the value of his work in creating a framework into which personal observations can be placed, he has been successful. This is a tool for visual awareness, but not a design methodology [p. 22].

CITY LIVING—A PATHOGENIC EXPERIENCE?

It is a common belief that factors associated with living in the city cause a variety of forms of social pathology as well as several types of physical pathology. In the limited space available, we cannot begin to discuss all the types of social pathology that in all likelihood are caused by aspects of the urban environment. Take, for example, crime in urban areas. This form of social pathology receives a great deal of attention and has been extensively researched. Studies of the relationship between certain kinds of built environments and crime were discussed in some detail in an earlier chapter. In these studies the urban environment was considered to be the independent variable and crime rates or types the dependent variable. Other researchers have used the crime rate as the independent variable and determined the effects of high crime rates in an area on the behavior of noncriminals living in that area. Thus investigators have reported not only changing attitudes toward crime and criminals with increasing crime rates, but also more overt behavior changes, such as buying watchdogs, installing new locks and burglar alarms, and carrying tear gas pens and other weapons. Although crime is certainly a factor that is viewed as a threat by most city dwellers and may have pronounced effects on their behavior, a discussion of this topic is beyond the scope of this book. We will restrict our discussion here to several topics of more direct interest to environmental psychologists.

Only relatively recently has widespread interest been shown in the possible pathological qualities of city dwellers' everyday behavior. The numerous articles on this behavior—often based on no more than casual observation—suggest that urbanites do not care, that they lack spontaneity, that they have withdrawn behind a critical facade, that they exist in a perennial state of distrust and reserve, and on and on. As we shall see later in this chapter, such conclusions are often the result of comparing the behavior of urbanites with that of persons living in rural areas. However, what must be questioned is the interpretation of the behavior of city dwellers as pathological. Michelson (1970) points out in discussing the behavior of urbanites and the tendency of observers to label this behavior pathological:

> In glorifying the assumed open, trusting, and spontaneous posture of nonurban peoples, they treat what may well be a different pattern in cities as a harmful one. And harmful it may be, both absolutely and in certain circumstances, but labeling it as pathological is nonetheless a value laden decision, which may say as much about the labelers as those labeled [p. 149].

Regardless of whether such behavior patterns are pathological, investigations have shown a relationship between certain characteristics of the urban environment and mental illness, heart disease, and hypertension. One characteristic thought to be associated with these types of pathology is high population density, which leads to the experience of overcrowding. Overcrowding and research relating to this topic will be discussed in detail in Chapter 6; here we will briefly consider overcrowding as a cause of pathology.

There is no shortage of "expert" opinion on the effects of overcrowding, and articles about its many expected adverse effects appear frequently. These articles, generally, are scantily documented or are based on animal study data, correlational data, or opinion. Zlutnick and Altman (1972) reviewed the *Reader's Guide to Periodical Literature* for a ten-year period and, from a number of articles, derived 17 propositions concerning overcrowding or overpopulation that have been cited in the popular literature. The investigators grouped these popular conceptions in three categories on the basis of the types of undesirable effects attributed to overcrowding:

1. *Physical effects.* Starvation, pollution, slums, disease, physical malfunctions. . . .
2. *Social effects.* Poor education, poor physical and mental health facilities, crime, riots, war.
3. *Interpersonal and psychological effects.* Drug addiction, alcoholism, family disorganization, withdrawal, aggression, decreased quality of life [p. 49].

Although there are a few controlled experiments on the effects of overcrowding (these will be discussed in later chapters), most of the data supporting the popular conceptions of crowding effects come from animal and correlational studies. Animal studies have a number of limitations, and it is dangerous to generalize from these studies to human behavior.

Correlational studies attempt to establish relationships between population density and such indexes of social disorganization as crime rates, frequency of physical and mental illness, and so forth. As noted earlier, a number of studies have found high population densities to be associated with high crime rates. Other studies have shown that certain types of physical illness are found at higher rates in high population density areas. However, Hay and Wantman (1969) compared the rate of such diseases as hypertension and heart disease (both presumably associated with stress) in New York City with national samples and found that hypertension rates are only slightly higher in New York. Heart disease was found to be lower in New York than in the United States overall. As Srole (1972) states, "the assumption that the city is inherently pathogenic for certain degenerative somatic disorders apparently may have to be rejected" [pp. 578–579].

Of the number of investigations attempting to link population density with mental illness, most report a positive correlation (Faris & Dunham, 1965; Lantz, 1953; Chombart de Lauwe, 1959; and Hollingshead & Redlich, 1958). However, Srole (1972) questions the view that a heavily populated urban area is necessarily less "mentally healthy." He reviews research in this area and points out that differences between urban and rural mental health figures are often not statistically significant and can be explained on the basis of factors other than population density. Srole concludes that the available data suggests:

1. For *children* under certain special combinations of conditions, both the metropolitan and rural slums are more psychopathogenic than are the adjoining nonslum neighborhoods.
2. For *adults* seeking a change in environment, the metropolis under most (but not all) conditions is by and large a more therapeutic milieu than is the small community, especially for the many troubled escapee-deviants among them [p. 583].

Apparently, then, we cannot state with certainty that the high population density of urban areas leads to such pathological conditions as mental illness, hypertension, and heart disease.

In these investigations the independent variable is typically the number of residents per acre of ground or some other measure of area. Other variables, however, are directly associated with population density, but these have been considered separately as possible factors contributing to pathology in urban areas. For example, noise is often correlated with population density, and there is some indication that it increases the incidence of pathology. Farr (1967) reports that high noise levels increase the likelihood of diseases associated with tension, such as duodenal ulcers. Housing type is another example. Fanning (1967), in a study comparing the health of wives and children of armed service personnel living either in three-story or four-story apartment buildings or in self-contained houses, found that the death rate of the apartment dwellers was 57 percent greater than that of those living in houses. The effects of both noise and types of housing on behavior were discussed in Chapter 2 and will not be considered in any more detail here.

We pointed out earlier in this chapter that many slum residents are highly satisfied with their neighborhood because of the extensive social relationships they have formed there. We also noted that many slum dwellers have been forcibly relocated by urban renewal programs but that relatively little information is available on the effects of relocation. Researchers have found, however, that forcibly moving persons from areas to which they have become deeply attached often causes what has been called a "grief syndrome," which can result in crying spells and psychosomatic illnesses, such as intestinal disorders, vomiting, and nausea. Of course, many people do not feel any attachment to their neighborhood; indeed, some residents of slum areas openly welcome demolition of their neighborhoods for urban renewal.

The best summary for our brief discussion of the city as a source of pathology is that very little is known about the relationship between various physical conditions in the urban environment and either behavioral or physical pathology. As Michelson (1970) states, "Such conventionally pursued causes of pathology as housing conditions, high density, noise, and housing type reap uncertain results due to (1) very limited effects documented, (2) ambiguity of the physical referent, (3) the salience of intervening variables, and (4) the lack of precise definition of dependent pathologies. But they remain potentially meaningful" [p. 167]. It remains for future research to determine just how meaningful the relationship between the urban environment and pathology actually is.

THE BEHAVIOR OF URBANITES

We have previously pointed out that living in a city is thought to result in behavior patterns different from those found in more leisurely rural areas. The typical city dweller is often thought of as a person who does not appear to care about others, who lacks spontaneity, who has a rational, even calculating approach to his daily routine, and so forth—though as Michelson (1970, p. 149) has suggested, labeling this type of behavior pathological is a value judgment. Before considering research comparing the behavior of urbanites with the behavior of residents of rural or less heavily populated areas, we will discuss a theoretical framework that has been advanced in an attempt to explain the behavior of people living in cities.

THE CONCEPT OF SYSTEM OVERLOAD

It has become convenient to think of our complex technological society in terms of systems in which industries, organizations, machines, and even people are considered to be interdependent components (subsystems) working together to achieve some objective. Systems analysts study the relationships among the subsystems and the ways in which these relationships contribute to the purposes of the system. These analysts tend to think in terms of *inputs* to the system and *transformations* of the inputs into *outputs*. If we think of a person in these terms, environmental stimuli are inputs; transformations are effected by a number of behavioral subsystems (perception, cognitive functions, memory, motivation, and so on); and outputs are behavior (Heimstra & Ellingstad, 1972).

If there are too many inputs for the system, either human or nonhuman, to cope with, we then talk about *system overload*. For the human, information overload can serve as a source of stress (discussed in more detail in Chapter 6) and may modify his behavior in a number of ways. Because information overload cannot always be avoided in man-machine systems, or in any other systems of which man is an integral part, research has been conducted to determine how people handle information overload and how it affects behavior. In a summary of some of this research, Miller (1964) lists the following adjustment processes that humans tend to make in response to information overload:

1. Omission, which is not processing information if there is an overload.
2. Error, processing incorrectly and failing to correct for it.
3. Queuing, delaying responses during heavy load periods and catching up during any lulls that occur.
4. Filtering, systematic omission of certain types of information usually according to a priority scheme.

5. Approximation, a less precise response given because there is no time for details.
6. Multiple channels, making use of parallel subsystems if the system has them at its disposal.
7. Decentralization, a special case of multiple channels.
8. Escape, either leaving the situation or taking other steps which cut off the input of information [p. 93].

Although the research dealing with these mechanisms has been conducted in laboratories, Milgram (1970a) suggests that somewhat similar adaptive mechanisms are involved in the behavior of city dwellers. He feels that city life is made up of continuous encounters with input overload and argues that this overload "deforms daily life on several levels, impinging on role performance, the evolution of social norms, cognitive functioning, and the use of facilities" [p. 1462]. He discusses a number of responses adopted by city dwellers to deal with system overload. These include:

1. *Allocating less time to each input.* One way to adapt to some kinds of overload, such as encountering vast numbers of people each day, is to allow little time for these kinds of inputs. Thus, urban dwellers "conserve psychic energy by becoming acquainted with a far smaller proportion of people than their rural counterparts do, and by maintaining more superficial relationships even with these acquaintances."
2. *Disregarding low priority inputs.* Urban dwellers become selective; they invest their time and energy in carefully defined inputs while disregarding others. Thus, the urbanite walking down a street ignores such inputs as panhandlers and drunks.
3. *Redrawing boundaries in certain social transactions.* In this adaptive mechanism the burden of an overload is shifted to the other party in a social exchange. For example, "harried New York bus drivers once made change for customers, but now this responsibility has been shifted to the client, who must have the exact fare ready."
4. *Blocking inputs.* Milgram uses as an example of this process the tendency of city dwellers to have unlisted phone numbers or to leave their phones off the hook. He also points out that a more subtle example of this response is when a city dweller discourages other persons from initiating contact by wearing an unfriendly expression.

5. *Diminishing the intensity of inputs.* The person responding in this way establishes "filtering devices" to avoid developing deep or lasting involvements with other people.

6. *Creating specialized institutions.* Various kinds of institutions are developed by city dwellers to "absorb inputs that would otherwise swamp the individual." An example is the welfare departments that handle the needs of individuals who "would otherwise create an army of mendicants continuously importuning the pedestrian" [p. 1462].

Milgram's system overload concept is an interesting theoretical framework for explaining the behavior of the urbanite in a wide range of situations. In his article Milgram deals with a number of specific consequences of responses to system overload and discusses how these responses make for differences in the behavior seen in cities and in towns. Although several of the investigations he cites will be discussed in this chapter, readers who are interested in pursuing this topic in more depth should read Milgram's article.

SOME RESEARCH ON THE BEHAVIOR OF URBANITES

Although there have not been a tremendous number of studies dealing directly with the behavior of urbanites, those that do exist involve a variety of approaches and techniques. In some studies the behavior of residents of different cities has been compared (Feldman, 1968; Zimbardo, 1969); in other studies, such as that by Altman, Levine, Nadien, and Villena (reported in Milgram, 1970b), the behavior of city dwellers has been compared with that of residents of more rural areas. Several other investigations are studies of certain aspects of behavior thought to be characteristic of urban dwellers. Latané and Darley (1969), for example, studied bystander intervention under a number of different conditions, while Mann (1970) investigated the unique set of social rules and behavioral regularities associated with waiting lines.

All the above studies will be discussed in this section. However, many other investigations described in other parts of this text would also be appropriate for consideration here. For example, the studies dealing with the effects of high population density on behavior, which are covered in Chapter 6, are relevant, as are several of the studies discussed in previous chapters. The reader should keep in mind that the point in the text where a particular study is discussed is a somewhat arbitrary decision on the part of the authors and does not mean that the study would not be equally relevant elsewhere in the book. For example, although it might be convenient to discuss a certain behavior-environment interaction under the heading of "multiple family dwellings," that these dwellings are probably located in an urban area and their inhabitants' behavior affected by the urban environment would justify discussing the interaction under "the behavior of urbanites." Thus, much environmental psychology research is directly or indirectly concerned with the behavior of urbanites although usually not labeled as such.

Rural-Urban Differences in Behavior

If system overload, resulting from the conditions existing in cities, brings about adaptive behavior, then persons living in small towns should not be overloaded and consequently should not show the adaptive forms of behavior supposedly characteristic of city dwellers. Studies comparing the behavior of urbanites with that of small town residents under a number of different conditions would reveal whether differences in behavior do in fact exist. Unfortunately, though speculation about differences abounds, virtually no empirical research is available. Milgram (1970a) cites two unpublished investigations illustrating this kind of research and suggesting that additional research along the lines of these studies might be profitable.

One of these two studies is by Altman, Levine, Nadien, and Villena (1969), who compared the behavior of city and town dwellers in agreeing to extend a type of aid that increased their personal vulnerability and required some trust of strangers. In this study the investigators (two males and two females) each rang doorbells in New York and in small towns, explained that he had lost the address of a friend living nearby, and asked to use the telephone. The researchers made 100 requests in the city and 60 in small towns. The investigators had much greater success in gaining admittance in the small towns than they did in the city. Although the female researchers were admitted more often in both the city and the towns than were the male researchers, all four were at least twice as successful in gaining admittance in the small towns as in the city. Besides recording the number of admissions, the investigators observed qualitative differences in the behavior of the rural and urban residents. They reported that the small towners were much more friendly and less suspicious than the city dwellers, who, even if they did allow the investigators inside, appeared suspicious and ill at ease.

The other unpublished study, by McKenna and Morgenthau (1969), was designed, in part, to compare the willingness of urbanites to do favors for strangers with that of small towners. The favors requested entailed a small amount of time and inconvenience but, unlike the requests in the other study, could in no way be interpreted as posing any personal threat. The researchers telephoned a number of people living in Chicago, New York, and Philadelphia and in 37 small towns in the same states as the three cities. Half the calls went to housewives and the other half to salesgirls in women's apparel shops. The investigator phoning represented herself as a long distance caller who had been mistakenly connected with the respondent. The investigator began asking for information on various topics and then said, "Please hold on," and put the phone down. After nearly a minute she picked up the phone and asked for more information. The investigator assigned scores to the respondents on the basis of how cooperative they had been.

The results of the study showed that the housewives were less helpful than the salesgirls in both the cities and the towns. Milgram (1970a) points out, however, that "the absolute level of cooperativeness for urban subjects was found to be quite high, and does not accord with the stereotype of the urbanite as aloof, self-centered, and unwilling to help strangers" [p. 1465].

The results of these two studies can be discussed in terms of Milgram's system overload concept. One possible reason for the urbanite's reduced social involvement seen in these studies is the need to reduce system overload. Milgram points out that the "ultimate adaptation to an overloaded social environment is to totally disregard the needs, interests, and demands of those whom one does not define as relevant to the satisfaction of personal needs . . ." [p. 1462]. One example of this type of adaptation is the failure of urban bystanders to help a person in distress. A similar adaptation can be seen in less urgent situations, as illustrated in the study by Altman and his coworkers, in which many urbanites failed to lend a hand to a stranger at their doors. The McKenna and Morgenthau study also reveals adaptive behavior in that cooperation with the caller was a matter of social responsibility.

Milgram (1970b) stresses that we have very little objective documentation of the differences between urbanites and town dwellers. However, his urban overload concept does provide theoretical framework for further study of these differences. He states:

> The concept of overload helps to explain a wide variety of contrasts between city and town behavior: (1) the differences in *role enactment* (the urban dwellers' tendency to deal with one another in highly segmented, functional terms; the constricted time and services offered customers by sales personnel); (2) the evolution of *urban norms* quite different from traditional town values (such as the acceptance of noninvolvement, impersonality, and aloofness in urban life); (3) consequences for the urban dweller's *cognitive processes* (his inability to identify most of the people seen

daily; his screening of sensory stimuli; his development of blasé attitudes toward deviant or bizarre behavior; and his selectivity in responding to human demands); and (4) the far greater competition for scarce *facilities* in the city (the subway rush, the fight for taxis, traffic jams, standing in line to await services). I would suggest that contrasts between city and rural behavior probably reflect the responses of similar people to very different situations, rather than intrinsic differences between rural personalities and city personalities. The city is a situation to which individuals respond adaptively [pp. 161–162].

There are, of course, other studies that have, for one reason or another, compared the behavior of persons living in urban and rural areas. For example, Martin and Heimstra (1973) tested children in rural and urban areas on a perception of hazard test to determine the degree of risk perceived in a number of scenes depicting different levels of hazard—a child holding a gun, loading a gun, swallowing aspirin, and so forth. Children living in urban and rural areas perceived different amounts of hazard in different scenes. For example, children in rural areas saw more hazard in the gun scenes, in street scenes, and in scenes depicting various types of power tools than did children from urban areas. Other studies not actually considered to be environmental psychology research by the investigators are also relevant here, such as studies showing different rates of narcotic usage between rural and urban areas, of alcohol use, of suicide, and of mental illness.

Differences among Cities

We pointed out earlier that different cities have different atmospheres and that some effort has been made to determine how the atmosphere of a city is created and how the image of the city is developed in the minds of its residents and visitors. Some investigators have also been interested in the differences in behavior that might be demonstrated by the residents of various cities. One such investigation was that by Feldman (1968), who studied the behavior of residents of Boston, Paris, and Athens toward compatriots and foreigners. This study, which was quite complicated, consisted of five situations, or experiments, in which "native" or foreign experimenters (a Frenchman in Boston, for example) were involved in situations with residents of each of the cities. The situations included (1) asking a resident of the city for directions; (2) asking a resident to do a favor for a stranger by mailing a letter (half of the letters unstamped); (3) asking a resident if he had just dropped a dollar bill (or the foreign equivalent) to see whether he would falsely claim money from a stranger; (4) deliberately overpaying a clerk to see whether the mistake would be corrected; and (5) determining whether cab drivers overcharged strangers or took longer routes to obtain higher fares.

Feldman found that the more than 3000 subjects in the five experiments showed consistent differences in treatment of compatriots and foreigners. In the experiment in which directions were asked for, both the Parisian and the Athenian samples gave help more often at the request of fellow citizens than at the request of foreigners; in Boston there was little difference. In the experiment in which the subjects were asked to mail a letter for a stranger, there were no major differences in the way compatriots and foreigners were treated in Boston and Athens. Surprisingly, in view of the American stereotype of Parisians' behavior, the Parisian subjects treated foreigners significantly better than their own compatriots. Moreover, the Parisians were significantly more honest in resisting the temptation to claim money falsely and, again, were less likely to make the false claim if a foreigner was involved than if a compatriot was involved. However, the stereotype of the typical Parisian cab driver held up; they overcharged foreigners more often than their compatriots. This was not the case in Boston or Athens.

We can only briefly summarize the results of Feldman's study. The original article contains much more data on the behavior of the residents of the three cities and is well worth reading by anyone interested in this type of research.

Another investigation comparing the behavior of residents of different cities is that of Zimbardo (1969). He made arrangements for an automobile to be left for 64 hours near the Bronx campus of New York University and another car to be left near the Stanford University campus in Palo Alto, California, for the same number of hours. In both cases the investigators removed the license plates from the cars and left the hoods open. The cars were watched continuously for the 64 hours, and photographs were taken at various times. Zimbardo states:

> What happened in New York was unbelievable! Within ten minutes the 1959 Oldsmobile received its first auto strippers—a father, mother, and eight-year-old son. The mother appeared to be a lookout, while the son aided the father's search of the trunk, glove compartment, and motor. He handed his father the tools necessary to remove the battery and radiator. Total time of destructive contact: seven minutes [p. 287].

By the end of the first 26 hours, the car had been stripped of everything worthwhile. Then random destruction began. In less than three days, what remained was a battered, useless hunk of metal. Many of the people involved in the "contacts" were well-dressed, respectable-looking adults. "In startling contrast, the Palo Alto car not only emerged untouched, but when it began to rain, one passerby lowered the hood so that the motor would not get wet" [p. 290].

The studies described have been concerned primarily with comparing the behavior of urbanites with that of residents of rural areas or with comparing the behavior of residents of different cities. Other studies are investigations of a particular type of behavior thought to be associated with urban living. In concluding this chapter, we will consider two studies of this type—one dealing with bystander intervention and the other with behavior in waiting lines.

Studies of Bystander Intervention and Waiting Lines

We have already pointed out that one adaptive response to urban overload is to disregard the needs of others in circumstances ranging from intervening in an emergency to lending a hand to a stranger. An often cited example of bystanders' refusing to become involved in the needs of someone else even if the person urgently needs assistance is the 1964 Genovese murder case in Queens. A young woman was stabbed repeatedly, and, even though her cries for help were heard by many persons, not one came to her assistance or even called the police until after she was dead. This murder, as well as other instances in which bystanders failed to help someone in serious trouble, has led to a series of controlled investigations of bystander intervention.

Probably the best known of these studies are those by Latané and Darley (1969). These studies involved a number of different experimental conditions. However, they all involved situations that were contrived in such a way that the researchers could observe the reactions of "bystanders" (who were actually subjects in the studies although they were not aware of it) to various kinds of "emergencies." For example, in one study the subjects were in a supermarket where they were under the impression that they were to assist in a survey. They were placed in a room under a number of conditions. Some subjects were alone; some were joined by one or two more persons. The others were friends, or strangers, in on the experiment or not, and so forth.

Shortly after the subject entered the room, a loud crash occurred in an adjacent room, together with moans and cries, as though someone had been injured. The dependent variable in this study was whether the subject went to the assistance of the "injured" person and, if he did, how long it took him to do so. When the subjects were alone in the room, 70 percent of them intervened. However, under all the conditions in which more than one person was present, the percentage who intervened dropped sharply. Other studies involving faked emergencies and bystander intervention had the same results. The general conclusion drawn from these investigations is that the larger the number of bystanders, the less likelihood that any one of them will intervene in an emergency.

One characteristic of life in the city is the need to spend considerable time waiting in lines of one kind or another. Although operations researchers have recognized for some time that queues are inefficient and time consuming and have conducted research aimed at shortening and speeding up all kinds of waiting lines, only recently have psychologists become interested in the behavior of persons forced to wait in line.

Mann (1970) and his co-workers investigated the unique set of social rules and behavioral regularities associated with waiting lines. In a series of field experiments, they studied a number of waiting lines where people were queued for tickets for football games, plays, and so forth. In other studies they formed their own queues experimentally in libraries and in other settings. They considered a number of aspects of waiting lines—social structure, line jumping, and other kinds of behavior. The researchers found that the social structure of a waiting line is focused on preservation of a person's right to leave the line momentarily without losing his place. If he does not follow a clearly defined protocol when leaving, he may not be allowed back in the line. Mann points out that brief leaves of absence from the queue are accomplished by two universally recognized procedures:

> One technique is the "shift" system, in which the person joins the queue as part of a small group and takes his turn in spending one hour "on" to every three hours "off." . . . A second technique for taking a time out is designed especially for people at the end of the queue who came alone. They "stake a claim" by leaving some item of personal property such as a labeled box, folding chair, or sleeping bag. Indeed, during the early hours of queuing . . . the queue consisted of one part people to two parts inanimate objects [p. 392].

Although queue jumpers violate the basic norm of the queue, physical violence is rarely used to punish or eject the violator. Interestingly, the favorite hunting ground of the queue jumper is the rear of the waiting line rather than the front.

Another interesting form of behavior was noted in some lines. When it was known that there was a limited number of items available (100 tickets for a football game, for example), many more than 100 people typically lined up. In one study Mann asked every tenth person in a line to estimate how many people were ahead of him. Up to the point where the tickets were likely to run out, the person tended to overestimate the number ahead. In other words, if 100 tickets were available, people up to about 100 in the line would estimate that there were more people ahead of them than there really were. After the critical point of 100, the mood of the queuers began to change, and people constantly underestimated the number of persons ahead of them. The investigators called this the wish fulfillment hypothesis. The researchers also found that the longer the line, the stronger was its drawing power and that a rapidly growing line tended to draw bystanders into it.

SUMMARY

In this chapter we have been concerned with several aspects of the urban environment and their effects on behavior. Some aspects of this environment that directly or indirectly affect nearly all urban dwellers are collectively called the urban crisis—poverty, crime, pollution, and so on. In all surveys these factors are listed as sources of dissatisfaction with urban living. However, there are also a number of sources of satisfaction associated with urban living, even in slum neighborhoods. For example, many residents of slum areas have a strong sense of belonging. The physical area surrounding their homes is viewed as an integral part of the home and serves as a framework for a vast set of social ties. The social ties and the feeling of belonging are important factors in determining whether residents of slum neighborhoods like or dislike living there. Residential satisfaction in suburban areas is determined by other factors. Among these are good physical facilities; good schools; friendly neighbors; relative safety from crime; access to stores, jobs, and so on; good environmental quality; and little congestion.

Researchers have also been interested in how residents of a city actually view the city—in the kind of image a city holds for its residents. Two popular techniques for charting these images of a city involve asking residents to construct mental maps by actually drawing a map of the city, and asking residents to view and attempt to identify scenes from the city. These mental maps have revealed that the physical elements of a city can conveniently be classified into five types, which Lynch (1960) calls paths, edges, districts, nodes, and landmarks. Mapping techniques of this sort have also led to a better understanding of the manner in which people view the cities in which they live.

A number of investigators have been concerned with the effects that living in cities may have on behavior and health. Studies have shown a relationship between certain characteristics of the urban environment, such as high population density, and such pathologies as mental illness, heart disease, and hypertension. However, Srole (1972), in a comprehensive review of the literature in this area, questions whether these relationships are as firmly established as they were once thought to be.

Other studies have compared the behavior of urban residents with that of residents of more rural areas to determine the nature and magnitude of any possible differences. Although the typical city dweller is generally thought to be a person who does not care about others, who lacks spontaneity, who has a calculating approach to daily living, and so forth, it is difficult to study systematically these kinds of behavior. The studies that have been conducted indicate that there are differences in behavior between urban and rural residents but that there is no basis for labeling one or the other type of behavior more or less "normal." Although theory is lacking in this area, Milgram (1970a) has attempted to explain the behavior of city dwellers in terms of system overload, where city life is viewed as a continuous encounter with input overload. According to this theory, much of the behavior of urbanites can be considered to be adaptive behavior designed to reduce the overload.

Comparisons have also been made between the behavior of residents of different cities. It has been shown that there are differences among cities in how the residents treat strangers in such matters as lending assistance and being honest in their dealings. Similarly, the behavior of residents of various cities may differ considerably in the manner in which they treat someone else's property, such as an automobile. In one study a car left in New York City was virtually demolished by residents within 24 hours while a car left under similar circumstances in Palo Alto was unharmed.

Although no attempt was made to deal exhaustively with urban environments and human behavior, the studies presented in this chapter are representative of the type of research being conducted by environmental psychologists in this area. It should be apparent that we still know very little about effects of living in a city. Indeed, much of what we "know" is based on speculation rather than on empirical research. The number of studies in this field is increasing, but considering how many millions of persons live in cities, certainly a great deal more research should be undertaken.

CHAPTER FIVE

THE NATURAL ENVIRONMENT

AND BEHAVIOR

In the preceding chapters we have been concerned with the man-made, or built, environment and with some of the ways in which this type of environment may influence human behavior. Thus, we have seen how rooms, houses, buildings, institutions, and cities may directly or indirectly affect the behavior of their occupants or residents. Although much of the research in environmental psychology has been concerned with the built environment and its effects on behavior, some researchers have been interested in the relationship between the *natural environment* and behavior. In this chapter we will discuss some of the theories and research on this relationship.

It would be convenient to think of the natural environment as the non-man-made environment, but doing so would result in a more restricted definition than we have in mind. As used in this chapter, the term "natural environment" means not only geographic regions and wilderness areas that, essentially, are natural areas and parks, but also large and small recreation areas, which usually have many man-made features. These recreation areas, however, are simulated natural environments in that they are built to give people some contact with trees, open space, streams, and so forth, which are viewed as components of the natural environment. Spending an hour or two in an urban park with its ponds and trees means, for many city dwellers, contact with natural environment in contrast to the built environment of buildings, streets, automobiles, and so on. This is the case even if the pond is man-made and the trees were carefully planted in orderly rows.

TYPES OF INTERACTIONS BETWEEN MAN AND THE NATURAL ENVIRONMENT

Man interacts with the natural environment in many ways and at many levels. In general, however, we can think of these interactions as falling into two general categories: *temporary* interactions and *permanent* interactions. For example, a visit to a national park or wilderness area, or to a regional park or recreation area, for most persons would involve a temporary interaction; for park rangers and other persons associated with these areas, a more permanent interaction would be involved. As we shall see, these temporary interactions are actively sought by many individuals and are thought to give them satisfaction or pleasure. We shall also see, however, that the motivation underlying this pursuit of the natural environment by millions of persons annually is not clearly understood and may be quite complex.

We all interact with the natural environment on a more permanent basis, although the nature and intensity of this interaction vary according to individual circumstance. We live in geographical regions that may be characterized by extreme heat or cold, by droughts or frequent floods, by tornadoes, hurricanes, or earthquakes, or by combinations of these. Each region also has distinctive terrain features, such as mountains, plains, or deserts. Although the relationships between these terrain and climatic features and behavior have not been clearly demonstrated, many environmental psychologists assume that such relationships do exist. We will discuss these permanent interactions in detail later in the chapter. At this point we will consider one of the most important of the temporary types of interactions—that encountered in outdoor recreation.

OUTDOOR RECREATION

Only a few years ago articles on the psychological aspects of outdoor recreation were relatively rare. However, interest has recently been increasing in the motivations for participating in outdoor recreation and the satisfaction associated with it. This increased attention is probably due to two primary factors. The first is that certain types of outdoor recreation facilities, such as national parks and wilderness areas, have in many instances already reached the saturation point in numbers of users, yet user demand continues to increase. Because the parks and wilderness areas are limited in supply and are not reproducible, the management system must decide how to cope with the demand. At the one extreme the management can let the use continue unabated; at the other they can severely restrict the use of the areas. Neither option is feasible, so managerial action somewhere between these extremes is required. To make these decisions, the management must have considerable information on the characteristics of the users, including their motivations for coming to the area, their perceived requirements of an area, and the types of interactions associated with a particular area that produce maximum user satisfaction. Although researchers have been attempting to gather information about these kinds of user characteristics, much more needs to be known before decisions about managing the park and wilderness areas can be made with any real confidence.

The other reason for the increased interest in behavior and outdoor recreation is the steadily growing amount of leisure time available to many segments of our society. Already some organizations have instituted the four-day work week, and a shorter work week has become an important negotiation point in many labor contracts. Although total leisure time might increase in various other ways (lowering the retirement age, for example), millions of people now appear to have more leisure time than ever before and may have even more in the near future.

There is a close relationship, of course, between leisure and recreation, whether indoor or outdoor. As leisure time increases, those who prefer some form of outdoor recreation will increase the demands on existing facilities and new ones of many kinds will have to be constructed. Some research on the behavior of the users of these facilities is being conducted that will hopefully provide useful information to the managers of existing outdoor recreation areas and the designers of new ones.

CATEGORIES OF OUTDOOR RECREATION

The range of outdoor recreation activities is, of course, wide, and they take place in a number of different areas. One of the schemes for classifying these areas is that of Clawson (1966):

> At one extreme are the user-oriented areas: close to where people live, suitable for use after school and after work, individually often rather small and not too demanding as to physical charac-

teristics, ready location is their prime requirement. Farther out lie the intermediate use areas: designed primarily for day-long recreation use, generally within an hour's travel time of most users, on the best sites available, they present much more flexibility in location and in resource qualities required. At the other extreme are the resource-based areas, whose superb and unusual physical or historical characteristics make them desirable in spite of a frequently inconvenient location for most users. The first require or are best suited to daily leisure, the second to weekend leisure, and the third to vacation time [p. 253].

In this chapter we will be primarily concerned with the last type of areas, those that Clawson categorizes as resource based. These include the national parks and wilderness regions, which serve as an important source of interactions with the natural environment for millions of people each year. However, as we shall see, the other types of areas are also important; for many people user-oriented and intermediate use areas are the primary source of temporary interaction with the natural environment.

THE KINDS OF BEHAVIOR STUDIED

Much of the research on the behavior of users of outdoor recreation areas and facilities has been applied research—that is, research designed to answer specific "real world" questions. Typically, the questions were raised by management personnel confronted with the need to make decisions about present and future use of outdoor recreation areas.

Some of the information required is straightforward and not particularly difficult to obtain. For example, the behavior of users of the various types of recreational areas can be observed and data obtained on the use of such facilities as campsites, trails, and lakes. Users can be questioned about what they did or did not do during a visit to a recreational area, and a relatively accurate idea of the overt behavior patterns of the typical user can be obtained. Other types of needed data, however, are not so easily collected. For instance, management personnel are interested in what factors associated with the user and the environment are most important in determining whether the outdoor recreation experience is satisfactory or unsatisfactory. Thus, several investigations have been conducted to determine the characteristics of wilderness areas that are considered to be critical aspects of the "wilderness experience." In this type of study, the researcher must isolate various affective states of the users—moods and feelings, attitudes, aesthetic experiences, and so forth—and relate them to the physical characteristics of the wilderness area.

By far the most common research method used in this type of study is to interview or give questionnaires to the users of an outdoor recreation area either while they are there or shortly after they leave. Although the survey instruments vary depending upon the objectives of the study, many are designed to elicit the attitudes or feelings of the respondents about their recreation experience. Other techniques have also been used with some degree of success. For example, Craik (1972) developed a landscape adjective check list that was used by subjects to describe a large number of different landscape scenes. Other investigators have used various types of representations of an area, such as a map (Lucas, 1964), in attempting to determine users' perceived requirements of a wilderness area. In general, however, the survey has been the primary method used in research in this field.

NATIONAL PARKS AND WILDERNESS AREAS

One of the major sources of temporary interactions between man and the natural environment are the national parks and wilderness areas. Annually, millions of persons visit these areas and engage in a variety of activities—fishing, backpacking, camping, hiking, horseback riding, and many others. Each year the number of persons visiting these areas increases substantially, and many parks and wilderness areas have already reached the saturation point. The problem promises to become even more critical. Since World War II the use of wilderness areas has increased about 10 percent per year, and there is no reason to expect that this growth rate will decrease. Indeed, Stankey (1972) points out that it may even increase:

> Simple projections do not tell the whole story. Wilderness users tend to be disproportionately drawn from higher-income groups, professional and technical occupational categories, urban areas, and the college and postgraduate ranks. Moreover, these characteristics apply to a steadily increasing proportion of the population. If indeed some casual relationship exists between any or all of these variables and wilderness use, then the possibility of future increases in wilderness use is further enhanced [p. 90].

Because of the tremendous increase in the use of national parks and wilderness areas, the persons responsible for their management have been faced with a number of crucial decisions. The key issues revolve around the question of how much change can be made in these areas to accommodate more visitors without changing the "wilderness experience" they seek.

Management's need for more information on which to base decisions has led to research on the characteristics of the users of the areas, the characteristics of the natural environment that are important to the users, and the interactions between man and the natural environment that occur in these areas. In this section we will discuss some of this research.

CHARACTERISTICS OF THE USERS

Surveys show that people in every socioeconomic class and occupation visit national parks and wilderness areas. However, as already pointed out, the users tend to be atypical socioeconomically when compared with the population as a whole. A disproportionate percentage of the users have a college or postgraduate degree, belong to one of the professions, and have an above average income. Consider, for example, the results of a survey conducted at Yellowstone National Park by McDonald and Clark (1968). Nearly 3000 visitors were given questionnaires at different points in the park. Although the questionnaires were designed to obtain data about the users' reactions to the park, data were also obtained on the visitors' occupations and education. Some of the 57 occupations identified are shown in Table 5-1. Note that although there were fluctuations across the summer, teachers and students made up a fairly large segment of the visitor population. Of all the visitors interviewed, 68 percent had at least some college education, a finding implied by the occupations listed in the table. This percentage of college educated is, of course, much higher than that found in the general population. McDonald and Clark's finding is similar to that of Gilligan (1962), who reports that about 80 percent of all visitors to a wilderness area had a college education and that 27 percent of these even had some postgraduate training.

Table 5-1. Percentage of visitors' occupations by month

Occupation	June	July	August
Teacher	7.88	6.07	7.97
Student	5.76	2.80	7.97
Labor	6.97	7.48	5.18
Engineering	5.45	6.54	7.17
Business	9.09	9.81	8.37
Military-government	5.76	3.74	7.17
Agriculture	3.33	3.27	5.18
Retired	6.67	5.14	4.38

Obtaining information about the occupations and educational backgrounds of park and wilderness users is, of course, relatively simple.

Information on other characteristics, however, is more important for management decisions and is more difficult to obtain. For example, "wilderness" is largely a function of human perception, and management must know the factors associated with a given area that cause it to be perceived as wilderness. Similarly, the relationship between various physical characteristics of an area and the affective states of its users needs to be determined. What motivates so many people to visit these areas? Why are some areas so much more popular than others? What do the recreational "purists" look for in an area in contrast to the ordinary users? Answers to these and many other questions are needed for proper management of parks and wilderness regions. Unfortunately, some of the questions are difficult to answer. Take, for example, the question of why people visit these areas.

Motivations of the Users

We know that each year many millions of people visit national parks and wilderness areas and that this number increases each year. We also know a good deal about the characteristics of these visitors—where they come from, their age, education, occupation, and so forth. What is not nearly so clear, however, is why they come to the parks and wilderness areas. Generally, when asked why they came to a particular area, a majority of the visitors give such reasons as wanting to get away from the city, seeking peace and tranquility, seeking a change in the everyday routine, and getting away from it all. Although replies such as these may partly answer the question of why they visit the park or wilderness area, the reasons for the need to "get away from it all" have not been systematically studied. Driver (1972) suggests that environmental stress encountered in urban areas may create needs of this sort and that recreation in parks and similar areas may serve as a means of coping with environmental stress.

The concept of environmental stress is discussed in some detail in the next chapter and will not be considered to any extent here. Briefly, a number of features associated with urban living are stressful, and increasing numbers of people are exposed to these stresses each year. In the literature dealing with stress and behavior, the theme of temporary escape as a mechanism for coping with stress is pervasive. Driver is suggesting that recreation areas provide temporary means of escaping from the stress encountered in everyday urban living and that these escapes enable people to recover somewhat from the effects of the stress.

The view that outdoor recreation has stress-mediating value raises an interesting question, however. If outdoor recreation serves as a temporary escape from the stresses of city living, what will happen as the stresses encountered in the recreation areas become more pronounced? For example, one source of stress usually associated with city living is high population density, which results in the experience of overcrowding. High population density as a source of stress is discussed in the next chapter, as is the concept of overcrowding. As we shall see, the experience of being crowded is greatly dependent upon situational variables; a person who does not experience overcrowding on a city street may experience it when forced to share a campsite in a national park or when encountering another backpacker on a wilderness trail. Traffic jams in national parks and crowded campgrounds may be a more significant source of stress than the stresses associated with the city. More and more visitors are complaining about the congestion in recreation areas, and, although management is trying to alleviate this condition, the task is difficult if not impossible. If visiting recreation areas becomes a matter of escaping from one stress-provoking condition to another condition that is equally stressful, the popularity of the parks and wilderness regions may decline.

In addition to suggesting that recreation areas serve as a means for escaping from stress, Driver suggests some other reasons that people visit these areas. He states:

> Recreational engagements provide interesting and sometimes the only opportunities for the gratification of other human needs. These would include the following: to develop, maintain, or protect a self-image (this need seems particularly true for the elderly who select types of recreation that protect or enhance their "age" image); to retain and develop social identities or more simply just to affiliate; to gain esteem, including the reduction of status incongruity; to display, apply, and develop skills or to achieve; to exercise power, for example, in motorboating, snowmobiling, or hunting; to satisfy exploratory and curiosity drives; to engage in creative self-fulfillment; or to achieve some satisfactory degree of closure on or mastery of other problem-need states of the individual [p. 237].

The above represents a substantial list of needs that may be fulfilled by a visit to a national park or wilderness area. As we have emphasized, however, just why people visit these areas in such large numbers remains something of a mystery. Although research aimed at uncovering the motivations of users presents the investigator with a number of problems, it is an important area that requires a good deal more systematic study before we have a satisfactory answer.

Perceived Requirements of Parks and Wilderness Areas

Just what do people look for or expect when they visit a national park or wilderness area? What features serve as sources of satisfaction, and what features do visitors find unsatisfactory? In other words, what do visitors perceive as requirements of an area in order for them to feel satisfaction about their interactions with the natural environment? Answers to these questions are of considerable importance to management personnel in making decisions about providing a particular type of recreation experience.

A number of studies have been conducted to answer these questions. One of the most comprehensive investigations was carried out by Stankey (1972), who examined the attitudes of wilderness users toward features of the areas that were considered important. He interviewed over 600 visitors to four wilderness areas, the Bob Marshall Wilderness in Montana, the Bridger Wilderness in Wyoming, the High Uintas Primitive Area in Utah, and the Boundary Waters Canoe Area in Minnesota.

Each respondent was asked to rate 14 items or statements, *in the context of wilderness,* on a five-point scale ranging from "very undesirable" to "very desirable." For example, the item "solitude—not seeing many other people except those in your own party" might be rated "very desirable" and would be given a score of 5 on the scale. The responses were scored so that an individual with very strong purist attitudes toward the wilderness would score high and persons with less strong attitudes would score lower. The possible range of total scores was between 70 and 14. On the basis of their scores, the respondents were classified into four groups: strong purists, moderate purists, neutralists, and nonpurists. Although comparisons were made between the responses of the various groups, Stankey considered the strong purists (scores between 60 and 70 on the scale) to be the users most relevant for wilderness management decisions. We cannot summarize all the findings of this study. Instead we will consider in some detail one of the more important perceived wilderness attributes indicated by the users—the attribute of solitude.

When the respondents were asked about the importance of solitude as a feature of the wilderness, 82 percent of the overall sample responded in a positive fashion, while 96 percent of the purists thought it a highly desirable feature. Thus, this characteristic of the wilderness would seem to be very important to the users. The attitude toward solitude is, however, more complex than one might think. In a detailed analysis of factors important in generating the feeling of solitude, Stankey points out that if a person truly desires solitude, one might expect to find him traveling alone in the wilderness. However, in the study only 2 percent of the respondents were traveling by themselves. Solitude, even in the mind of the purist, apparently involves a situation in which contacts with *other* groups are minimal; interaction with members of one's own party does not infringe upon the feeling of solitude. (Actually, for many people social interaction with members of other groups around a campfire or in other circumstances also seems to be an important and positive part of the wilderness experience, although only about one in ten of the purists thought social interaction an integral part of the experience.)

The visitors were asked whether they would be bothered by (1) meeting many people on the trail and (2) meeting no one all day. About 25 percent of the respondents other than the purists indicated that they enjoyed encountering others on the trail, but only 10 percent of the purists felt this way. About three out of four of the purists stated that they would enjoy meeting no one all day, whereas only 3 percent of the purists indicated that this would not bother them.

Few or no encounters thus seems to be an important dimension of the wilderness experience for purists. However, other factors associated with solitude are as important as frequency of encounters. For example, Lucas (1964) found that canoeists felt their solitude more threatened when they encountered a single motorboat than they did when they encountered several other canoes. Wilderness users are also typically more disturbed by large groups of people than by small ones. The location of the encounter is another important variable. For example, both the purists and the nonpurists seem to prefer trail encounters to encounters in the vicinity of their camps; the majority of both groups agree that the wilderness campsite should provide complete solitude. When the respondents in Stankey's study were asked to consider a situation in which several other parties arrived after camp had been set up, most purists indicated that they would be disturbed. A number stated that they would attempt to find another campsite or would cut their visit short.

Another aspect of solitude, which does not actually involve encounters but is also important, is the evidence of previous use of a wilderness area by other visitors. Two obvious indications of previous use are litter and campsite deterioration. It is not surprising that the purists in Stankey's study expressed strong dissatisfaction with campsites that showed wear and tear and with finding litter in the wilderness.

In a somewhat similar study by Shafer and Mietz (1972), five phrases or statements were selected that were thought to represent what an individual may enjoy most about a wilderness experience. The statements described the qualities of a recreational experience—physical, emotional, aesthetic, educational, and social. Thus, a physical experience involved the opportunity for physical exercise and exertion that stimulated the body, an emotional experience was identified by such physical reactions as the thrill of experiencing new sensations and exploring wild regions, and so forth.

Each of the five statements about wilderness values was printed on separate cards, and the cards were arranged in sets of two into all possible combinations, for a total of ten sets. A total of 76 hikers from two wilderness areas were asked to select the statement in each set describing the value that was more important to them. The results showed that aesthetic experiences were most important, with emotional experiences a close second. These were about ten times more important than social values, which came last. Physical experiences were third, while educational experiences were fourth.

The results of this study suggest that the most critical perceived attributes of a wilderness area are those that result in aesthetic experiences. Although it is difficult to distinguish between aesthetic experience and emotional experience (both of which rate high as requirements), it has been suggested that, at least in the wilderness context, emotional experiences are identified by physical reactions, while aesthetic experiences are more related to mental appreciation. Obviously, these experiences are closely allied and may occur during the same recreational activity. Thus, one may have an emotional experience when a rainbow trout strikes and simultaneously derive aesthetic satisfaction from the surroundings.

Very little is known about the characteristics of a natural environment that result in an aesthetic response. Litton (1972) attempted to define the aesthetic dimensions of the landscape and to establish appropriate "aesthetic criteria." He considers unity, vividness, and variety to be basic criteria and emphasizes that these are not discrete but overlap. According to Litton, *"unity* is that quality of wholeness in which all parts cohere, not merely as an assembly but as a single harmonious unit" [p. 284], while *"vividness* is that quality in the landscape which gives distinction and makes it visually striking" [p. 285]. *"Variety,* in simple form, can be defined as an index to how many different objects and relationships are found in a landscape" [p. 286]. Craik (1972) appraised the objectivity of these dimensions by developing rating scales and having subjects rate various landscapes. He concluded, "The results of this appraisal of the objectivity of a system of landscape dimensions are encouraging" [p. 306]. The importance of the aesthetic experience for the wilderness user would seem to justify considerably more research on it.

Other factors involved in determining whether an area is perceived as wilderness were examined in studies by Muriam and Amons (1968) and Lucas (1964). In the former study 108 subjects were interviewed in three wilderness areas of Montana that differed considerably in isolation and access. The researchers identified among the subjects basically two types of temporary users—one group consisting of hikers and horseback riders and the second consisting of roadside campers. When asked to define what they considered wilderness, the hikers and riders included such criteria as undeveloped natural country, difficulty of access, few people, and the absence of improvements brought about by civilization. The hikers interviewed in the largest, most accessible area (Glacier National Park) were quite specific in stating that a person had to be at least three miles from the nearest road or guided nature tour to consider himself in the wilderness. To the campers, the wilderness began at the edge of the campground.

In the Lucas study users of a wilderness area in northern Minnesota were surveyed. Upon leaving the area, the respondents were shown a map of it and were asked to indicate where they had been and where they would draw the boundary between wilderness and nonwilderness on the map. Generally, the users who engaged in the more purist activities (canoeing, for example) indicated a much smaller area than did the more casual users (the motorboaters and weekend campers, for example).

Implications of Perceived Requirements for Management Personnel. We have seen that several characteristics of a park or wilderness area are important in determining whether the area is perceived as wilderness by the users. One example of such a feature is perceived solitude. In Stankey's study solitude was rated very high by both the purists and the nonpurists. Similarly, in the Shafer and Mietz study, the respondents rated social experience lowest as a wilderness value. Indirect evidence of high usage of an area, such as litter and deteriorated campsites, also tends to result in dissatisfaction.

These findings have important implications for management personnel. It is apparent that the desired wilderness environment would involve a low intensity of use. Possibly, through design, schedules of use, and other modifications, the total use of some wilderness areas can be maintained at present levels and most users can be given at least a satisfactory experience of solitude. However, in all likelihood, use limitations will eventually have to be imposed to maintain a satisfactory recreational experience for those who do use the areas. Some would argue that the problem of maintaining a feeling of solitude is not so serious as it appears to be because the perception of solitude will change as the population increases. Stankey points out:

> A standard argument for not using visitor attitudes as a means of formulating wilderness management strategies is that public attitudes as to what constitutes solitude, the pristine, or the natural will become less discriminating as population rises, urban densities increase, and so forth.

The idea that attitudes about what is "pure wilderness" will weaken in the future might be a classic example of a self-fulfilling prophecy. If we orient wilderness management along a line designed to accommodate gradually less-demanding tastes, we will almost certainly attract a clientele that, in time, will hold a less demanding concept of wilderness [pp. 113–114].

Many other features of wilderness areas, of course, seem to contribute to the overall satisfaction of the users and so are important to consider in management and decisions. For example, the absence of man-made features (except for trails) seems to be an important factor. If an area has roads and trails, many users feel that these should be restricted to backpackers or to horseback riders, with no motorized vehicles permitted. Many other such requirements of the physical aspects of an area appear to be important to users. Even the size of the area is important; if an area is not large enough (even though it meets most of the other requirements), it is not as satisfactory as a larger area. Requirements also depend upon the type of wilderness area involved. Thus, in areas where the most important activity centers around water, the purists use canoes and, if they had their way, would ban all motorboat activity. Obviously, just what features of an area contribute most to an aesthetic or emotional experience depend upon the personal characteristics of the individual using the area.

Nonetheless, some specific features found to be aesthetically satisfying were determined by Shafer and Mietz in their interviews with the hikers in the two wilderness areas they surveyed (see Figure 5-1). The hikers felt that the most scenic enjoyment was obtained from trails that

(1) include large rock outcrops where the hikers can observe the surrounding landscape; (2) go through natural openings in forest stands where there is variability in lighting, color, temperature, and the distance one can see through the forest; and (3) follow stream courses whenever possible so that waterfalls and rushing water are part of the natural beauty along the trail [p. 214].

The hikers also reported that forest stands having a mixture of pine and white birch were more appealing aesthetically than pure stands of pine but that "at other times a pure stand of majestic old culls may be far more desirable. From an aesthetic viewpoint, trails should be located on grades that will prevent erosion from water and heavy use. Overall, the respondents wanted variation in trail scenery more than anything else" [p. 214].

Figure 5-1. Wilderness hikers strongly prefer trails that include large rock outcrops, go through natural openings in forest stands, and follow stream courses containing waterfalls and rushing water. Photo courtesy of the South Dakota Department of Highways, Pierre, South Dakota.

Individual Differences in Perceived Requirements. Clearly, all the studies we have discussed on the preferences of national park and wilderness users show that the users differ considerably in their perceived requirements of an area. Thus, one type of user may be disturbed by encountering another backpacker on a wilderness trail, while another type of user may welcome the social contact. That users perceive virtually all the features of these areas differently and respond to them differently is obvious from Stankey's study, for he was able to classify users into several different groups according to their responses to items about features of a wilderness area.

Relatively little is known, however, about the basis for differences in perceived requirements of wilderness areas. It is relatively safe to state that these differences are due to the backgrounds and experiences of the users, but saying so does not tell us very much. For example, what kinds of past experiences are important in determining whether a person is a purist or a nonpurist in his attitudes toward the wilderness? Are personality factors related to perceived requirements of wilderness areas?

One study that supplies some answers is that by Cicchetti (1972). Through sophisticated statistical techniques, he attempted to analyze the relationship between the preferences and behavioral patterns of wilderness users and such factors as (1) age, sex, income, and education and (2) childhood residential and recreational experience. Using Stankey's purist score, Cicchetti was able to relate a number of these variables to users' purist scores. The details of this study are too technical to discuss in full, but we will mention some of the relationships he established.

Cicchetti found that the older a person was when he first visited a wilderness, the higher was his purist score. This direct relationship was also true for the variable of education; for each year of education beyond the eighth grade, the purism score increased by about .65 points. It would seem, then, that with greater age and education the individual needs a more pristine or remote wilderness experience. In some cases relationships between other variables were also found. For example, in the Bridger area male visitors tended to rank higher in purism than did women visitors.

Childhood residence and recreational experiences were also found to affect purism scores. In general, visitors who grew up in a small town or in a rural area had lower purism scores than did users who grew up in urban areas. Cicchetti suggests that rural residence leads to the development of a utilitarian view of the wilderness—that is, the trees or other resources of a wilderness area are valuable and should be exploited. The users who said that they had hiked frequently as children scored higher on the purism scale than did the users who had not. Such other types of childhood experiences as camping also had a positive effect on the score.

We have already indicated that solitude appears to be the most important attribute of a wilderness area as perceived by users. In relating some of the above variables to this wilderness value, Cicchetti reports that the results of his study:

> seem to indicate that the visitor who is older when he first visits a wilderness, who had considerable auto camping and hiking experience as a child, who has a discriminating view of the wilderness, and who did not grow up in a small town is the one likely to be most upset by congestion. He may even cut short his planned trip and return home [p. 158].

An obvious source of individual differences in responses to features of the natural environment is, of course, the nature of the interaction with the environment that the user expects or seeks. Although this factor has been implicit in our discussion up to this point, its importance cannot be overemphasized. Obviously, if a visitor expects to encounter other parties in a wilderness area, he will not be as disturbed as he would be if he did not expect encounters. A user's expectancy, or set, is thus an important determinant of the degree to which he will be satisfied or dissatisfied with his wilderness experience. Similarly, the user's objective in visiting an area will determine to a great extent his satisfaction with the area. Thus, the same user visiting a particular wilderness area on two occasions with two different objectives in mind may be highly satisfied on one visit and highly dissatisfied on the other. Consider, for example, a user who visits an area in the spring for several days of backpacking and then visits the same area in the fall for several days of deer hunting. He may walk on the identical trails, but his perceived requirements are quite different. While on the spring hike, he may consider various terrain features from an aesthetic point of view and find them very satisfying; he may view the same features during the fall hunt as a nuisance because, for various reasons, they interfere with effective hunting. Similarly, he may not be bothered by meeting other hikers in the spring, but encountering other hunters in the fall may be annoying. Both trips, however, may be satisfying—the spring trip because of the aesthetic experiences (the primary objective) and the fall trip because of success in bagging a deer. For most hunters, though they may prefer hunting in a natural environment where they can enjoy the scenery, the overwhelming criterion of a satisfying or dissatisfying interaction with the natural environment is whether or not they were successful in obtaining the game they were seeking.

A number of other studies along the same lines as those reported in this section have been conducted. Although the findings of all these studies differ somewhat, depending on the particular wilderness area involved and the purpose of the survey, we do have some idea of users' perceptions of the wilderness. As the use of wilderness areas increases, it will be essential that those responsible for the management of these areas use this information if the perceived requirements of the wilderness users are to be met.

In this section we have concentrated on wilderness areas rather than on national parks. Although the perceived requirements for wilderness areas and national parks differ somewhat, the approaches to studying the requirements are quite similar. Moreover, the motivations for visiting the parks are quite similar to those involved in wilderness use. Consequently, instead of discussing studies focusing on park users' behavior, we will now consider man's interactions with the natural environment in other kinds of outdoor recreation.

SOME OTHER TEMPORARY INTERACTIONS

Many of the millions of persons who visit national parks and wilderness areas each year, as well as millions of others, engage in many other forms of temporary interactions with the natural environment. We pointed out earlier that our definition of the natural environment is quite broad and includes a number of environments in which man-built features are present and may even predominate. Some of these environments can be considered simulated natural environments in that they provide the user with what he feels is at least an approximation of some features of natural environments. An example is the elaborate outdoor recreation facilities that have been developed for residential neighborhoods and communities. For many persons, the recreation opportunities offered by these facilities, such as swimming, golfing, hiking, boating, and tennis, serve as either a primary or the only source of interaction with what they consider a natural environment.

There are, of course, many recreational activities that allow participants to "get outdoors" and, at least to some extent, temporarily interact with the environment. Some examples are skiing, boating, and snowmobiling; and all of these have increased tremendously in the last few years. Large numbers of people also engage in hunting or fishing, hiking, rock collecting, spelunking, mountain climbing, scuba diving, or simply driving in the country. The last may in fact be an important man-environment interaction that is not generally recognized. As Suholet (1973) points out, the highway can serve as open space and thus provide opportunities for significant interactions between man and the natural environment (see Figure 5-2).

Another important type of outdoor activity generally ignored by those concerned with outdoor recreation is gardening. Vogt (1966) points out:

> Gardening—conservatively—must involve over twenty million people, a number approaching the numbers of hunters and fishermen combined, exceeding those in attendance at major-league baseball games, and vastly exceeding the numbers of those who own motors and boats and who are such a pampered fraction of outdoor recreationists. In view of the day-to-day relationship of gardening to the way people live and would like to live, and therefore the impact it could—and should—have on the future development of our society, it is to be regretted that gardeners have not been given the consideration they merit in thinking about the future of the American environment [pp. 383–384].

All the above activities and many more are important sources of outdoor recreation. The wilderness purists may scoff at these kinds of natural

Figure 5-2.   One type of interaction with the natural environment enjoyed by millions is simply driving in the country. Although in many parts of the country highways cannot be considered open space, in other areas, such as that shown, highways provide an opportunity for interactions with the natural environment. Photo courtesy of the South Dakota Department of Highways, Pierre, South Dakota.

environment interactions, but it should be kept in mind that the purists represent only a small percentage of the persons who value and achieve satisfaction from outdoor recreation of one kind or another.

MOTIVATIONS OF THE USERS

The motivations of the persons enjoying the many kinds of temporary interactions listed above vary tremendously. However, the motives for visiting national parks and wilderness areas can be considered the same as those for engaging in other types of outdoor recreation. Thus, outdoor recreation may serve as a temporary escape from stress. Such outdoor recreation activities may also fulfill all the needs listed on page 124—to develop and maintain a self-image, to develop a social identity, to affiliate, to gain esteem, to develop and apply skills, and so forth. Readers interested in a detailed analysis of recreational behavior should read Driver and Tocher (1970), who deal with this issue in great depth.

One motivation for outdoor recreation is not written about a great deal but may be quite important. Many types of outdoor recreation involve the risk of injury or death. It has been frequently pointed out that American culture has always prized and even rewarded behavior that involves taking risks of one kind or another. Indeed, in our society a man is often defined as someone who has courage or who takes a chance. Thus, many persons may consciously seek outdoor recreation that has a high level of risk to satisfy a social value or need.

As we emphasized earlier, the motivations of users of any outdoor recreation area, whether it is a wilderness area or a neighborhood park, are complex. Although the motivations involved in outdoor recreation have been subjected to study in recent years, much more remains to be learned before we have a reasonably complete understanding of this kind of behavior.

PERCEIVED REQUIREMENTS

We have pointed out that users of national parks and wilderness areas (particularly the latter) have some very definite requirements of these areas. To the extent that these perceived requirements are met, the wilderness experience can be considered satisfying. One of the key elements of the satisfactory wilderness experience is solitude. Aesthetic, emotional, and other experiences are also important. As one might expect, perceived requirements are associated with other types of recreation areas as well.

Outdoor recreation areas were earlier classified as user-oriented areas, intermediate use areas, and resource-based areas. The first type is best suited to daily leisure, the second to weekend leisure, and the third to vacation time. Thus, accessibility is an important requirement for the first two types but may be an undesirable feature of the resource-based areas, or wilderness areas, where inaccessibility may be considered as contributing to solitude and, consequently, to the satisfaction of the experience. Landscape is typically of less concern to those visiting the user-oriented and intermediate use areas than to the users of the resource-based areas, where landscape is important for the aesthetic experience. Similarly, those using the first two types of areas expect to encounter a considerable number of man-built features and facilities, while these are undesirable to users of the wilderness areas.

In other words, the perceived requirements of the types of areas depend greatly upon the objectives of the person using the areas—a point we have emphasized previously. We cannot discuss or even summarize the requirements associated with the various types of outdoor recreation areas because of their number and diversity. What the users perceive as requirements of a ski area differ considerably from the requirements of a hiking area, which, in turn, are different from those of a hunting area. However, participants in each type of outdoor recreation establish requirements for an outdoor recreation experience, and, to the extent that these requirements are met, the experience will be perceived as satisfactory.

THE RECREATION EXPERIENCE

In concluding our discussion of man's temporary interactions with the natural environment, we should point out that we have emphasized only a small part of what can be considered the total recreation experience. In discussing outdoor recreation, Clawson (1966) notes that the outdoor recreation experience, particularly that involving the resource-based areas, has five distinct phases. The first of these phases Clawson calls the anticipation or planning phase, in which the family or group decides when and where to go, what to do in the area, what to take, and so forth. This phase may involve a number of months, as in the case of planning an extended visit to a national park or wilderness area, or only a few minutes, as in the case of planning to visit a local recreation area. For many persons, this phase, as the name indicates, is a time of pleasant anticipation and is an important part of the recreation experience. Many hours may be spent discussing the proposed trip, buying equipment, perhaps making financial sacrifices so that the family or group can afford the trip, adjusting work schedules, applying for vacation, and so forth. Although the actual interaction with the natural environment may be some time away, the behavior of the participants will already be modified to a considerable extent during the planning phase [p. 254].

The second phase of the recreation experience is the travel to the site of the recreation. This trip may involve considerable time and money. Many persons find the travel experience itself a pleasurable and satisfying part of the recreation, although others regard it less highly. The third phase is the on-site experience, which we have concentrated on in the preceding pages. The trip back home from the site is the fourth phase of the recreation experience. Although the beginning and end points are usually the same as are involved in travel to the site, the mood and attitudes of the travelers may be quite different during this trip. This aspect of the recreation experience has not been subjected to study, but most readers will agree that their feelings are quite different when returning from an outdoor recreation area than when traveling to it. In discussing the last phase—recollection—Clawson states: "Recollection is the last, and possibly the most important, phase of the total experience. It is altogether possible that more total satisfactions or values arise here than in all the other phases combined" [p. 254].

Clawson emphasizes that the whole experience must be considered as a package deal and that the demand for outdoor recreation can be studied meaningfully only in terms of the whole experience. Although we have concentrated on the on-site experience—and most of the available research findings deal with that phase—the other phases are also important. As Clawson points out: "The recreationist will balance up his total satisfaction from the whole experience against its total costs; the dirty restroom will loom as large for some persons as the fine new park museum" [p. 256].

PERMANENT INTERACTIONS BETWEEN MAN AND THE NATURAL ENVIRONMENT

In the preceding pages we have been concerned with a number of kinds of interactions between man and his natural environment. These interactions take place in a wide variety of outdoor recreational areas, ranging from wilderness regions to local parks and recreational facilities. Although the duration of these interactions may vary from only an hour or so to several weeks or even longer, they can be considered temporary interactions. In this section we will examine more permanent types of interactions that typically involve years or even entire lifetimes.

In previous chapters we dealt in some detail with the relationships between the built environment and behavior. In this context we discussed, as an expanding system, rooms, houses, buildings, institutions, and cities and their effects on behavior. These environments, however, are part of what we will call the geographic environment, which may also influence behavior.

THE GEOGRAPHIC ENVIRONMENT AND BEHAVIOR

By "geographic environment" we mean the natural physical characteristics of a region, such as its geology, climate, and possible natural hazards, such as floods, blizzards, hurricanes, tornadoes, and earthquakes. Psychologists in the past considered the geographic environment to be of little significance as a determinant of behavior, but the growing interest in man-environment relationships has been accompanied by an increase in the attention paid to the geographic environment as a potential influence on man's behavior.

For many years anthropologists, historians, geographers, and others have been writing about the influence of physical environmental variables on human activities. These writers, who have been called *environmental determinists*, contend that there are important factors in the geographical environment that affect the customs and character of people exposed to particular environments. Thus, environmental determinists argue that such national traits as bravery, laziness, and superstition may be determined by various geographical factors. This view is in contrast to the view of those who tend to think of man as the active agent in interactions with the natural environment. These theorists minimize the influence of the environment on behavior and, rather than thinking of the environment as shaping the organism, think of the organism as shaping the environment. Many psychologists and social scientists hold this view; members of the design professions are more likely to hold the former view.

The available data do not support the view of the environmental determinists, for relationships between national traits (which are not easily identified) and geographic characteristics are far from firmly established. Perhaps the most convincing data come from anthropological studies, such as those reported by Barry, Child, and Bacon (1959), who found some evidence that the type of subsistence economy determined by geographic environment may have a significant effect upon child-rearing practices. Societies in which accumulating and caring for food sources are necessary apparently emphasize the development of such traits as obedience and responsibility. In hunting and fishing societies, on the other hand, personal achievement and self-reliance tend to be stressed.

A great deal of evidence, of course, supports the view that man has a considerable influence upon his physical environment. His activities can and often do result in temporary and, frequently, permanent damage to the geographical environment. As mentioned previously, man and his interactions with the environment can be studied from two points of view. One way is to view man's behavior as the dependent variable and some aspect of the physical environment as the independent variable. This approach would be the logical way of studying such interactions from the point of view of the environmental determinist. However, man-environment interactions can also involve situations in which man's behavior is the independent variable and changes in the physical environment brought about by his activities are the dependent variable. This type of interaction is of more concern to conservationists and others who are concerned with the changes that man makes in his natural environment. Although environmental psychologists are also concerned with this problem, we have limited our discussion in this text to the situations in which man's behavior is thought to be influenced by the natural environment.

THE KINDS OF BEHAVIOR STUDIED

One can easily think of a variety of human activities that are directly or indirectly influenced by the geographical environment in which a person resides. The kinds of clothes that a person buys will be determined, to some extent, by the region in which he lives, as will the leisure activities in which he engages. A person's job, the type of house he desires, and the type of automobile he buys may all be a function of the particular geographic environment involved. Obviously, the environment of a region has a great deal to do with the economy of the region, which, in turn, directly influences the behavior of the residents. Typically, however, these kinds of environment-behavior relationships have been of more interest to economists than to environmental psychologists.

Environmental psychologists have, instead, been chiefly interested in man's comprehension and perception of his geographical environment. The sparse research in this area that has been reported deals, for example, with residents' attitudes toward such natural hazards as floods or earthquakes. Similarly, some studies have dealt with how physical features of regions are perceived by residents of these areas. Researchers have asked, for example: What are the characteristics of a region that influence decisions on residential choice and migration? What characteristics tend to make living in a particular region a satisfactory experience? An unsatisfactory experience?

Obviously, researchers attempting to study the effects of geographic environments on behavior are dealing with an extremely complicated type of independent variable. Although a particular geographic environment may encompass other physical environments, such as buildings and cities, it is still only part of a person's total environment. In other words, it is difficult to use some feature of the geographic environment as an independent variable without having it confounded with a variety of other variables, all of which may influence the behavior of the person. These studies are further complicated by the fact that all the persons living in a particular region are not equally exposed to its geographic environment. Some residents are "closer to nature" than others, so that the environment may have a much more profound effect on their behavior.

Figure 5-3. The geographic environment affects various individuals in different ways. Thus, the rancher whose livelihood is affected by a blizzard will develop attitudes and feelings about the geographic environment different from those of city dwellers who might be inconvenienced by the blizzard or of others who find the results of a major storm a source of satisfaction and a means of interacting with the natural environment. Photos by Don Polovich. Courtesy of the *Rapid City Journal.*

Differential Effects of the Geographic Environment

When we consider the kinds of behavior that may be affected by permanent interactions with the natural environment, it is important to keep in mind that the environment may differentially affect individuals living in a particular region (see Figure 5-3). For example, consider the effect of the natural environment on farmers or ranchers and on city dwellers in the same general geographic region. Both types of individuals are exposed to basically the same climatic conditions but have a very different attitude toward the weather. Though the city dweller may complain about a long hot spell and having to water his lawn frequently or running up his electric bill because of using his air conditioner, at worst the weather is a source of inconvenience and annoyance. The hot weather, however, may jeopardize the rancher's or farmer's livestock or crops. The weather in this case is not just an inconvenience; his livelihood may be threatened. As Heimstra and McDonald (1973) point out:

> One of the reported differences in rural-versus-urban lives most referred to by urban people is their amazement at the many references rural people make to the weather. However, the entire rural community in an agricultural economy is dependent on the weather. If there is not enough rain, crops don't grow; if there is too much rain at the time of harvest, crops are lost; if it freezes or if it's too hot, income is lost. This affects not only the farmer but the machinery suppliers, warehouses, agricultural production, grocery stores, banks, realtors, car salesmen, and so forth [p. 315].

THE PERCEPTION OF A GEOGRAPHIC ENVIRONMENT

Persons seeking employment often list on their résumés a regional preference as well as their qualifications and job requirements. One person may indicate a preference for the Southwest, another may state that he is seeking employment in the Northwest or the Great Plains region, while still another may simply state that he would prefer a position in a region where he has access to mountains or to some other feature of the geographic environment. Some individuals will suffer economic loss to live in a specific geographic environment.

Obviously, a person's perception of a region is an important factor in determining whether he will establish residence there or, if he already lives in the region, whether he will remain there. Residential choice or migration decisions, of course, are typically based on many other variables as well. For most individuals, economic factors are more important than geographic factors, particularly during periods of tight job markets, as in recent years. Thus, one does not see nearly so many regional preference statements in employment bulletins as was the case a few years ago, when a seller's market prevailed. However, if asked, most people would be able to list a number of features of the geographic environment that they perceive as desirable or undesirable.

How a person perceives his geographic environment depends on a variety of factors. A person's degree of dependence upon the environment partly determines his attitude toward such environmental features as weather. As we suggested earlier, the manner in which a farmer perceives a given region may be quite different from the manner in which it is perceived by a city dweller. Similarly, a person in the construction industry, where his opportunity to work is often dependent on climatic conditions, is more aware of the environment than the typical office worker. Any person's list, then, of features of the environment perceived as desirable or undesirable will depend to a considerable extent on the direct impact of the geographic environment on his activities and means of making a living.

Personal characteristics are also important in determining how the environment is perceived. Aesthetic preferences for mountains, the desert, or some other terrain feature play an important role for many persons, as do attitudes and beliefs. For example, attitudes on overpopulation, industrialization, or pollution can result in satisfaction or dissatisfaction with a particular region.

Numerous factors, then, contribute to a person's satisfaction with a given region and determine whether migration from the region is undertaken or seriously considered. However, in considering the behavioral aspects of migration, an important point must be kept in mind. Wolpert (1966) says of migration:

> Common explanations for these movements revolve around the attractions of new economic and social opportunities, climes, or landscapes and repulsion from areas of limited opportunity or negative milieus. . . . Yet the migration record is filled with cases of reshuffling exchanges between similar environments. Thus deterministic hypotheses based upon economic, climatic, aesthetic, and other causes are only partial and do not correspond to any inherent determinism in migration behavior [p. 92].

Wolpert goes on to discuss a rather complicated model in which migration is viewed as an adjustment to environmental stress. He suggests that "in addition to the push and pull forces which may be latent in the migrational decision, the triggering off of that decision may frequently be associated with a stress impetus" [p. 95].

Considerably more research is required before all the factors associated with geographic environment satisfaction, residence choice, and migration are understood. However, some studies have been conducted that deal with somewhat more specific aspects of the geographic environment. We will now consider research on the perception of natural hazards associated with various geographic regions.

The Perception of Natural Hazards

As Burton (1972) notes, there appears to be a persistent tendency for people to concentrate in regions subject to various types of natural hazards. He further points out that, despite the recurrence of floods, droughts, earthquakes, and other hazards, people not only occupy these regions in large numbers but also tend to move back into these areas after a disaster has taken place. The hazardous areas are quickly resettled, and new buildings are often more elaborate and expensive than those that were destroyed. Burton states: "The pattern seems to be universal. It occurs in widely different cultures and in relation to a variety of hazard events. How can this behavior be described and what is the explanation for it?" [p. 184]. As we shall see, describing and explaining this behavior are difficult tasks and have met with only limited success.

Burton suggests that the tendency of persons to remain in or move back to areas with a high likelihood of natural hazards is due to a complex set of interwoven factors and that this kind of behavior occurs "sometimes as a result of one set of circumstances, sometimes as a result of a quite different set" [p. 185]. Analysis of the factors involved indicates that this behavior may be due to one (or a combination) of three primary factors: (1) the comparative economic advantage of hazard areas, (2) the affected individuals' apparent lack of perception of threat or lack of concern, and (3) what Burton refers to as problems of institutional and social rigidities. Although our concern in this chapter is with the second factor, we will briefly mention the other two.

Hazard areas, in many instances, have economic advantages greater for the residents than those offered elsewhere. For example, a flood plain may be more fertile than other areas or may offer advantages for con-

Figure 5-4.   Perception of the many types of natural hazards depends upon a number of factors. Even the same general class of disaster may create different perceptions and feelings. A flood that damages crops and buildings but causes no loss of life may be perceived quite differently from a flood like the one whose results are shown in this photograph, where more than 200 lives were lost. Photo courtesy of the *Rapid City Journal.*

struction of industries or transportation systems. Thus, the opportunity for earning a livelihood may be better in the hazard area than in other regions. Concerning the problem of institutional and social rigidities, Burton suggests that frequently "the institutional arrangements in a society operate to keep people in the same place and to protect existing short-term interests by reinforcing the status quo and by failing to offer means whereby individuals may extricate themselves from an unpleasant situation" [p. 187]. For example, in some instances payments are given to victims of a disaster with the stipulation that they rebuild on the same site.

Burton and co-workers (Barker & Burton, 1969; Burton, 1962, 1965, 1972; Burton & Kates, 1964; Burton, Kates, Mather, & Snead, 1965; Burton, Kates, & White, 1968; Golant & Burton, 1969) and others (Kates,

1962; Saarinen, 1966) have been primarily concerned with the second factor listed above—the apparent lack of perception of threat or lack of concern of individuals living in hazardous regions. These researchers, as well as others, have studied the manner in which persons perceive hazard, their awareness of the probable consequences of natural hazards, their attitudes and beliefs about hazards, and the variations in individual responses to natural hazards. We cannot summarize all these investigations, but we will consider several to illustrate the techniques used and the kinds of results obtained.

Kates (1962) investigated the comprehension of flood hazards by residents of flood plains. He interviewed residents of six urban areas on which extensive data on past flooding were available. His interviews revealed a positive relationship between past experience with flooding and expectation of future flooding and also found that the adoption of protective measures was related to previous experience with flooding. Nonetheless, many persons who had previously experienced one or more floods declared that they did not expect future floods. Such expectations are based on attitudes or beliefs. Although some residents believe that floods are in fact repetitive events and will probably occur again, they may feel that for special reasons they will not be struck again. Others do not view floods as repetitive events and feel that circumstances are such that their regions will not be flooded again. They may base this expectation on existing or contemplated flood control programs or on faith in God.

Thus, the interesting feature of studies such as those conducted by Kates is that many persons' comprehension of the flood hazard does not correspond to reality. When a region has been flooded on a regular basis for many years, it would seem logical that most residents would expect future flooding, particularly if no flood prevention programs have been undertaken. Yet many residents of such a region will, when asked, indicate that they do not expect another flood.

Burton, Kates, and White (1968) studied the responses obtained from many interviews dealing with natural hazards. They found that the responses of residents of hazard areas to questions about their susceptibility to hazards fall into one of two general categories. Some responses can be classified as those that "eliminate the hazard," while the other responses can be categorized as those that "eliminate the uncertainty." Each of these categories has two subcategories. The responses that fall in the category of "eliminating the hazard" are broken down into (1) those that deny or denigrate the existence of the hazard ("It can't happen here") and (2) those that deny or denigrate its recurrence ("Lightning never strikes twice in the same spot"). The responses categorized as those that "eliminate the uncertainty" are broken down into (1) those that make the uncertainty determinate and knowable

("Floods only occur every ten years") and (2) those that transfer the uncertainty to a higher authority ("God will take care of us"). It is apparent that residents of regions susceptible to natural hazards have built up elaborate systems of attitudes and beliefs that, in their own minds, justify their remaining in the hazard areas.

Although floods, earthquakes, hurricanes, and similar abrupt and devastating events are obvious examples of natural hazards, other natural events can also be thought of as hazards. Take, for example, droughts. Droughts are, like the other hazards, largely unpredictable and unpreventable. Moreover, large numbers of persons live in areas susceptible to drought, which may adversely affect their livelihoods. The effects of this type of natural hazard on behavior have not been extensively studied, though Saarinen (1966) conducted a comprehensive investigation of the expectations and attitudes of residents of arid regions of the Great Plains. He selected six counties in four states (Nebraska, Oklahoma, Kansas, and Colorado) that were quite similar on a Drought Index and interviewed a number of persons in each of the six areas. In terms of actual frequency of droughts, residents of all the areas tended to underestimate the frequency of occurrence. However, residents of the most arid counties tended to place a higher likelihood on the occurrence of drought in the future and, more specifically, to anticipate a drought in the next year.

To probe the adjustment of the residents to their semiarid environment more deeply, Saarinen administered to respondents not only the standard cards of the Thematic Apperception Test (TAT) but also several specially designed TAT cards involving pictures of the arid environment. The TAT is a projective test that requires a person to make up a story about each picture in the test set and is designed to reveal to a trained examiner the various drives, needs, and conflicts that make up the subject's personality structure. It is assumed that in making up the story about each picture, the subject will project his own personality into the situation and reveal aspects of his personality that he might not reveal directly to the interviewer. Analysis of the subject's responses to tests of this type involves a great deal of detail and is beyond the scope of this text. However, Saarinen did find interesting variations among the persons who took his test. Certainly this approach has considerable potential in studies of man's response to natural hazards in his environment.

In summary, then, residents of areas subject to natural hazards display what might appear to nonresidents to be some rather strange attitudes and beliefs about their regions. Typically, the threat of future occurrence of the hazard tends to be underestimated based on the statistical probability of the event's recurring. It would seem that the residents construct a rather elaborate system of beliefs and attitudes that, in their own minds, reduces the threat present in the environment. It should be kept in mind, however, that the perception of hazard in the geographic environment is subject to considerable individual variation and that, at least to some extent, the relevance of a natural hazard (in terms of direct impact on an individual) and the expected frequency of occurrence are related to the manner in which the hazard is perceived.

In discussing man's temporary and permanent interactions with his environment, we have limited our discussion to field studies, generally of the survey type. Virtually all of the most relevant research has been of this sort. However, some laboratory studies have been conducted that were designed to study certain aspects of man's interaction with his natural environment. In concluding this chapter, we will briefly mention several of these investigations.

LABORATORY RESEARCH

Because man must work and sometimes wage war in extreme heat and cold, various government agencies, including the military branches, have been interested in how these temperature extremes affect performance. Although there has been some field work on this topic, much of the research has taken place in laboratory settings, where careful control has been exerted over the independent variable (heat or cold) and various measures of performance obtained when subjects were exposed to the variable.

Physiological changes take place, of course, when humans are subjected to either extreme heat or extreme cold. Behavioral changes also occur. For example, Mackworth (1961) related performance on a number of tasks to heat stress. Subjects were exposed to hot atmospheres for several hours, rectal temperatures were obtained, and the subjects then performed the tasks. In general, as rectal temperature increased, performance on the various tasks decreased. In other studies, however, somewhat different findings were obtained, with performance on some tasks improving under high temperature conditions. Poulton (1970) suggests that as body temperature begins to increase, errors will also increase because the person's level of arousal is lowered. However, when body temperature is sufficiently raised, arousal level will increase, and, consequently, performance will improve on some types of tasks. Although this arousal level concept of heat effects has not been verified, it does fit in nicely with the results of other studies dealing more directly with arousal and performance.

Much of the laboratory work that has been conducted has not dealt with behavior but with other types of response to heat. Considerable research has been conducted, for example, on the factors involved in acclimatization to heat. Physiological changes, such as blood circulation, have also been studied in detail. These topics, however, are more appropriately discussed in physiology books.

A variety of studies have also been conducted on the effects of varying degrees of cold. Early studies were concerned primarily with the effects of cold hands on certain types of tasks involving dexterity. As might be expected, dexterity decreases as finger temperature decreases. A study by Poulton, Hitchings, and Brooke (1965) dealt with the effects of lowered body temperature on performance. In this study the subjects were sailors standing watch on the open bridge of a ship during the winter. Each of 16 subjects was required to monitor several lights and to report the appearance of a very dim light that came on at irregular intervals. When the subject observed this faint signal, he depressed a large key with the palm or side of his gloved hand. In the arctic cold (as compared to performance in a moderate climate), performance deteriorated, leading the researchers to conclude that as the body cools, the efficiency of the brain is impaired. Other studies have also shown a decrement in performance on various kinds of tasks under conditions of cold.

As was the case with heat research, numerous studies have dealt with physiological changes during exposure to cold and with man's ability to acclimatize to cold. There is evidence that persons who live in cold climates produce more heat when resting than do persons in warmer climates and that persons living in cold climates have an increased blood supply in their extremities. Other studies also have revealed various types of acclimatization effects. Again, however, such studies, though of interest to environmental psychologists, are more appropriately discussed in other types of textbooks.

CHAPTER SIX

THE ENVIRONMENT
AS A SOURCE OF THREAT

THE CONCEPT OF STRESS

Such terms as "stress" and "stressor" are part of our everyday vocabulary. Unfortunately, however, they mean different things to different people, not only laymen but also researchers. Where one researcher uses the term "stress," another might use "anxiety," still another might use "frustration," and a fourth might use "conflict." All may be referring to the same phenomenon (Lazarus, 1966, p. 2). Since there is no agreed-upon terminology in the study of stress, any definition of terms here will necessarily be somewhat arbitrary.

In the literature in this field, two kinds of stress are often distinguished—*systemic* and *psychological* stress. The concept of systemic stress was first introduced into the biological sciences by Hans Selye in 1936, and since that time thousands of articles and numerous books have been published on this topic. Basically, systemic stress is a situation in which an organism's tissue systems react to or are damaged by certain types of noxious stimulation. Selye refers to these noxious stimulating conditions as *stressors*; *stress* is the reaction of the organism's system to the stressors. In much of the research on systemic stress, some type of aversive stimulus, such as a chemical agent, heat, or cold, is introduced and manipulated and the effects of this manipulation on various of the subject's biologic systems determined.

Many types of stimulus situations do not, however, involve physical stressors, such as those typically used in systemic stress studies, but will also result in responses considered to be reflections of a *stress state* in the organism. These stimulus conditions often involve psychological factors that serve as stressors. Although the human organism may encounter situations involving physical stressors and systemic stress, he is much more likely to encounter psychological stressors. Whereas in systemic stress conditions the stress response is physical changes in the organism's biologic systems, the response in psychological stress situations is often quite different (though physical changes may also occur).

Let us briefly consider the conditions that produce psychological stress reactions and the nature of these reactions. Appley and Trumbull (1967) point out that the stimulus conditions involved in psychological stress are

characterized as new, intense, rapidly changing, sudden or unexpected, including (but not requiring) approach to the upper thresholds of tolerability. At the same time, stimulus deficit, absence of expected stimulation, highly persistent stimulation, and fatigue-producing and boredom-producing settings, among others, have also been described as stressful, as have stimuli leading to cognitive misperception, stimuli susceptible to hallucination, and stimuli calling for conflicting responses [p. 5].

Obviously, then, many situations can be thought of as involving psychological stress. Although, as we have pointed out, there is a great deal of disagreement among researchers in this field, all the above have been used by investigators as operational means for defining and producing psychological stress.

Possibly a simpler way of viewing the complex of stimulus situations that result in psychological stress is in terms of a characteristic common to nearly all these situations. As Lazarus points out, "Psychological-stress analysis . . . is distinguished from other types of stress analysis by the intervening variable of threat. Threat implies a state in which the individual anticipates a confrontation with a harmful condition of some sort" [p. 25]. Thus, many investigators feel that a stimulus situation involving the threat or anticipation of future harm may result in psychological stress. It should be pointed out that whether the situation actually is or can be harmful to the individual is irrelevant as long as the individual perceives it as threatening. It is also important to keep in mind that the term "harm" does not imply only physical damage of some sort. A situation can be seen as threatening and potentially harmful if it may involve embarrassment, loss of face, financial loss, and so forth.

In research on psychological stress, a number of types of reactions or responses have been used as indexes of stress. Lazarus suggests that these dependent variables fall into four major categories: reports of *disturbed affect, motor-behavioral reactions, changes in the adequacy of various types of cognitive functions,* and *physiological changes.* Disturbances in affective states, such as anxiety, anger, and depression, are common stress responses, as are certain types of motor behavior, such as increased muscle tension, disturbances in speech, facial expressions, bodily posture, and loss of sphincter control. Changes in cognitive functioning are another response to stress; there "is an extensive literature on the effects of stress on perception, thought, judgment, problem solving, perceptual and motor skills, and social adaptation" [Lazarus, 1966, p. 7].

A wide range of physiological and psychophysiological measures have been used as indexes of stress states. Among these indexes are changes in blood composition, particularly in regard to eosinophils, increases in 17-ketosteroids in the urine, changes in adrenal gland functioning, increases or decreases in the weight of various glands, changes in heart rate, galvanic skin response (GSR), and critical flicker fusion.

It cannot be overemphasized, however, that the capacity of any situation to produce such stress reactions is very much dependent upon the characteristics of the person or persons involved. Situations that are perceived by some as threatening will be perceived quite differently by others. Moreover, the past experience of an individual with the particular situation will determine, to a great extent, his perception of the situation. Thus, with repeated exposure to a situation, *adaptation* may occur; the situation is no longer seen to be as threatening as it once was, and either no stress reaction takes place or it is considerably modified.

That individuals differ in the ways in which they perceive specific situations or stimulus conditions often makes research on psychological stress difficult. One cannot assume that all subjects perceive the stimulus conditions in the same way. Yet even if all subjects did perceive the situation similarly, personality factors and past experiences would determine to a great extent the stress reaction shown.

THE ENVIRONMENT AS A SOURCE OF THREAT

Considering the tremendous range of activities in which man engages, one can assume that many of these activities place a person in situations that he perceives as threatening and that, consequently, are stressful. Such situations may be encountered in the home, on the job, at play, in many social interactions—indeed, in virtually any situation where man interacts with the environment. A significant part of the content of books in many areas of psychology deals with what can be considered environmental stress and man's reactions in stressful situations. For example, much of abnormal psychology is concerned with stress reactions, as is much of industrial psychology, social psychology, and marriage counseling.

In this chapter we will be concerned with some of the stressors associated with our increasingly complex urban society. The many basic social problems that can be viewed as stressors include overcrowding, urban decay, educational deterioration, inadequate health services, crime, racial discrimination, and many more. Such environmental factors as air, water, and noise pollution can also be considered stressors because many people view them as a threat or potential source of harm. It is these sorts of problems that are of particular interest to environmental psychologists. We cannot discuss all of them, but we will consider several in some detail to illustrate the complexity of these problems and the approaches used by investigators to understand them better and to help solve them.

OVERCROWDING

One major social problem that many view as a serious threat is the ever increasing world population. We read and hear a great deal about the approaching world-wide population disaster and the associated predictions about starving millions and "standing room only" for man. Although we have not yet reached this stage in the United States, parts of the world are approaching it, and certainly in many areas in this country the population density and consequent overcrowding are such that they are viewed as a major problem.

Although the term "overcrowding" is a common one and we use it frequently, it requires definition. In discussions of population problems, two terms are frequently used: *population density* and *overcrowding*. Population density is the number of people or other types of animals occupying a given unit of space. "Space" in this case may refer to a room, a building, a city, or any other definable unit. Although this is a simple definition of population density—there are those who discuss inside density, outside density, social density, spatial density, and so forth—the definition presented here is adequate for our purpose. When the population density reaches a high level, it is common to say that overcrowding has taken place. Thus, at some point along the population density continuum, the condition of overcrowding is assumed to occur.

Though it may be convenient to define overcrowding objectively as a level of population density, overcrowding is more appropriately thought of in more subjective terms. We have emphasized that a person's past experience and personality are important factors in determining how he perceives a particular situation. Thus, when population density increases and people are forced to live closer and closer to one another, at some point a person will feel overcrowded and will perceive the situation as involving some degree of threat and, consequently, will experience stress. However, the point at which the subjective experience of overcrowding occurs will depend upon both the characteristics of the person involved and the specific situation. Thus, some individuals may not feel overcrowded in the very high population density areas encountered in many cities, while others experience overcrowding if they encounter a few other people in a camping area high in the mountains. On the other hand, the same person who does not feel overcrowded in the city may experience overcrowding when, on a camping trip, he is forced to share a campsite with others. This may occur even when the population densities of the two situations are quite different.

In a more formal analysis, Zlutnick and Altman (1972) list the variables associated with overcrowding under three main headings. In the first group are *situational variables,* which include factors associated with a particular setting, such as the number of people per unit of space within a room or residence (inside density); the people per unit of space outside the room or residence, as in the neighborhood (outside density); the duration of exposure to the situation; and characteristics of the setting, such as type of room, the way in which the space is laid out, and so forth. These and other situational variables help determine whether the experience of overcrowding takes place.

The second category consists of *interpersonal determinants* of crowding. One of these, which is probably of primary importance, is the ability of a person to control interactions with others. People control interactions with others in a variety of ways, ranging from locking themselves in a room to avoid interacting with others as completely as possible to subtle nonverbal behavior, such as turning away or assuming some type of bodily posture that may discourage interactions with others. As Zlutnick and Altman point out: "a whole spectrum of techniques is used to pace relations with other people. One hypothesis is that when these control mechanisms break down, especially in high-density situations, a condition commonly described as crowding may exist" [p. 52].

The third group of variables are *psychological factors.* As pointed out, the past experience and the personality of a person are important in determining whether he experiences crowding in a particular situation. Among the many additional factors that may help to determine whether he feels crowded are his expectations of a particular situation in what he considers an optimum density and his perceived ability to control interactions.

The effects of overcrowding on human behavior have been relatively little researched. However, a substantial number of investigations have been conducted on the effects of population density on animal behavior (particularly rodents); and these studies may have some implications for human behavior. Consequently, we will consider in some detail the findings of animal studies, though it must be kept in mind that rodents are far from perfect models of humans, so that generalizations from rodents to man must be made with a great deal of caution.

POPULATION DENSITY STUDIES WITH ANIMALS

There is considerable evidence that the population size of many mammalian species, especially rodents, is self-limiting. Once a particular population density is reached, the animals' reproductive capabilities are modified to the extent that the population either remains stable or decreases. Much of the population density research on animals has been designed to explain why this self-limiting phenomenon occurs.

One popular explanation is based on the concept of social stress. It is generally agreed that as population density increases, the animals are subjected to more and more contact with other animals and that at some point these social contacts become stressful. Thus, the high population density condition is considered a stressor that creates various behavioral and physical changes in the animals.

These reactions may be dramatic and easily observable or subtle and observable only under carefully controlled conditions. An example of a dramatic reaction associated with high population densities is the mass migration of lemmings. However, the behavior of animals subjected to high population densities may also involve more aggressive behavior than normal, various forms of "aberrant" sexual behavior, the devouring of young by their mothers, and other types of behavior that, for the animals involved, can be considered unusual or abnormal. Physical changes also occur, with various internal organs modified and endocrine functions disturbed. Thus, under stressful conditions the adrenal glands enlarge and are hyperactive, as is the pituitary gland, while the gonads may atrophy and become hypoactive. In discussing the pituitary-adrenal-gonadal effects of stressors, Thiessen and Rodgers (1961) point out:

> If population density were a stressor, it would be inversely related to gonadal activity and therefore to reproductive behavior, as well as to other factors affecting survival. Such relationships could account for the apparently self-limiting nature of density of population and would help to account for the triphasic population cycle. Under conditions of low density of population and in otherwise favorable circumstances, gonadal and reproductive activity would be high, resulting in an expanding population. The increasing population density, acting as an increasing stressor, would eventually reduce reproduction to the point that deaths would match births. The population would reach equilibrium at that point and would enter the second phase of the population cycle. Such stability would be maintained until the population was subjected to an additional stressor, such as increased daylight or increased cold occurring with seasonal change. The additional stressor could destroy the equilibrium and precipitate a more or less rapid decline of population, partially by its effects on reproduction rate and partially by other lethal effects of the increased stress [pp. 441–442].

We will not attempt to summarize all the studies in this area. Rather, we will describe several investigations that are representative of the approaches used by researchers studying the effects of increased population on animals. In general, these studies are either field studies, in which the investigator attempts to study the animals under natural or nearly natural conditions, or laboratory studies, in which the animals are studied under carefully controlled conditions.

Field Studies

At one time it was customary to explain population changes among small mammals as the result of cycles in the environment—temperature and rainfall, predator populations, or disease cycles, for example—or of available food and shelter. Although these may be important factors in some instances, a study by Calhoun (1952) showed that other aspects of the environment may be even more important in limiting population.

In this study Calhoun observed rats in a 10,000-square-foot pen for 28 months. During this time the colony grew from a few individuals to about 150 and then leveled off at this number. Of particular interest in this study was that the population remained at this level even though Calhoun estimated that there was enough food as well as space for several thousand rats. According to the observed reproductive rate, at least 5000 adult rats might have been expected. However, the population remained at about 150 because of the extremely high infant mortality rate. Even with only 150 adults in the pen, stress from social interaction led to such a disruption of maternal behavior that most of the young rats did not survive. Calhoun states:

> As the population increased in numbers there was an increase in frequency, intensity, and complexity of behavioral adjustments necessitated among and between groups of rats. This forced more and more rats to be characterized by social instability with the accompanying result of lowering the biotic potential to the point where there was a balance between natality and mortality—all this in the continued presence of a superabundance of food and unused space available for harborage [p. 141].

Although Calhoun does not report any physical changes in the rats as their population reached its peak of about 150, other studies have shown that there is a definite relationship between population density and adrenal weight in natural populations of Norway rats. Christian and Davis (1956), for example, studied rats from 21 Baltimore city blocks. These researchers pointed out that "each city block is effectively an island and its rats form a discrete population unit since immigration and emigration of rats is negligible or absent" [p. 476]. In all the blocks studied, ample food was available from garbage cans, and there was adequate harborage on each block.

At the start of the investigation, considerable information from previous studies was available on the population characteristics of the various blocks. These data and data from live trappings allowed the investigators to assign each of the blocks to a particular population cycle stage. These stages, which are illustrated in Figure 6-1, were labeled the low stationary stage, the low increasing stage, the high increasing stage, the high stationary stage, and the decreasing stage. Thus, if a longitudinal study had been conducted on a single block, it would be expected that the rat population in that block would proceed through each of the stages shown in Figure 6-1. In the Christian and Davis study, however, a number of blocks were sampled and it was determined whether rats in a particular block were at the low stationary stage, the low increasing stage, or at one of the other stages.

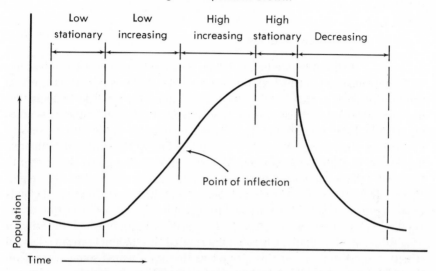

Figure 6-1.   Hypothetical population growth curve. In the Christian and Davis study, each population of rats was placed in one of the five population stages at the time of collection of each sample. From Christian, J. J., & Davis, D. E. The relationship between adrenal weights and population status of urban Norway rats. *Journal of Mammalogy,* 1956, **37,** 475–486. Reproduced by permission of the *Journal of Mammalogy.*

Rats from all the blocks were trapped and killed, and the weights of a number of organs were determined. Although the weight of the adrenal gland was of primary interest, the weights of the thymus, thyroid, and pituitary glands were also obtained. No changes were found in the weights of the thymus, pituitary, and thyroid glands. However, a progressive increase was found in the adrenal gland weights, starting with the low increasing population, progressing through the high increasing and high stationary stages, and ending with an overall 18 percent increase in adrenal weights in the decreasing population. To the extent that adrenal weight correlates with adrenal activity, the results of this investigation indicate that stress increases as the population cycle progresses. Since ample food supplies were available, it appears that social factors rather than purely biological factors were of primary importance in determining the difference in adrenal gland weights.

A number of other field studies have found population density to be associated with changes in adrenal weights and with other physiological indexes assumed to reflect stress. In all these studies the absence of food shortages and other environmental stressors suggests that social stressors brought about by a high population density were responsible for the stress reactions.

Laboratory Studies

Laboratory studies, in which the population density can be carefully controlled and in which extraneous variables that might serve as stressors can be either eliminated or controlled, have supported the field findings that increased population density serves as a stressor. In these investigations adrenal glands have been found to enlarge as population density increased. Changes in other organs have also been noted. One of the studies demonstrating the relationship between population size and adrenal gland size is that of Christian (1955). He placed weanling mice in groups of one, four, six, eight, 16, and 32 for one week. The animals were then killed and their adrenal glands weighed. Adrenal weights showed a linear relationship to the logarithm of the population size in all cases except the groups of 32 mice, in which the adrenal weights declined. Initially, Christian interpreted this finding to mean a "social structure deterioration" at this group size that represented some decrease in stress. However, later work by Christian showed that the decrease in adrenal weight at this population level was due to a loss in the lipid content of the cortical cells of the gland, which indicates intense activation of the adrenocortex. Thus, the trend of increased adrenal activity with increased population density held for all the limits tested.

Physiological changes reflecting a stress reaction in the animal undoubtedly take place when population density reaches a certain level. However, as we have indicated, stress reactions may also be reflected by changes in behavior. Although there is considerably more research on the physical types of stress reactions resulting from high population density, a classic study by Calhoun (1962) reveals a good deal about the behavioral changes that may be associated with this type of stressor.

Calhoun partitioned a 10 X 14 foot room into four pens, as shown in Figure 6-2. Each of the pens was a complete dwelling unit for rats and included a water bottle, a food hopper, and an elevated artificial burrow reached by a spiral staircase. The pens were separated by electrified partitions that had ramps built over them, so that the rats had access to all pens. The behavior of the rats was observed through a window in the ceiling of the room. The rat population was held constant at 80 rats by leaving in the pens only enough infant rats to replace the older ones that died.

As can be seen in Figure 6-2, there was no ramp between pens 1 and 4. These pens were reached by only one ramp each, while pens 2 and 3 were reached by two ramps each. Thus, because of the number of ramps entering the pens, numbers 1 and 4 could be considered end pens and 2 and

3 middle pens. Because of the number of ramps available and for other reasons, pens 2 and 3 had higher population densities than pens 1 and 4. The female members of the population tended to distribute themselves about equally in the four pens, while the male animals concentrated in pens 2 and 3. Pens 1 and 4 each contained a dominant male that would tolerate only a few other males that respected his dominance. The collection together of animals in unusually large numbers, as happened in pens 2 and 3, is called a *behavioral sink.* As Calhoun points out, "The unhealthy connotations of the term are not accidental: a behavioral sink does act to aggravate all forms of pathology that can be found within a group" [p. 144].

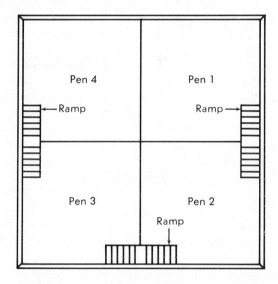

Figure 6-2.   A top view of the pen arrangement used by Calhoun to study overcrowding in rats. Note that ramps connect all pens but 1 and 4. From Heimstra, N. W., & McDonald, A. L. *Psychology and contemporary problems.* Monterey, Calif.: Brooks/Cole, 1973.

Bizarre forms of behavior began to develop quite rapidly, particularly among the animals in the behavioral sinks. The behavior of both the male and the female rats was affected. The females became less adept at building nests and eventually stopped building them altogether. Moreover, rather than transporting their pups from one place to another, which is normal behavior, the females simply picked pups up and dropped them at different places in the pen. During estrous periods the female rats were almost continually pursued by packs of males. There was a very high rate of mortality among these females during pregnancy and parturition.

A variety of different types of behavior was demonstrated by the male rats. The aggressive, dominant males were the most normal, but sometimes even these animals would go berserk and attack females, juveniles, and submissive males. Some of the nondominant males displayed homosexual behavior because they could not discriminate between appropriate and inappropriate sex partners. Other males became completely passive and moved through the pens ignoring other rats and being ignored in turn. Though they were fat and sleek with no scars, their social disorientation was virtually complete.

Possibly the strangest type of behavior was demonstrated by the male rats Calhoun called "probers." These rats, which always lived in the middle pens, were hyperactive and hypersexual. They were always on the alert for an estrous female, and if they could not find one in their own pen, they would lie in wait for a female on the top of a ramp leading to another pen. These animals were also homosexual, and some were cannibalistic.

Marsden (1972) describes another study conducted in Calhoun's laboratory that is somewhat similar to the earlier study. In this investigation eight mice were introduced into what Marsden, basing his judgment on food supplies and living accommodations, describes as a "potential mouse utopia." Four of the mice were males and four females. The utopia was closely observed as the mouse population increased, exceeded what was considered to be the optimum population, and approached the maximum. As this happened, "processes evolved that resulted in the emergence of proportionally more and more divergent types of animals, animals deviating strongly from the ideal of how a normal mouse should behave—that is, a male being occupier and defender of his personal space and the procreator of his species and a female bearer and rearer of healthy young" [p. 9].

The abnormal behavior patterns were first seen in male mice. Males that had been ejected from their usual living quarters now lived on the open floor in large groups of similar individuals. They moved to food and water but then returned to their groups. Normal mouse behavior disappeared, and they withdrew almost completely from normal social interactions.

The grouped withdrawn males on the floor were the first deviants to emerge as the population density increased. A second type appeared shortly afterward. These were solitary withdrawn males that lived alone on the floor at the base of food hoppers or on top of them. There was also a third type of deviant males, which Marsden called the "Beautiful Ones," since they were fat, sleek, and well groomed and had few if any wounds. They lived in the quarters that were available but did not participate in sex activities or compete for territory. These mice actually appeared to be less involved in social activities than either the grouped or the solitary withdrawns. Apparently this type was unstressed; tests of adrenal enzymes showed that the Beautiful Ones had a lower level of the enzyme than did the withdrawn mice.

The population of mice reached a maximum of about 2000, which was about half of the theoretical maximum but well above what was considered to be the optimum number. When the number of mice reached about 2000, the population began to decrease steadily. Indeed, as this chapter is being written, Calhoun has just reported that the last mouse in this mouse utopia has died.

It is apparent from these studies, and from several others that we have not discussed, that social pressure brought about by high population density will result in drastic behavior changes as well as in stress reactions manifested by physiological changes in the animal.

Combinations of Stressors

In laboratory studies as well as in many field studies, researchers try to eliminate or control variables other than the independent variable that might affect the subjects. Although such efforts are a necessary experimental procedure, they remove the studies even further from the real world, in which numerous variables interact and affect the organism. Thus, we know that high population density is a stressor and causes a variety of reactions. What happens, however, in high population density situations when additional stressors are added?

Relatively little research has been conducted on the effects of population density in combination with other stressors. However, to illustrate the dramatic effects that combinations of stressors can have, let us briefly consider research in which social stressors associated with population density are combined with chemical stressors.

Amphetamine sulfate is a central nervous system stimulant that a significant number of persons have begun to use for its mood-changing characteristics. In addition to this illicit use, the drug has become widely used for treating certain types of behavioral disorders in children. When administered to a research subject, such as a mouse or a rat, it will generally result in hyperactivity and other behavior changes.

A number of years ago amphetamine was found to be much more lethal to mice placed together in groups of three or four than to isolated animals. For example, an LD 50 (lethal dose for 50 percent of the subjects) may be about 125 mg/kg for mice that are treated with the drug and placed in isolation. However, the LD 50 for mice treated and placed in groups is only about 10 mg/kg.

If we injected mice with about 50 mg/kg of amphetamine and placed them in isolation, we would observe a number of behavioral effects. Most of the mice would be hyperactive; some would develop strange behavior patterns, such as biting the wire of the cages or rapidly moving their heads back and forth. In general, we would be able to see that these mice behave differently from untreated mice. Very few would die, however. On the other hand, if we were to give a number of mice 50 mg/kg doses and then place them in groups of four in small cages, the behavioral changes shown by these mice in comparison to nontreated controls would be startling. Almost immediately the mice would begin to ricochet around their cages at a tremendous speed. Occasionally, when mice ran into one another, they would adopt a defensive posture by standing on their hind legs and holding their front legs in a boxing position. Almost at once the running would be resumed. Within a few minutes all the amphetamine-treated mice in the group condition would go into convulsions and die.

The lethality of this combination of population density and amphetamine can even be increased by adding other stressors. For example, mice treated with amphetamine and placed in groups will die at an even lower dosage level when heat stress in the form of a hot testing room is added. Other variables decrease the lethality. A study by Mast and Heimstra (1962) showed, for example, that prior social experience will modify the death rate of amphetamine-treated mice placed in group conditions. Mice that had been reared in group conditions had a lower mortality rate after drug treatment than did mice reared in isolation. Obviously, then, many factors will modify the stress effects of population density.

It is tempting, of course, to make, on the basis of the findings of population density studies with animals, dire predictions about the eventual fate of humans if population pressures become too great. As we have pointed out, however, the rodent is far from a perfect model of the human, and any generalizations from findings of animal studies to human behavior must be made with great caution. Clough (1965) points out:

> As might be expected, the ideas devised to explain animal cycles —especially the finding that life in crowded conditions can have profound physiological effects—are now being used to discuss human population problems. But, in my view, there are too many basic differences to justify much of this speculation. For one thing, historically, human populations have shown only a steadily increasing growth over thousands of years—or no significant change in the case of some isolated peoples. There has never been the regular, short-term rise and fall seen in the rodent popula-

tions. For another difference, although it is probably true that humans crowded into urban centers are plagued by certain mental and physical diseases of civilization, their birth rates are not greatly inhibited (if at all) nor their mortality rates increased. In fact, the birth rates are comparatively high among the people who live with the poorest conditions of nutrition, housing, and, perhaps, even emotional and mental hardships [pp. 204–205].

OVERCROWDING AND HUMAN BEHAVIOR

We have pointed out that rigorous empirical data are scarce on the effects of overcrowding on human behavior. At several points in the text, we have discussed studies relevant to this section and will not consider them again. For example, some of the research on the relationship between population density and physical and mental disease was discussed in Chapter 4. Similarly, some of the investigations in the same chapter dealing with life in the city would be appropriate here, as would the studies comparing the behavior of urbanites with rural residents. However, we will conclude our discussion of population density by considering a few laboratory investigations concerned with overcrowding and its effects on behavior.

In laboratory studies of overcrowding, the experimental method of observing behavior is typically employed. Recall that researchers using this method manipulate some aspect of the environment (an independent variable) and observe the effect of this manipulation on some form of behavior (the dependent variable). Usually, in studies of overcrowding, population density is the independent variable, while a variety of different types of behavior may serve as the dependent variable. Relatively few studies of this type have been conducted, but the increasing interest in overcrowding should lead to more and more such investigations.

Typically, in the studies that have been reported, the subjects are exposed to varying degrees of crowdedness and then asked to rate their feelings while under these conditions. A person may be asked to complete an anxiety scale, a stress scale of some type, a hostility scale, or one of a variety of other scales designed to measure his affective state. The differences among the ratings obtained under the various conditions of crowdedness are then compared. Measures of performance on tasks are seldom obtained.

Smith and Haythorn (1972) used 56 naval enlisted men as subjects in a study of the effects of long-term isolation on behavior. The subjects were isolated in groups of two or three for 21 days. Although the primary independent variable in this study was the group size, the investigators were also interested in a number of other variables, including crowding. Thus, a number of the groups were tested under conditions of isolation and confinement that allowed about 70 cubic feet of usable space per man, while other groups were confined in test rooms with 200 cubic feet per man. The design, then, involved two-man groups under high and low crowded conditions and three-man groups under high and low crowded conditions. A variety of dependent variables were employed, both physiological and psychological.

Among the psychological measures were several tests designed to measure stress, anxiety, and hostility. The measure of stress indicated that the groups were highly similar during the first nine days of confinement. However, during the remainder of the time in confinement, crowdedness appeared to have a greater effect on the three-man groups than on the two-man groups. The three-man groups in the high crowded condition showed the highest level of stress, while the three-man groups in the low crowded condition showed the least stress. The two-man groups scored somewhere in between. Measures of anxiety showed that the two-man groups under both conditions of crowding and the three-man groups under the high crowded condition were about the same but that the three-man groups under the low crowded condition were considerably less anxious than the other groups. A surprising finding of this study is that greater hostility toward partners was revealed by subjects in less crowded groups than by crowded subjects.

An investigation by Baxter and Deanovich (1970) was designed to determine the anxiety-arousing properties of inappropriate crowding. The subjects in this study were 48 female volunteers from a psychology class. They were tested under two conditions. Under the crowded condition the subject was seated in a chair and the experimenter (another woman) placed her chair very close to the subject's. Under the spaced condition the experimenter placed her chair at the end of a table at some distance from the subject's.

The subjects were presented with the Make a Picture Story Test, consisting of eight settings containing two doll figures and accompanied by a brief narrative describing each of the settings. The subjects were asked to rate the amount of anxiety felt by the dolls in the different settings. The results indicated that the crowded subjects projected more anxiety in their ratings of the scenes than did the uncrowded subjects. The effects became more pronounced during the latter half of the experimental period.

Griffith and Veitch (1971) investigated the effects of hot and crowded conditions on behavior. They tested subjects in an environmental chamber under a normal temperature condition and under a hot condition. The subjects were also tested under different population densities (small or large groups of subjects together in a test room). Several behavioral measures were used. Under the high temperature and high population density conditions, the subjects who were asked to evaluate a stranger on the basis of his responses on a questionnaire indicated more dislike for the stranger than did the subjects under the other conditions. The mood of the subjects was also found to be negatively affected by the high temperature and high population density conditions.

Studies such as those reported above suggest that crowding affects how a person feels. However, it is difficult to infer from such studies how overt behavior may be affected by crowding. Laboratory studies have generally not found differences in performance among subjects exposed to various degrees of crowding. For example, Freedman (1971) and his co-workers gave subjects a variety of intellectual tasks to perform that varied in complexity and took several hours to complete. The subjects performed these tasks under different conditions of crowding. The results revealed no performance differences on any of the tasks as a result of crowding.

THE EFFECTS OF CROWDING—AN OVERVIEW

It should be apparent from the material presented in this section that empirical data are scarce on the effect of crowding on human behavior. Although there are a great many guesses and predictions about what will happen to people in high population density conditions in which overcrowding is experienced, most of these predictions are based on research conducted with rodents. Studies with rodents have shown that these animals, when subjected to high population density conditions, will demonstrate marked changes in behavior as well as physiological changes that indicate the animals are being subjected to a great deal of stress. Other studies have shown that rodent populations are self-limiting; when a certain population density is reached, the population will level off and then decrease—supposedly because of social stressors that interfere with reproductive behavior. Though it is tempting to generalize from such findings to humans—and many such generalizations have been made—there is no indication that overcrowding does in fact have similar effects at the human level.

As was pointed out in Chapter 4, overcrowding has also been said to cause physical and mental illness. Data supporting these assertions have typically been obtained in investigations in which some index of population density is correlated with an index of mental health problems or frequency of a particular physical condition, such as heart disease or hypertension. A number of studies have shown correlations suggesting that a relationship exists between these variables. However, attempting to establish causal factors with correlational data is difficult, so that we cannot be certain that population density in itself causes a higher rate of mental or physical disorders. Srole (1972) has questioned the view that urbanization leads to higher rates of mental health disorders and such physical disorders as heart disease. He presents an impressive argument for the view that differences actually do not exist between high population density areas and lower density areas in incidence of the mental and physical disorders once thought to be associated with the high density areas.

Controlled laboratory studies of the effects of crowding on human behavior are scarce. The few that have been conducted suggest that crowding may affect how a person feels by increasing anxiety and influencing other affective states. However, there are few laboratory data suggesting that crowding results in any significant changes in performance on intellectual or other types of tasks.

It would appear, then, that although there is considerable speculation about the possible negative effects of crowding on human behavior, data supporting these speculations are lacking. We obviously need to conduct much more research, both in the field and in the laboratory, before we have even a basic understanding of what changes in human behavior we can expect as a result of crowding.

POLLUTION AND ITS BEHAVIORAL EFFECTS

In viewing the environment as a source of threat, up to this point we have been concerned with overcrowding as a potential stressor. There are, of course, many other aspects of the built and natural environments that some people perceive as threatening. For example, our society is based on an increasingly complex technology, which in many ways tends to pollute the environment. Pollution—air, noise, water, and other types—is seen by many individuals as a threat to both their physical and their psychological health. The existence of pollution in an individual's environment, then, can serve as a stressor. Again, however, it must be kept in mind that whether pollution or, for that matter, any other aspect of the environment is perceived as a threat depends upon the personal characteristics of the individual involved. One person, because of his past experience and personality, may view a particular type of pollution as a serious threat, while another person may hardly be aware that it exists.

Although a few people have been concerned about pollution for many years, only recently has the concern of some segments of the public about pollution problems brought about a reaction from the government. Part of this reaction was the formation of the Environmental Protection Agency, which is charged with controlling and eventually reducing pollution of various kinds. Although the success of the efforts of this agency remains to be seen, that attempts are at least being made to halt and, hopefully, reverse the deterioration of the environment must be considered a giant step forward.

For the most part, research on pollution has been conducted by engineers interested in developing techniques that will reduce pollution and by physical and biological scientists interested in the effects of pollutants on the environment and on organisms exposed to the pollutants. Behavioral scientists have been slow in turning their attention to this problem although the psychological impact of pollution has long been recognized. Now, however, increasing numbers of psychologists, sociologists, and other behavioral scientists are becoming involved in research on pollution. Relatively little research has been conducted on the behavioral effects of pollution. Much of the work that has been done has dealt with attitudes toward pollution and with the effects of pollution on various affective states.

There are, of course, many different kinds of pollution, all of which are capable of eliciting strong negative feelings in various people. Some kinds of pollution, because of the obvious threat to health, will bring about a reaction in nearly everyone involved as soon as they are aware that a danger exists. Thus, an accidental release of nerve gas or some other dangerous pollutant would draw an immediate response from persons in the vicinity. At the time this was being written, an unusually high bacteria count was found in the drinking water of a large Eastern Seaboard resort city. The reaction, in this case to water pollution, was immediate and strong.

In this section, however, we will be concerned with what might be termed "chronic" pollutants, those to which people are exposed for long periods. Most types of air pollution are of this type, as is water pollution. Noise pollution has also become a chronic problem in many areas, as has pesticide pollution. These types of pollution generally do not have an immediate and dramatic impact on the individual. Usually, no immediate threat to health is perceived, and the pollution problem is viewed as an annoyance rather than as a physical threat. Many people are not even annoyed and appear quickly to adapt psychologically and biologically to a polluted environment. As will be pointed out later, man's reaction to pollution is a complex psychological phenomenon that is not easily explained.

AIR AND WATER POLLUTION

National polls and surveys consistently show that a significant percentage of the population express concern over the problem of air and water pollution. In a recent poll dealing with national priorities, over 50 percent of

Figure 6-3.   There are many types and degrees of pollution, and a person's reactions to pollution will depend upon the type and degree to which he is exposed. Though a person would probably have negative reactions when viewing a river covered with soap suds, as in the top photograph, his reactions would probably be considerably stronger if he were exposed to thousands of fish killed by a chemical in a river. Top photo courtesy of the *Sioux Falls Argus Leader.*

those surveyed named air and water pollution as one of the three most important domestic issues facing the government. One would assume, then, that the majority of persons in our society view pollution as a threat and feel strongly that something should be done about it. As we shall see, this is not the case.

Although virtually no research has been conducted on the effects of pollution on behavior, a number of studies have attempted to determine people's attitudes and feelings toward pollution. Most of these surveys have been conducted in regions where pollution is at a high level and where the attention of the public has been called to its existence by repeated media coverage. Some interesting findings have emerged from these studies.

As was pointed out in the chapter on methods in behavioral research, the results obtained from surveys and polls depend to a great extent on how the questions are worded. For example, if a surveyor asked his respondents, "Do you think that air pollution is a major health problem?" he could expect to get a very high percentage of positive responses. On the other hand, if the question were worded, "What do you consider to be a major health problem in this locale?" the response would probably be quite different. In fact, one common finding of the public opinion polls on air pollution is that very few people will *spontaneously* complain about air pollution even if they live in areas with extremely high levels of pollution. Thus, in several surveys conducted in areas with serious air pollution problems, when the respondents were asked whether the area was a healthy place to live, a high percentage said that it was. However, when the respondents in these same areas were asked whether they were bothered by smog, a significant percentage indicated that they were.

Thus, if the survey instrument is worded in a particular fashion, most people will indicate that they consider pollution to be a threat to health at worst and an annoyance at best. One might assume that one effect of pollution on behavior would be the development of a "let's do something about it" attitude on the part of the public. We have seen this development in relatively few individuals; they have been vocal and have been largely responsible for the action programs that have begun. However, most individuals do nothing even though they express concern about pollution when asked. Why?

There are probably a number of reasons for the lack of response in most of the public. Many people lack knowledge about the nature of pollution and have only a vague understanding of its possible ill effects. Although lack of understanding does not mean that intense opinions about pollution cannot be held (in fact, some of the strongest antipollution campaigners appear to know very little about the problem), it is often difficult to combat effectively a problem about which little is known.

Even if a person does feel strongly that something should be done about pollution, what can he do? Most people have no idea of who they can complain to or, if they do, may feel that their complaint will do no good. If one perceives his possible role in solving a pollution problem as having no effect, it is likely that no effort will be made.

Possibly one of the primary reasons that the public tends to do nothing about pollution problems is that it will clearly cost something to solve the problems. We have pollution because we depend on a highly complex technology; and any change in the technology that may reduce pollution is bound to result in some drastic changes in our life style. Most people appear to view the fight against pollution within a cost-payoff matrix of some sort. If the payoff appears great and the cost little, there seems to be a tendency to attempt to do something about the pollution problem. Thus, if a pollution source is traced to a particular industry, and closing or modifying the industry will have little economic impact on the region, the attitudes of the people living in the region toward the pollution caused by the industry are likely to be negative. On the other hand, if closing the industry will result in the loss of many jobs and a serious impact on the economy, the attitudes of the people in the region toward the pollution problems will likely be quite different. In other words, the cost seems to be considerably greater than the perceived payoff. Though the cost is often measured in financial terms—increased taxes, for example—in some instances the cost may be such that people are involved in a very direct fashion.

The results of various surveys make it seem safe to state that many are concerned, or at least express concern, about pollution. Though this concern is infrequently translated into action of any type, we do on occasion see forms of behavior that may be motivated by attitudes toward pollution. For example, there have been a number of demonstrations whose stated purposes have been to call attention to pollution problems. Moreover, more people are now leaving California each day than are moving into the state. Many of those who leave say that their primary reason for the move is California's air pollution.

Other forms of behavior may be a direct result of pollution, but they are hard to identify. Obviously, if a high level of pollution results in physical distress of some type, such as burning eyes or difficulty in breathing, associated behavioral changes will occur that can be blamed on the pollution. If a person's agricultural crops or other property is damaged, we can expect some behavior changes. It has become customary for some residents of areas with high air pollution to get away from the smog occasionally for weekends. Thus, pollution may be modifying recreational behavior to some extent, although it is quite probable that if smog were not present, other reasons would exist for getting away.

Possibly the safest conclusion that can be drawn at present on the effects of pollution on behavior is that we do not know how behavior is affected. As pointed out previously, behavioral scientists are just beginning to express an interest in this area, and very few data currently exist upon which to base any conclusions. Though some information is available on attitudes toward pollution and on gross behavioral responses, such as demonstrations and emigration, pollution likely influences behavior in a number of subtle ways. Different approaches to studying the problem will probably have to be used before we can understand these subtle modifications. Laboratory research, in which a particular variable associated with pollution can be studied in some detail while other variables are controlled, may be such an approach.

An example of such a laboratory study is one conducted by Swan (1970), who used as subjects a number of high school students living in Detroit. Each subject was presented with a series of slides showing various urban environments and asked to report what environmental problem he observed in each slide. The primary purpose of the study was to assess perceptual awareness of air pollution.

To accomplish this objective, each slide series represented a continuum of visible air quality ranging from relatively clean to highly polluted air. The number of slides in the continuum that a subject recognized as showing an air pollution problem was used as his measure of perceptual awareness of air quality. Swan found that perceptual awareness of air pollution was significantly less for students from low socioeconomic backgrounds. He speculates that such students had less chance to be out of the city and see natural sky colors and had come to accept the brownish-blue polluted atmosphere as normal. This conclusion raises an interesting question that has implications for research. As Swan points out, "it is difficult to determine if people are actually perceptually aware of polluted air in their environment or if they are more likely to base their responses to public opinion surveys on media coverage of the issue" [p. 68]. It makes a considerable difference in how we interpret the data from attitude surveys if we know that the responses are based on direct perceptions or on information obtained from the media.

Other types of laboratory studies can contribute important information on the effects of pollution on behavior. Animal studies, for example, have been conducted in which various types of animals are exposed to extremely high levels of air pollution and the effects of this pollution on their behavior and general health determined. It is difficult, of course, to conduct studies of this kind on humans, although it is possible in laboratory situations to study the effects of some aspect of pollution on a person. Thus, in a study reported by Jones (1972), smog was manufactured in the laboratory, and the effects of various components of the smog on the eye were determined. The subjects wore eye masks through which the smog was introduced. The psychophysical method of limits was used, with the subjects being exposed to increasingly stronger concentrations of smog during a series of trials. The point at which a subject indicated eye irritation was considered the threshold for a particular concentration and type of smog. Using this technique, Jones found that the presence of hydrocarbon in smog is the best single predictor of eye irritation and that formaldehyde is close behind.

In this section we have been primarily concerned with air pollution. Much of what has been said about this type of pollution is also applicable to the problem of water pollution. Surveys have shown that people are concerned about water pollution, but, as is the case with air pollution, most people are uncertain of what they can do about the problem. There have been strong reactions from some individuals and groups that have led to efforts by the Environmental Protection Agency to do something about the problem. However, very little research has been conducted on the effects of water pollution on behavior.

NOISE POLLUTION

When we use the term "sound," we are referring to both a form of physical energy and what we hear. In other words, sound can be thought of as having both physical and psychological dimensions. As physical energy it consists of variations in air pressure that are caused by some type of vibrating body that has set air molecules in motion. We can measure this energy with various types of meters and specify, with considerable accuracy, the physical makeup of a particular sound. As what we hear, sound can also be studied as a psychological phenomenon. Measurement in this case is much less precise. Though the physical attributes of sound are related to its perceived attributes —that is, what we hear or experience when exposed to a sound—how the sound is perceived depends upon a variety of factors. We will discuss some of these factors later in this section.

Among the countless sounds to which we are exposed on a regular basis are some that are unwanted. They may be unwanted because they produce physiological or psychological damage or because they interfere with such activities as communications, work, rest, recreation, and sleep. When for these or other reasons a sound is unwanted, we refer to it as *noise*. We have seen that air pollution degrades the quality of life, disrupts activities, and sometimes serves as a threat to health. Noise is an environmental pollutant that is generated in a different fashion but has similar effects.

Noise pollution is becoming an increasingly serious problem in our society for several reasons. First, each year the number of new noise sources increases tremendously. Although transportation noise is the major source of complaint—and this problem grows yearly—numerous other new sources of noise, ranging from washing machines to construction equipment, appear each year. A second reason that noise pollution is becoming more of a problem is that demographic changes are causing more of the population to be exposed to noise sources. As more and more people move into urban regions, increases in population density significantly increase the number of people exposed to noise pollution.

Noise pollution promises to remain a serious problem. We have noise pollution because it is generally cheaper to produce noisy products by noisy means than quiet products by quiet means. Thus, the noise producers lack economic incentive to lessen their noise output. The American public is also generally unaware of the nature and magnitude of the noise pollution problem. Although there are presently some government efforts to reduce the noise problem, until the public becomes aroused and demands action, it will not be forthcoming in any real fashion.

The Nature of Sound

When we talk about noise, we are, of course, talking about a particular type of sound that for various reasons is unwanted. As we have indicated, sound can be considered in terms of its physical characteristics and its psychological characteristics. Physically, sound has two characteristics, frequency and intensity.

Vibrating bodies cause air molecules to be alternately pushed together (positive pressure) and pulled apart (negative pressure), resulting in a wave of positive pressure moving through the air immediately followed by a wave of negative pressure. This is the sound wave that is the physical stimulus for hearing. The back and forth movement of the air molecules can be represented graphically with sine waves, as shown in Figure 6-4.

The *frequency* of a sound wave is indicated in cycles per second (cps) or, in more recent usage, *hertz* per second (Hz). In Figure 6-4 the middle sine wave has a frequency twice that of the upper sine wave. Frequency, in cps or Hz, is a physical quality of sound. The frequency of a sound wave is primarily responsible for the psychological dimension of hearing that we refer to as *pitch*. In other words, how high or low a sound is perceived to be is primarily due to its frequency.

The *intensity* of a sound wave is the amplitude of the wave (see Figure 6-4). Note that in the figure the middle and bottom sine waves have the

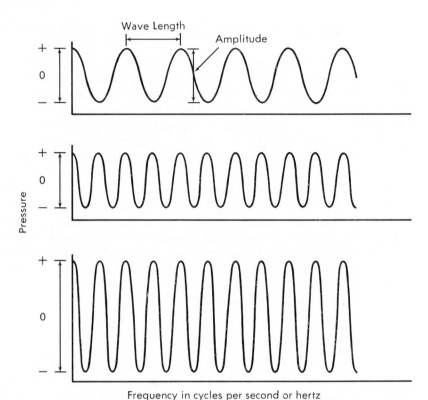

Figure 6-4.   Three sine waves that have different frequencies and amplitudes. The amplitude is the same for the top two sine waves, but the frequencies are different. The bottom sine wave has the same frequency (cycles per given period of time) as the middle wave, but it has twice the amplitude. From Heimstra, N. W., & Ellingstad, V. S. *Human behavior: A systems approach.* Monterey, Calif.: Brooks/Cole, 1972.

same frequency but the amplitude of the bottom wave is twice that of the middle wave. The psychological correlate of intensity (amplitude) is *loudness*. Thus, a particular sound wave will result in the auditory sensation of pitch, which is related to its frequency, and loudness, which is related to its amplitude.

The physical and psychological dimensions of sound are more complex than indicated above. For example, a change in intensity may also produce a perceived change in pitch, and a change in frequency may result in a change in perceived loudness. Moreover, we rarely encounter the pure tones illustrated in Figure 6-4. Normally, tones are complex and made up of a number of frequencies. This mixture of frequencies leads to a third psychological dimension of sound, called *timbre* or *tonal quality*.

The range of sound intensities to which man responds is so great that intensity is measured on a very large scale called the *decibel scale*. The decibel is a ratio indicating the relative difference in intensity between two sounds. However, this ratio has meaning only if everyone uses the same reference value. The reference value selected is .0002 dynes per square centimeter (a dyne is a unit of pressure), which is about the lowest change in pressure to which the ear is sensitive. It should also be kept in mind that the decibel scale is a logarithmic scale, which means that if one sound is 100 decibels more intense than another sound, it is 10 billion times more powerful. The sound pressure (decibel) levels of a number of sounds are shown in Figure 6-5. On this scale the pain threshold is reached somewhere around 125–135 decibels. In other words, sound pressure around this level actually causes a person to experience a painful sensation.

When Is Sound Unwanted?

The manner in which a sound is perceived depends upon a number of factors. As mentioned previously, the psychological dimensions of sound —pitch, loudness, and timbre—depend upon the physical attributes of frequency and intensity and the mixture of different frequencies. When certain physical characteristics are present in a sound, it is more likely to be perceived as unwanted than when these characteristics are absent. However, other factors, such as situational variables, are also important. Thus, a particular sound might be considered unwanted in a church but not in a bar. Similarly, a sound may not be unwanted in the afternoon but may be considered noise at 2 A.M. Personality and past experience are also important variables in determining how a sound is perceived. A good deal of research has been conducted on all these variables.

As Kryter (1970) points out, the use of the word "noise" for unwanted sound sometimes results in confusion because there are two general categories of unwantedness. Very often, it is not the sound itself that is unwanted but the information that the sound conveys. For example, if we were awakened at night by a sound that we knew indicated the presence of an intruder, the information, not the sound, would be unwanted. Thus, we would not consider these sounds to be noise in the way we consider other kinds of sounds unwanted in a particular situation to be noise. People quite consistently judge the latter types of sounds to be unwanted, annoying, or objectionable, and it is these kinds of sounds that cause noise pollution.

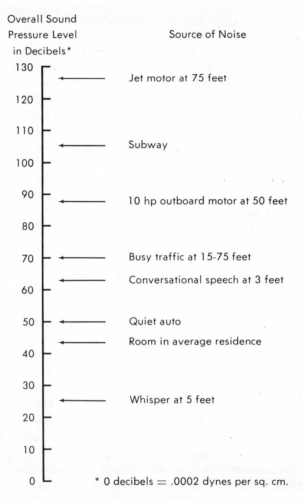

Figure 6-5.   Sound pressure levels for a number of different sounds. From Heimstra, N. W., & Ellingstad, V. S. *Human behavior: A systems approach.* Monterey, Calif.: Brooks/Cole, 1972.

Of the physical characteristics of a sound that result in its being perceived as noise, *loudness* appears to be most important. However, *frequency* is also a factor; high pitched sounds are more likely to be considered unwanted than sounds with a lower pitch. Similarly, an *intermittent* sound is usually considered unwanted more often than a continuous sound of the same frequency and intensity. Duration, increases and decreases in intensity, spectrum content, and other physical characteristics are also associated with the degree of perceived noisiness of a given sound.

As one might expect, a variety of situational factors are important in determining whether a sound is perceived as noise. It would be impossible to list all the situational factors, but we can make some generalizations. When a sound interferes with some ongoing activity, the sound tends to be perceived as unwanted even though its physical characteristics may be such that normally it would not be considered noise. When some sound interferes with speech communication, for example, the sound is highly likely to be viewed as unwanted. When sleep is disturbed by a sound, the sound is even more likely to be considered unwanted. Sounds may interfere with a person's concentration, relaxation, work, and so forth. In general, then, when a sound interferes with some activity, it becomes a noise.

The individual's personality and past experience also interact with the situation and the characteristics of a sound to determine whether it will be considered unwanted. Research indicates, for example, that extroverts and introverts respond to sounds in a different fashion. There is some evidence that complaints about noise come disproportionately from neurotic people and that the individuals who are most annoyed by noise may have difficulties in personal adjustment. Attitudes, which are based on the past experience of the individual, play an important role in perceived noisiness. The attitude of the listener toward the source of a sound is critical in determining whether the sound is perceived as noise. Thus, the sound of a neighbor's lawn mower may not bother a person, while the sound of a motorcycle might.

Obviously, then, whether a sound is perceived as unwanted and, consequently, as noise is a complex affair and dependent upon a variety of variables that have just been touched upon in this section. Engineers are increasingly called upon to predict whether the sound of a piece of equipment, a new highway, or a new airport will be perceived as noise by the persons exposed to the sound. These predictions, at best, are often educated guesses, since the data needed to make the predictions with a high degree of accuracy are unavailable.

Noise Pollution and Behavior

A considerable amount of research has dealt with the effects of noise on human behavior. Much of this work has concerned the already discussed relationship between the physical characteristics of sound, situational variables, and personality variables and the perceived noisiness of various sounds. Typically, in these studies the variables listed above serve as the independent variables; the dependent variable is some indication of the annoyance or perceived noisiness elicited by a particular sound. The dependent variable is generally measured by a rating scale of some type.

Other studies have been concerned with community reaction to noise, generally that associated with aircraft or other types of transportation. These studies have usually measured attitudes toward the noise and the "bother" that is generated. Some investigations have attempted to correlate exposure to noise with hearing impairment, psychological disturbances, and various other health problems. Finally, a large number of laboratory studies have been conducted to determine the effects of noise on the performance of a variety of tasks. We will briefly summarize the findings of each of these types of studies.

Community Reaction to Noise. Studies have shown that it is difficult to predict community response to noise because so many variables are involved. As was the case with air pollution, a significant percentage of people in a community exposed to high noise levels will indicate that they consider noise a problem. They will generally give as a reason that the noise interferes with their talking, sleep, and so forth. Typically, however, they do not try to have something done about the noise unless it is very loud. If the noise level reaches 90 db or thereabouts, most people will react vigorously with complaints and threats of action.

Investigations of community attitudes toward noise and the factors that will modify the attitudes have been relatively numerous. As might be expected, when the noise source is a major economic factor in the community, attitudes toward the noise are more favorable than when it is not. Many other situational and personal factors, such as the type of annoyance developed by the noise and when the noise occurs, will determine the attitude toward noise pollution. Research also suggests that more favorable attitudes toward noise can be established, sometimes by rather simple methods. For example, letters to citizens explaining a noise source and discussing its necessity were shown, in one study, to reduce significantly the percentage of people who considered the noise an inconvenience. Similar findings have been reported near military air bases when the public was made aware of the importance of the base and the efforts being made by the pilots for the comfort and safety of the citizens.

Even though studies do show that members of a community often have negative attitudes toward noise pollution, these attitudes are rarely translated into action. Perhaps the best summary of community reaction to noise is that there is very little reaction. Though we do on occasion read or hear about a group taking legal action against some noise source, such as an airport or an industry, considering the magnitude of the problem, the reactions are certainly minimal.

The Effects of Noise on Performance.   A large number of studies have dealt with the effects of noise on the performance of various types of tasks, but the findings are ambiguous. The results of some investigations show that noise has a detrimental effect on performance, other studies show no effect, and still other studies reveal that noise facilitates performance. What has become apparent is that the effects of noise on performance depend upon the characteristics of the noise, of the task, and of the individual. The frequency and intensity of the noise, as well as other physical characteristics, help determine the effect of the noise on behavior. Intermittency appears to be a particularly important physical variable; in several studies in our laboratory (Warner & Heimstra, 1971, 1972, 1973), intermittent noise with a 30 percent on-off ratio (1.5 seconds on, 3.5 seconds off) facilitated performance on a number of tasks. Task variables important in determining noise effects include such factors as how difficult the task is, whether it requires constant alertness, whether it is largely psychomotor or primarily mental, and how long the task takes. Personal variables include both transient and relatively permanent factors. A person's mood or motivation at a particular time is an important determinant of noise effects, as are personality, age, sex, and attitudes. The predictability of the noise and whether a person can control its termination influence the annoyance level of the noise and its effect on behavior (Reim, Glass, & Singer, 1972; Glass & Singer, 1972). However, all the variables associated with the noise, the task, and the person interact in unpredictable ways and make it difficult to state accurately the effects of noise on performance.

Noise and Health.   Long exposure to high intensity noise does result in hearing loss. Because this fact has been well established, the government has set standards for permissible noise exposures. For example, under these standards the permissible sound level for an eight-hour work day is 90 db. A person may be exposed to 100 db for only two hours per day and to 110 db for only one-half hour. Though most people are now protected when they are at work, they are often exposed to noise levels that exceed the permissible exposure limits in other settings. For example, in discotheques and at rock concerts, music is often played for long periods at levels of around 110 db and sometimes as high as 120 db. Several studies have shown that persons who spend a good deal of time listening to music in these settings suffer either temporary or permanent hearing damage.

There have been reports that long exposure to noise may result in mental health problems for some persons, but this conclusion is not well documented. There is also some evidence that there may be health differences among groups subjected to different noise exposures. A European study reports correlations between cardiovascular irregularities and intense occupational noise exposure, and a study in Russia found that adults living near airports had a higher morbidity rate than did persons living some distance away. Additional European studies suggest that long exposure to noise may have still other effects on health.

In the United States the prevailing view among noise experts is that man's tolerance to noise is high and that he can adapt to present noise conditions without harmful physical effects. This view has been challenged, however, by researchers in the U.S. Public Health Service. Antigaglia and Cohen (1970) state:

> There is no question that noise or sound can cause physiologic changes. At issue is whether long-term repetitive exposures to noise can induce physical changes that are eventually degrading to the health of the individual. The position of the United States experts that noise has no ill effects is difficult to defend at this time in view of the absence of systematic study and objective data in this area. For example, epidemiological surveys concerned with the incidence of acute and chronic ailments in different work groups have never been undertaken in this country and are greatly needed. Such information could corroborate or refute findings from the European literature which . . . suggest apparent associations between noise and adverse health effects.

BEHAVIORAL EFFECTS OF POLLUTION—AN OVERVIEW

Clearly, we can make no definitive statements about the behavioral effects of pollution. In all likelihood pollution affects behavior; but only recently have psychologists and other behavioral scientists turned their attention to this problem, and they have as yet made no significant progress in solving it. Although we know that many members of society have negative attitudes toward pollution, research has not established why people who are bothered by air, water, or noise pollution tend not to complain, to move away from the area, or to take any other action that might alleviate the problem.

As Maloney and Ward (1973) point out in discussing their research in this area, "most people say they are willing to do a great deal to help curb pollution problems and are fairly emotional about it, but, in fact, they actually do fairly little and know even less" [p. 585].

Much of the research on the behavioral effects of pollution has been community surveys to determine the percentage of people who are bothered by a particular pollutant. Obtaining data of this type is relatively simple, but it does not tell us much about the behavioral effects of the pollution. If people are in fact bothered, however, it is probably safe to say that their behavior has been modified in some fashion, perhaps in subtle ways that are difficult to measure. We might ask: What changes in life styles take place when chronic exposure to pollution is involved? Do social interactions, both within and outside family groups, change in any way? Is a person's affective state modified in any fashion? These questions and many others remain to be answered.

One point has become obvious through the research in this area. If meaningful answers are to be found to questions raised about pollution and behavior, highly sophisticated research techniques will be needed. It is apparent that the behavior-pollution interaction is extremely complex and influenced by many variables. The physical characteristics of the pollutant, the situation in which the person is exposed to the pollutant, and the characteristics of the person himself all interact in a complex way to determine just what behavioral effects occur. We are far from the point where the effects of a pollutant on behavior can be predicted.

In this section we have not emphasized the possible deleterious effects of the various types of pollution on health. If pollution does affect health, then it is obvious that behavioral effects will also occur. Thus, a person whose hearing has been permanently impaired by exposure to loud noises will behave somewhat differently from the way he did before the impairment occurred. However, aside from the demonstrated noise-induced hearing loss, there is still a question in the minds of many investigators about the health effects of air and noise pollution.

One conclusion that can be drawn about research on pollution and behavior is one with which the reader is already very familiar: More research is needed. Though increasing numbers of behavioral scientists are beginning to study this topic, considering the magnitude of the problem, the number is insignificant. The amount of money available for research in the field is also minimal. Hopefully, if one were to attempt to review the literature on pollution and behavior five years from now, there would be more to talk about. Certainly, however, at the rate research is being conducted at present there is no guarantee of that.

ADAPTATION TO THE ENVIRONMENT

We have seen in this and previous chapters that certain character-istics of the physical environment are perceived as threatening by some individ-uals and, consequently, serve as stressors. Though we have emphasized the characteristics of overcrowding and pollution in the present chapter, the con-cept of a stressful environment has been discussed at various other points in the text. For example, certain types of housing areas have high crime rates, which are stressful for many residents, as are various geographic environments where the probability of natural disasters occurring is quite high. A question of some interest to environmental researchers is how man is able to adapt to the various environmental conditions, many of which are stressful, in which he exists.

Psychologists and other scientists have known for many years that a sensory system is modified by the continuous presentation of stimuli. This process of modification is called adaptation. Although the physiological mechanisms underlying adaptation vary depending upon the sensory modality involved, adaptation as a general process occurs in all the senses when they are exposed to constant stimulation. However, some of the senses adapt much more than others. Though we usually think of adaptation as resulting in a lowering of the sensitivity of the receptors involved, adaptation is a two-way process that can involve either a heightened or a lowered performance of the receptors. For example, when the eye becomes dark-adapted, the receptors become much more efficient during the course of adaptation. A light that would not be detected before adaptation is easily detected after adaptation has taken place. However, in the case of cutaneous adaptation, the receptors become less efficient. Thus, while one may feel a sweater on his body when he first puts it on, in a short time he will no longer feel it. Taste and smell also adapt rapidly.

Most research on adaptation has involved simple dimensions of sensory intensity, such as brightness of light, temperature, and odor, and has been conducted under carefully controlled laboratory conditions. Adaptation to a real world environment is undoubtedly much more complex because of the multidimensional characteristics of the stimuli involved. When attempting to generalize from the findings of laboratory studies on adaptation to the real world, a question raised by Wohlwill (1970) must be kept in mind: "How do they apply with reference to such stimulus attributes as complexity, incon-gruity, ambiguity, or to the multidimensional character of such workaday experiences as that to which a commuter on the New York subways or the Los

Angeles freeways is subjected?" [p. 307]. Although we know that man is endowed with an excellent adaptive physiology and that he does adapt to many kinds of built and natural environments, there are a great many questions about this process to which we do not have answers.

One question has to do with the characteristics or dimensions of the stimuli that are important in the adaptation process. Intensity of stimulation is, of course, an important dimension and has been of concern to designers for some time, as shown by their attempts to provide specified levels of noise and illumination. Wohlwill (1966) points out other dimensions of stimulation that may be important: complexity, variation, surprisingness, and incongruity. But how does an investigator measure and manipulate such dimensions as surprisingness and complexity to study adaptation to them? Because this task is so difficult, we do not have a great deal of information about these aspects of the physical environment and about adaptation to them.

Another key question has to do with the limits of adaptability. Both common sense and some empirical data indicate that there are limits, but as yet we know relatively little about them or about the behavior to be expected when the limits are reached. It is generally assumed that there is an optimal level of stimulation along the stimulus dimensions listed above and that too little or too much may have detrimental effects. Indeed, sensory deprivation research, in which subjects are deliberately deprived of much of their normal sensory experience, has shown that under these conditions hallucinations and other behavioral effects occur. Typically, however, environmental conditions are such that excessive stimulation occurs rather than too little. When these excessive limits are reached, in some cases physical or mental illness may occur. In other situations more subtle effects—nervousness, irritability, and so forth—are likely to occur. Undoubtedly, there are significant individual differences in level of tolerance to stimulation, but, again, relatively little is known about this topic.

A last question is that of long-term adaptation effects. Wohlwill (1966) asks: "What are the long-range effects of exposure to a given environment featured by a particular level of intensity, complexity, incongruity, etc. of stimulation?" [p. 36]. He then goes on to question "whether, in spite of the individual's capacity to adapt to an astonishingly wide range of environmental conditions, such prolonged exposure to stimulus environments falling near the extreme of the complexity or intensity dimension, for instance, may not leave its mark nevertheless." This type of exposure probably does have a variety of behavioral effects. Recall, for example, our earlier discussion of system overload encountered by persons living in cities and the adaptive responses that are thought to develop to reduce the overload. According to the system overload theory, many of the types of behavior thought to characterize urbanites can be considered to be adaptive responses that have developed because of long exposure to excessive stimulation.

Adaptation to the environment, then, is a process that obviously does occur, but we know very little about it. Since adaptation may result in a wide range of behavior, this topic should be an important area of research for those interested in behavior-environment relationships. Although various researchers are beginning to pay some attention to the problem, questions like those asked above still do not have answers.

EPILOGUE

ENVIRONMENTAL PSYCHOLOGY: WHERE DOES IT GO FROM HERE?

As pointed out earlier, environmental psychology is an emerging field of inquiry with subject matter not yet completely defined. Researchers from many disciplines have contributed scientific findings to the field, but, as stated, more research is needed. Though a relatively broad layer of empirical research underlies the current knowledge in this field, it is a thin layer. At this stage of the development of the field, we might legitimately ask: Where does it go from here? In the next few years will environmental psychology expand and become firmly established as a scientific field, or will it be looked back on as a fad, never fulfilling its early promise?

While no crystal ball will answer this question, it does appear to us that several developments are necessary to firmly establish environmental psychology. First, as we have pointed out, there is only a thin layer of research upon which this field is based. Consequently, if environmental psychology is to develop, more depth must be achieved in this layer of research. Equally important, this research must be such that the findings can be used by environmental decision makers in areas ranging from the design of buildings and other

189

built environments to the use of wilderness areas. Environmental psychology originated from a concern over the relationships between man and his physical environment, and, if it does not provide solutions to problems arising from these relationships, it probably will not survive. The future of environmental psychology centers on two key questions: Will there be more research in the field? Will the research findings be used? A third question: Will public attitudes toward the environment change, and, if so, will such changes affect the development of this field?

An increased level of research in environmental psychology will depend upon a variety of factors, ranging from additional funding to changing the existing attitudes of psychologists toward research of this kind. All research is expensive, and research in environmental psychology is no exception. Though present research programs in many areas suffer from funding cutbacks, in many instances the programs are still viable. Most areas of research in environmental psychology, however, have never had adequate financial support, and current research grants and contracts are meager, so it is difficult for established investigators in environmental psychology to continue research programs that have been in existence for some time, and new investigators are discouraged from entering the field. Unless additional money becomes available, we will not soon see a marked increase in research in environmental psychology.

Funding is critical, but research also takes manpower, and relatively few psychologists are now interested in conducting investigations in environmental psychology. As Craik (1973) points out: "In light of the number of fronts currently under investigation along the behavior-environment interface, it is evident that the field could tolerate a significant increase in research manpower, yet still retain its status as an undermanned behavior setting . . . " [p. 412]. This may change if the funding problem is alleviated.

But we may see more psychologists entering environmental psychology. First, graduate training programs are now available for students to obtain advanced degrees. Though these programs are rare, training only a few students, a general trend in many graduate programs may result in substantial numbers of graduates who can contribute to environmental psychology. Increasingly, graduate programs recognize that traditional training has not prepared students for real world settings—for research relevant to the pressing problems of modern society. Students must be exposed to research methods other than the strict experimental approach, where all but one variable is controlled; also, attitudes toward real world problem-solving research must be changed. No longer is "applied research" an area for students who could not succeed in "pure" or "basic" research. In the near future there should be many new Ph.D.'s interested in conducting research in environmental psychology.

Will the research findings be used? The answer centers on the interactions of three groups: the researchers in environmental psychology, the potential users of research findings (architects, planners, government agencies), and the ultimate users of the environment, the general public.

Presently a problem exists for environmental decision makers. If they desire to consider the behavioral effects of their decisions, the behavioral data for intelligent planning probably do not exist. However, Ward and Grant (1970) suggest:

> Another and greater problem has been that the designer has not known what sort of data he needed in the first place, let alone whether or not it existed. A third problem, the greatest of all, is that if the designer has known what sort of data would be useful and if, as has increasingly been the case in recent years, the data has been found to be available, the designer has not known how to incorporate it into his decision-making processes [p. 2].

The solution to these problems defines additional areas of responsibility for future behavioral scientists in environmental research. First, the researcher must aid environmental planners to determine what information applies to the problem. For instance, will planners need measures of attitude or measures of activity? Which attitudes or activities represent the effects of planning decisions? These types of questions demand answers before data can be collected. Second, the researcher must not only design his investigations to answer relevant questions; he must also transform his findings into a form digestible to the planners. The researcher must present more than anecdotal observations or results of statistical manipulations of data to influence persons in environmental design or management. Finally, the researcher must disseminate his findings among those who may need his information.

In addition to cooperating with environmental decision makers in formulating new methods of design and management based on research results, the future environmental researcher must act as a sounding board or representative for the ultimate users of pre-existing built and natural environmental facilities. At present designers and managers are not responsible for behavioral effects their decisions may have. Therefore, the behavioral scientist involved in environmental research must provide feedback to decision makers on the behavioral success or failure of their design practices. This obligation can be met by rigorously evaluating existing environments—for example, public housing projects, parks, suburban developments, city transportation systems—to determine the needs and desires of environmental consumers. This information, in turn, must be communicated to the decision makers. Finally, public acceptance of such research investigations will increase as the public becomes more aware of the influence the environment has on daily life.

The attitude of the general public toward the environment and environmental problems will influence the future development of environmental psychology. The field has reached its current state because of public concern about the deterioration of the physical environment, population problems, and other problems discussed in this text. Public interest and concern, however, can change abruptly, and if this happens, the support for all environmental sciences, including environmental psychology, will diminish. The public seems to feel that efforts directed at protecting the environment are worthwhile so long as there is no significant impact on their own behavior. Efforts of government agencies will have pronounced effects on behavior, however, and if these effects are too dramatic, then environmentalists may be condemned instead of applauded.

Where does environmental psychology go from here? We have not answered the question. But we have pointed out what must happen if the field is to expand significantly over the next few years. Funding, manpower, application of research findings, and public attitude are critical. Environmental psychology has made and will make contributions to help solve some of the pressing problems confronting society today. Increasing recognition of this fact will result in a steady development of the field.

REFERENCES

Acking, C. A., & Küller, R. *Factors in the perception of the human environment: Semantic ratings of interiors from colour slides.* Lund, Sweden: Department of Theoretical and Applied Aesthetics, Lund Institute of Technology, 1967.

Acking, C. A., & Küller, R. The perception of an interior as a function of its colour. *Ergonomics,* 1972, **15,** 645–654.

Altman, D., Levine, M., Nadien, M., & Villena, J. Trust of the stranger in the city and the small town. Unpublished research, Graduate Center, City University of New York, 1969.

Altman, I. Territorial behavior in humans: An analysis of the concept. In L. Pastalan & D. H. Carson (Eds.), *Spatial behavior of older people.* Ann Arbor: University of Michigan–Wayne State Press, 1970.

Altman, I., & Haythorn, W. W. The ecology of isolated groups. *Behavioral Science,* 1967, **12,** 169–182.

Altman, J. W. *Psychological and social adjustment in a simulated shelter.* Santa Barbara, Calif.: American Institute for Research, 1960.

193

Antigaglia, M. D., & Cohen, A. Extra-auditory effects of noise as a health hazard. *American Industrial Hygiene Association Journal,* 1970, **31,** 277–281.

Appley, M. H., & Trumbull, R. On the concept of psychological stress. In M. H. Appley & R. Trumbull (Eds.), *Psychological stress.* New York: Appleton-Century-Crofts, 1967.

Babbie, E. R. *Survey research methods.* Belmont, Calif.: Wadsworth, 1973.

Barker, M., & Burton, I. *Differential response to stress in natural and social environments: An application of a modified Rosenzweig Picture-Frustration Test.* (Natural Hazard Research Working Paper No. 5.) Toronto: Department of Geography, University of Toronto, 1969.

Barry, H. A., Child, I. L., & Bacon, M. K. Relation of child rearing to subsistence economy. *American Anthropologist,* 1959, **61,** 51–64.

Barton, M., Mishkin, D., & Spivack, M. *Behavior patterns related to spatially differentiated areas of psychiatric ward day room.* (Environmental Analysis and Design Research Report Series 5.) Cambridge, Mass.: Laboratory of Community Psychiatry, Harvard Medical School, 1971.

Baxter, J. C., & Deanovich, B. S. Anxiety arousing effects of inappropriate crowding. *Journal of Consulting and Clinical Psychology,* 1970, **35,** 174–178.

Bell, G., Randall, E., & Roeder, J. *Urban environments and human behavior: An annotated bibliography.* Stroudsburg, Pa.: Dowden, Hutchinson & Ross, 1973.

Bennett, C. A., & Rey, P. What's so hot about red? *Human Factors,* 1972, **14,** 149–154.

Berry, P. C. Effect of colored illumination upon perceived temperature. *Journal of Applied Psychology,* 1961, **45,** 248–250.

Betchel, R. B. An investigation of the movement response to environment. In C. W. Taylor, R. Bailey, & C. H. H. Branch (Eds.), *Second National Conference on Architectural Psychology.* Salt Lake City: University of Utah Press, 1967.

Brookes, M. H., & Kaplan, A. The office environment: Space planning and affective behavior. *Human Factors,* 1972, **14,** 373–391.

Burton, I. *Types of agricultural occupance of flood plains in the United States.* (Department of Geography Research Paper No. 75.) Chicago: University of Chicago Press, 1962.

Burton, I. Flood damage reduction in Canada. *Geographical Bulletin,* 1965, **7,** 161–185.

Burton, I. Cultural and personality variables in the perception of natural hazards. In J. F. Wohlwill & D. H. Carson (Eds.), *Environment and the social sciences: Perspectives and applications.* Washington, D. C.: American Psychological Association, 1972.

Burton, I., & Kates, R. W. The perception of natural hazards in resource management. *Natural Resources Journal,* 1964, **3,** 412–441.

Burton, I., Kates, R. W., Mather, R., Jr., & Snead, R. E. *The shores of megalopolis: Coastal occupance and human adjustments to flood hazard.* (Publications in Climatology, 18, No. 3.) Elmer, N. J.: Thornthwaite, 1965.

Burton, I., Kates, R. W., & White, G. F. *The human ecology of extreme geophysical events.* (Natural Hazard Research Working Paper No. 1.) Toronto: Department of Geography, University of Toronto, 1968.

Calhoun, J. B. The social aspects of population dynamics. *Journal of Mammology,* 1952, **33,** 139–159.

Calhoun, J. B. Population density and social pathology. *Scientific American,* 1962, **206,** 139–148.

Caplow, T., & Forman, R. Neighborhood interaction in a homogeneous community. *American Sociological Review,* 1950, **15,** 357–366.

Chombart de Lauwe, Y. M. J. *Psychopathologie sociale de l'enfant inadapté.* Paris: Centre National de la Recherche Scientifique, 1959.

Christian, J. J. Effects of population size on the adrenal glands and reproductive organs of male white mice. *American Journal of Physiology,* 1955, **181,** 477–480.

Christian, J. J., & Davis, D. E. The relationship between adrenal weights and population status of urban Norway rats. *Journal of Mammology,* 1956, **37,** 475–486.

Cicchetti, C. J. A multivariate statistical analysis of wilderness users in the United States. In John V. Krutilla (Ed.), *Natural environments: Studies in theoretical and applied analysis.* Baltimore: Johns Hopkins University Press, 1972.

Clawson, M. Economics and environmental impacts on increasing leisure activities. In F. D. Darling (Ed.), *Future environments of North America.* Garden City, N. Y.: Natural History Press, 1966.

Clough, G. C. Lemmings and population problems. *American Scientist,* 1965, **53,** 199–212.

Craik, K. H. Environmental psychology. In *New directions in psychology,* Vol. 4. New York: Holt, 1970.

Craik, K. H. Appraising the objectivity of landscape dimensions. In John V. Krutilla (Ed.), *Natural environments: Studies in theoretical and applied analysis.* Baltimore: Johns Hopkins University Press, 1972.

Craik, K. H. Environmental psychology. In P. H. Mussen & M. R. Rosenzweig (Eds.), *Annual review of psychology.* Palo Alto, Calif.: Annual Reviews, 1973.

Driver, B. L. Potential contributions of psychology to recreation resource management. In J. F. Wohlwill & D. H. Carson (Eds.), *Environment and the social sciences: Perspectives and applications.* Washington, D. C.: American Psychological Association, 1972.

Driver, B. L., & Tocher, S. R. Toward a behavioral interpretation of planning, with implications for planning. In B. L. Driver (Ed.), *Elements of outdoor recreation planning.* Ann Arbor, Mich.: University Microfilms, 1970.

Ellingstad, V. S., & Heimstra, N. W. *Methods in the study of human behavior.* Monterey, Calif.: Brooks/Cole, 1974.

Esser, A. H. (Ed.) *Behavior and environment: Use of space by animals and men.* New York: Plenum, 1971.

Fanning, D. M. Families in flats. *British Medical Journal,* 1967, **18,** 382–386.

Faris, R., & Dunham, H. W. *Mental disorders in urban areas.* Chicago: Phoenix Books, 1965. (Originally published: 1939.)

Farr, L. E. Medical consequences of environmental noises. *Journal of the American Medical Association,* 1967, **202,** 171–174.

Feldman, R. E. Response to compatriot and foreigner who seek assistance. *Journal of Personality and Social Psychology,* 1968, **10,** 202–214.

Festinger, L., Schachter, S., & Back, K. *Social pressures in informal groups.* Stanford, Calif.: Stanford University Press, 1950.

Fitch, J. M. The aesthetics of function. *Annals of the New York Academy of Sciences,* 1965, **128,** 706–714.

Freedman, J. Population density and human performance and aggressiveness. In A. Damon (Ed.), *Physiological anthropology.* Cambridge, Mass.: Harvard University Press, 1971.

Fried, M., & Gleicher, P. Some sources of residential satisfaction in an urban slum. In J. F. Wohlwill & D. H. Carson (Eds.), *Environment and the social sciences: Perspectives and applications.* Washington, D. C.: American Psychological Association, 1972.

Fucigna, J. T. The ergonomics of offices. *Ergonomics,* 1967, **10,** 589–604.

Gilligan, J. P. (Ed.) *Wilderness and recreation.* (Study Report No. 3.) Washington, D. C.: Outdoor Recreation Resources Review Commission, 1962.

Glaser, D. Architectural factors in isolation promotion in prisons. In J. F. Wohlwill & D. H. Carson (Eds.), *Environment and the social sciences: Perspectives and applications.* Washington, D. C.: American Psychological Association, 1972.

Glass, D., & Singer, J. *Urban stress.* New York: Academic Press, 1972.

Golant, S., & Burton, I. *The meaning of a hazard—Application of the semantic differential.* (Natural Hazard Research Working Paper No. 7.) Toronto: Department of Geography, University of Toronto, 1969.

Grandjean, E., Hunting, W., Wotzka, G., & Scharer, R. An ergonomic investigation of multipurpose chairs. *Human Factors,* 1973, **15**(3), 247–255.

Griffith, W., & Veitch, R. Hot and crowded: Influences of population density and temperature on interpersonal affective behavior. *Journal of Personality and Social Psychology,* 1971, **17,** 92–99.

Gump, P. V., & James, E. V. *Patient behavior in wards of traditional and of modern design.* Topeka, Kan.: Environmental Research Foundation, 1970.

Hall, E. T. *The silent language.* Garden City, N. Y.: Doubleday, 1959.

Hall, E. T. *The hidden dimension.* Garden City, N. Y.: Doubleday, 1966.

Hay, D. G., & Wantman, M. J. *Selected chronic diseases: Estimates of prevalence and of physicians' service, New York City.* New York: Center for Social Research, Graduate Center, City University of New York, 1969.

Heimstra, N. W., & Ellingstad, V. S. *Human behavior: A systems approach.* Monterey, Calif.: Brooks/Cole, 1972.

Heimstra, N. W., & McDonald, A. L. *Psychology and contemporary problems.* Monterey, Calif.: Brooks/Cole, 1973.

Hollingshead, A. B., & Redlich, F. C. *Social class and mental illness.* New York: Wiley, 1958.

Hollingshead, A. B., & Rogler, L. Attitudes towards public housing in Puerto Rico. In L. Duhl (Ed.), *The urban condition.* New York: Basic Books, 1963.

Honikman, B. An investigation of the relationship between construing of the environment and its physical form. *Environmental design: Research and practice.* Environmental Design Research Association, 3/AR8, Los Angeles, 1972.

Horowitz, M. J., Duff, D. J., & Stratton, L. O. Personal space and the body-buffer zone. *Archives of General Psychiatry,* 1964, **11,** 651–656.

Ittelson, W. H., & Kilpatrick, F. P. Experiments in perception. *Scientific American,* 1951, **185,** 50–55.

Ittelson, W. H., Proshansky, H. M., & Rivlin, L. G. The environmental psychology of the psychiatric ward. In H. M. Proshansky, W. H.

Ittelson, & L. G. Rivlin (Eds.), *Environmental psychology: Man and his physical setting.* New York: Holt, 1970.

Ittelson, W. H., Proshansky, H. M., & Rivlin, L. G. Bedroom size and social interaction of the psychiatric ward. In J. F. Wohlwill & D. H. Carson (Eds.), *Environment and the social sciences: Perspectives and applications.* Washington, D. C.: American Psychological Association, 1972.

Jaco, E. G. Evaluation of nursing and patient care in a circular and rectangular hospital unit. (Final Report.) Hill Family Foundation, St. Paul, Minnesota, 1967.

Jones, M. H. Pain thresholds for smog components. In J. F. Wohlwill & D. H. Carson (Eds.), *Environment and the social sciences: Perspectives and applications.* Washington, D. C.: American Psychological Association, 1972.

Kaplan, S., & Wendt, J. Preference and the visual environment: Complexity and some alternatives. *Environmental design: Research and practice.* Environmental Design Research Association, 3/AR8, Los Angeles, 1972.

Kates, R. W. *Hazard and choice perception in flood plain management.* (Department of Geography Research Paper No. 78.) Chicago: University of Chicago Press, 1962.

Kryter, K. D. *The effects of noise on man.* New York: Academic Press, 1970.

Kumove, L. A preliminary study of the social implication of high density living conditions. Toronto: Social Planning Council of Metropolitan Toronto, 1966. (Mimeographed)

Kuper, L. (Ed.) *Living in towns.* London: Cresset Press, 1953.

Lantz, H. R. Population density and psychiatric diagnosis. *Sociology and Social Research,* 1953, **37**, 322–327.

Latané, B., & Darley, J. M. Bystander "apathy." *American Scientist,* 1969, **57**(2), 244–268.

Lazarus, R. S. *Psychological stress and the coping process.* New York: McGraw-Hill, 1966.

Lett, E. E., Clark, W., & Altman, I. *A propositional inventory of research on interpersonal distance.* Bethesda, Md.: Naval Medical Research Institute Research Report No. 1, 1969.

Lewis, O. A poor family moves to a housing project. In H. M. Proshansky, W. H. Ittelson, & L. G. Rivlin (Eds.), *Environmental psychology: Man and his physical setting.* New York: Holt, 1970.

Lippert, S. Travel in nursing units. *Human Factors,* 1971, **13**, 269–282.

Litton, R. B. Aesthetic dimensions of the landscape. In John V. Krutilla (Ed.), *Natural environments: Studies in theoretical and applied analysis.* Baltimore: Johns Hopkins University Press, 1972.

Lucas, R. C. User concepts of wilderness and their implications for resource management. In *Western resources conference book—New horizons: Issues and methodology.* Boulder: University of Colorado Press, 1964.

Lynch, K. *The image of the city.* Cambridge, Mass.: MIT Press, 1960.

Mackworth, N. H. Researches on the measurement of human performance. In H. W. Sinaiko (Ed.), *Selected papers on human factors in the design and use of control systems.* New York: Dover Books, 1961.

Maloney, M. P., & Ward, M. P. Ecology: Let's hear from the people. *American Psychologist,* 1973, **28,** 583–586.

Mann, L. The social psychology of waiting lines. *American Scientist,* 1970, **58,** 390–398.

Manning, P. *Office design: A study of environment.* Liverpool: Pilkington Research Unit, 1965.

Marsden, H. M. Crowding and animal behavior. In J. F. Wohlwill & D. H. Carson (Eds.), *Environment and the social sciences: Perspectives and applications.* Washington, D. C.: American Psychological Association, 1972.

Martin, G. L., & Heimstra, N. W. The perception of hazard by children. *The Journal of Safety Research,* 1973, **5,** 238–246.

Mast, T. M., & Heimstra, N. W. Prior social experience and amphetamine toxicity in mice. *Psychological Reports,* 1962, **11,** 809–812.

McCormick, E. J. *Human factors engineering.* (3rd ed.) New York: McGraw-Hill, 1970.

McDonald, A. L., & Clark, N. Evaluation of the interpretive program for Yellowstone National Park. Report prepared for National Park Service, 1968.

McKenna, W., & Morgenthau, S. Urban-rural differences in social interaction: A study of helping behavior. Unpublished research, Graduate Center, City University of New York, 1969.

Mehrabian, A., & Diamond, S. G. Effects of furniture arrangement, props, and personality on social interaction. *Journal of Personality and Social Psychology,* 1971, **20,** 18–30.

Michelson, W. *Man and his urban environment: A sociological approach.* Reading, Mass.: Addison-Wesley, 1970.

Milgram, S. The experience of living in cities. *Science,* 1970, **167**(3924), 1461–1468. (a)

Milgram, S. The experience of living in cities: A psychological analysis. In F. F. Korten, S. W. Cook, & J. I. Lacey (Eds.), *Psychology and the problems of society*. Washington, D. C.: American Psychological Association, 1970. (b)

Milgram, S. A psychological map of New York City. *American Scientist,* 1972, **60**(2,) 194–200.

Miller, J. G. Adjusting to overloads of information. In D. McK. Rioch & E. A. Weinstein (Eds.), *Disorders of communication*. Baltimore: Williams & Wilkins, 1964.

Muriam, L., & Amons, R. Wilderness areas and management in three Montana areas. *Journal of Forestry,* 1968, **66,** 390–395.

Naftalin, A. The urban problem and action research. In F. F. Korten, S. W. Cook, & J. I. Lacey (Eds.), *Psychology and the problems of society*. Washington, D. C.: American Psychological Association, 1970.

Nemecek, J., & Grandjean, E. Results of an ergonomic investigation of large-space offices. *Human Factors,* 1973, **15,** 111–124.

Newman, O. *Architectural design for crime prevention*. Washington, D. C.: United States Department of Justice, National Institute of Law Enforcement and Criminal Justice, 1973. (a)

Newman, O. A theory of defensible space. *Intellectual Digest,* 1973, **3**(7), 57–64. (b)

Nowlis, V. Research with the mood adjective check list. In S. S. Tomkins & C. E. Izard (Eds.), *Affect, cognition, and personality*. New York: Springer, 1965.

Osgood, C. E., Suci, G. J., & Tannenbaum, P. H. *The measurement of meaning*. Urbana: University of Illinois Press, 1957.

Osmond, H. Function as the basis of psychiatric ward design. In H. M. Proshansky, W. H. Ittelson, & L. G. Rivlin (Eds.), *Environmental psychology: Man and his physical setting*. New York: Holt, 1970.

Poulton, E. C. *Environment and human efficiency*. Springfield, Ill.: Charles C Thomas, 1970.

Poulton, E. C., Hitchings, N. B., & Brooke, R. B. Effect of cold and rain upon the vigilance of lookouts. *Ergonomics,* 1965, **8,** 163–168.

Propst, R. L. The Action Office. *Human Factors,* 1966, **8,** 299–306.

Proshansky, H. M., Ittelson, W. H., & Rivlin, L. G. (Eds.) *Environmental psychology: Man and his physical setting*. New York: Holt, 1970.

Rand, G. Pre-Copernican views of the city. *Architectural Forum,* 1969, **131,** 76–81.

Reim, B., Glass, D., & Singer, J. Behavioral consequences of exposure to uncontrollable and unpredictable noise. *Journal of Applied Social Psychology,* 1972, **2,** 44–56.

Richardson, E. The physical setting and its influence on learning. In *The environment of learning.* New York: Weybright and Talley, 1967.

Roder, W. Attitudes and knowledge on the Topeka flood plain. In G. F. White (Ed.), *Papers on flood problems.* (Department of Geography Research Paper No. 70.) Chicago: University of Chicago Press, 1961.

Ronco, P. G. Human factors applied to hospital patient care. *Human Factors,* 1972, **14,** 461–470.

Rosengren, W. R., & DeVault, S. The sociology of time and space in an obstetrical hospital. In E. Freidson (Ed.), *The hospital in modern society.* New York: Free Press, 1963.

Rozelle, R. M., & Bazer, J. C. Meaning and value in conceptualizing the city. *Journal of the American Institute of Planners,* 1972, **38,** 116–122.

Saarinen, T. F. *Perception of drought hazard on the Great Plains.* (Department of Geography Research Paper No. 106.) Chicago: University of Chicago Press, 1966.

Shafer, E. L., Jr., & Mietz, J. Aesthetic and emotional experiences rate high with Northeast wilderness hikers. In J. F. Wohlwill & D. H. Carson (Eds.), *Environment and the social sciences: Perspectives and applications.* Washington, D. C.: American Psychological Association, 1972.

Skinner, B. F. *Science and human behavior.* New York: Macmillan, 1953.

Smith, S., & Haythorn, W. Effects of compatibility, crowding, group size, and leadership seniority on stress, anxiety, hostility, and annoyance in isolated groups. *Journal of Personality and Social Psychology,* 1972, **22,** 67–79.

Sommer, R. Studies in personal space. *Sociometry,* 1959, **22,** 247–260.

Sommer, R. The distances for comfortable conversation: A further study. *Sociometry,* 1962, **25,** 111–116.

Sommer, R. *Personal space: The behavioral basis of design.* Englewood Cliffs, N. J.: Prentice-Hall, 1969.

Sommer, R. *Design awareness.* San Francisco: Rinehart, 1972.

Srivastava, R. K., & Peel, T. S. *Human movement as a function of color stimulation.* Topeka, Kan.: Environmental Research Foundation, 1968.

Srole, L. Urbanization and mental health: Some reformulations. *American Scientist,* 1972, **60,** 576–583.

Stankey, G. H. A strategy for the definition and management of wilderness quality. In John V. Krutilla (Ed.), *Natural environments: Studies in theoretical and applied analysis.* Baltimore: Johns Hopkins University Press, 1972.

Suholet, D. The highway as open space. *Highway User,* March 1973.

Sundstrom, E., & Altman, I. *Relationships between dominance and territorial behavior: A field study in a youth rehabilitation setting.* Salt Lake City: University of Utah Press, 1972.

Swan, J. Response to air pollution: A study of attitudes and coping strategies of high school youth. *Environment and Behavior,* 1970, **2,** 127–152.

Thiessen, D. D., & Rodgers, D. A. Population density and endocrine function. *Psychological Bulletin,* 1961, **58,** 441–451.

Vogt, W. Population patterns and movements. In F. D. Darling (Ed.), *Future environments of North America.* Garden City, N. Y.: Natural History Press, 1966.

Ward, W. S., & Grant, D. P. Potentials for collaboration between human factors and architecture. *Human Factors Society Bulletin,* 1970, **13**(2), 1–3.

Warner, H. D., & Heimstra, N. W. Effects of intermittent noise on visual search tasks of varying complexity. *Perceptual and Motor Skills,* 1971, **32,** 219–226.

Warner, H. D., & Heimstra, N. W. Effects of noise intensity on visual target-detection performance. *Human Factors,* 1972, **14,** 181–185.

Warner, H. D., & Heimstra, N. W. Target-detection performance as a function of noise intensity and task difficulty. *Perceptual and Motor Skills,* 1973, **36,** 439–442.

Wells, B. W. P. Subjective responses to the lighting installation in a modern office building and their design implications. *Building Science,* 1965, **1,** 153–165.

Whyte, W. H., Jr. *The organization man.* Garden City, N. Y.: Doubleday Anchor Books, 1956.

Wildeblood, P. *Against the law.* New York: Messner, 1959.

Wohlwill, J. F. The physical environment: A problem for a psychology of stimulation. *Journal of Social Issues,* 1966, **22,** 29–38.

Wohlwill, J. F. The emerging discipline of environmental psychology. *American Psychologist,* 1970, **25**(4), 303–312.

Wolpert, J. Migration as an adjustment to environmental stress. *Journal of Social Issues,* 1966, **22,** 92–102.

Woodson, W. E., & Conover, D. W. *Human engineering guide for equipment designers.* Berkeley: University of California Press, 1966.

Yancey, W. L. Architecture, interaction, and social control: The case of a large-scale housing project. In J. F. Wohlwill & D. H. Carson (Eds.), *Environment and the social sciences: Perspectives and applications.* Washington, D. C.: American Psychological Association, 1972.

Yoshioka, G. A., & Athanasiou, R. Effect of site plan and social status variables on distance to friends' homes. *Proceedings of the 79th Annual Convention of the American Psychological Association,* 1971, **6,** 273–274.

Zehner, R. B. Neighborhood and community satisfaction: A report on new towns and less planned suburbs. In J. F. Wohlwill & D. H. Carson (Eds.), *Environment and the social sciences: Perspectives and applications.* Washington, D. C.: American Psychological Association, 1972.

Zimbardo, P. G. The human choices: Individuation, reason, and order versus deindividuation, impulse, and chaos. In W. J. Arnold & D. Levine (Eds.), *Nebraska symposium on motivation.* Lincoln: University of Nebraska Press, 1969.

Zlutnick, S., & Altman, I. Crowding and human behavior. In J. F. Wohlwill & D. H. Carson (Eds.), *Environment and the social sciences: Perspectives and applications.* Washington, D. C.: American Psychological Association, 1972.

INDEX

205